The Hill Road

The
Hill Road

Patrick O'Keeffe

Viking

VIKING
Published by the Penguin Group
Penguin Group (USA) Inc., 375 Hudson Street,
New York, New York 10014, USA
Penguin Group (Canada), 90 Eglinton Avenue East, Suite 700,
Toronto, Ontario, Canada M4P 2Y3
(a division of Pearson Penguin Canada Inc.)
Penguin Books Ltd, 80 Strand, London WC2R 0RL, England
Penguin Ireland, 25 St Stephen's Green, Dublin 2, Ireland
(a division of Penguin Books Ltd)
Penguin Books Australia Ltd, 250 Camberwell Road, Camberwell,
Victoria 3124, Australia
(a division of Pearson Australia Group Pty Ltd)
Penguin Books India Pvt Ltd, 11 Community Centre, Panchsheel Park,
New Delhi–110 017, India
Penguin Books (NZ), Cnr Airborne and Rosedale Roads, Albany,
Auckland 1310, New Zealand
(a division of Pearson New Zealand Ltd)
Penguin Books (South Africa) (Pty) Ltd, 24 Sturdee Avenue,
Rosebank, Johannesburg 2196, South Africa

Penguin Books Ltd, Registered Offices:
80 Strand, London WC2R 0RL, England

First American edition
Published in 2005 by Viking Penguin,
a member of Penguin Group (USA) Inc.

10   9   8   7   6   5   4   3   2   1

"That's Our Name" was published in different form under the title "Looby's Hill" in *DoubleTake* magazine, Winter 2001.

Publisher's Note
This is a work of fiction. Names, characters, places, and incidents either are the product of the author's imagination or are used fictitiously, and any resemblance to actual persons, living or dead, business establishments, events, or locales is entirely coincidental.

Library of Congress Cataloging-in-Publication Data
O'Keeffe, Patrick, 1963–
    The hill road / Patrick O'Keeffe.
        p.   cm.
    ISBN 0-670-03398-7
    1. Ireland—Social life and customs—Fiction.   2. Country life—Fiction.   I. Title.
    PR6115.K44H55 2005
    823'.92—dc22   2005040414

Printed in the United States of America
Set in Adobe Caslon
Designed by Daniel Lagin

To Charles Baxter

Acknowledgments

I am thankful to James Baker Hall and Mary Ann Taylor Hall for friendship and artistic support over many years; to my teachers Nicholas Delbanco and Eileen Pollack at the University of Michigan; to Louis Cicciarelli and Jill Holister, Bill Hogan, Alex Ralph and Lizzie Hutton, Sharon Pomerantz, Francesca Delbanco, Peggy Adler, David Morse and Carol Tell, Paul Barron, Ray McDaniel, Aric Knuth, Nancy Reisman and Rick Hilles, Tatiana Suspitsyna, Sejel, Valerie Laken and Rodney Rankin, Jamsie McNaughton and Trisha McElroy, David and Martha McElroy, Caroline Eisner, Keith Taylor, Michael Haskell and Kate Bell, Mike and Chris Reigert, Chris Hebert and Margaret Lazarus Dean, Deborah Moss, Mika De Roo and Jen, Whitney Baker and Mary Ann Fugate, Carrie Wood and Chris Looby, Paul Lewis and Jennifer Khoshbin, Randall Buskirk, Geoff Trumbo, Sue Bonner, Michael Johnson, Laurence X Tarpey, Dan Shumer and Alison, Mike and Chris Sullivan, Mike McCarthy, Matt Patterson, Warren, Quiz, Chris Rice and Sheryl, Kate Wheeler, Matt and Kathy Hughes, Jim O'Keeffe, Mike and Kathy Ryan, the McDonald family, Danny and Steve Hart, Jonathan Allison, Matt and Jen Higham, Diane Fleet, Paul McCauley, and Neil Giordano.

Thank you always, Mary Gilmartin.

For past financial assistance, I am grateful to the Hopwood, Cowden, and Chamberlain awards at the University of Michigan, and the Kentucky Arts Council for an Al Smith Fellowship in fiction writing.

With special thanks to my agent, Leigh Feldman, for her constant faith in this work, and to my editor, Paul Slovak, for his encouragement, intelligence, and vision.

Contents

The Hill Road

The Hill Road

JAMES NASH'S FORGE, OR SAINT NASH'S, AS MY FATHER, HIS friends, and my aunt Mary called it, stood in the shadow of Kilroan village, at a cross of three roads, where you turn right onto the hill road; it was a small hut, set back ten feet from the roadside, with a rust-eaten galvanized roof that was shaded by old and leafy sycamore. Beneath the sycamores were four abandoned milk churns, stained by rust patterns that looked like boiling rain clouds, and the grass and the weeds grew up around them like a jungle; but I used to break a stick from one of the sycamores, knock the grass and the weeds to one side, wait patiently for the bees to float off and the powder that clouded the air to settle before I sneaked under to kneel and examine these shiny patterns with awe.

In the forge yard itself were piles of worn-out horseshoes, and leaning against the forge wall were the large, heavy iron bands that were once fitted around the wooden wheels of old trap cars and common cars, and the men now tied their horses to these.

In the middle of the yard, directly in front of the forge door, was Mick Nash's anvil, which his son, James, didn't use, and on Saturday afternoons in early spring and late autumn, Rome Kelly, John Hogan, my father, and some few other farmers smoked their pipes and cigarettes, talked and laughed around this anvil, trying to make enough room so that each could put one foot up on it. Inside in the forge, James Nash tended to his own anvil: the fierce ringing, pounding, and hissing that went into one horseshoe, for shoeing a horse was mostly why the men went there, although they might have likewise brought a barrel needing hoops, a plow whose blade needed sharpening, or even an old pot or frying pan, with either a hole or a broken handle, which the blacksmith could mend in a slapdash way, to make it last for another couple of months. This time was at the end of something. Within a year or two, most of the farmers would buy tractors and master them overnight, like they were naturally born to this; they then disposed of their horses, and all the things the horses once dragged behind them were useless, although the blacksmith stayed on in business: He learned to fix and weld new implements such as transport boxes, pike lifters, muck spreaders, silage cutters, and trailers.

James Nash claimed to be the last man to see Albert Cagney, on a summer's night in 1917 or 1918; he was also the only man in Kilroan, on this same night, to see what he called "a blazing from the man above himself." I heard him tell it on a Saturday evening, in autumn, when he happened to walk out of his forge for a breath of fresh air and a smoke. He always wore a black patch over his left eye, which I'd heard the men say was from his youth, when a red-hot horseshoe he was hammering hopped off the anvil and landed there—that evening I had come out from under the trees, and I stood in the forge yard with my brother and sisters; our father was getting the pony shoed. The blacksmith said what he first remembered about the night were the buttons on Albert's British army uniform glinting in the moonlight, which was how he knew it was Albert, walking the road from the village toward the crossroads. The soldier stopped; the blacksmith and he chatted for five minutes or so, and about ten minutes after Albert had wished James Nash a good night, and Albert had headed back home along the hill road, the blacksmith's bedroom behind the forge filled with an unnaturally bright light, and he fell out of his bed, ran without a stitch on him into the crossroads to see above the hill road a small flame in the sky, in the shape of a huge tear, but with enough force in it to illuminate the darkened fields for miles around; in fact, so powerful was the light and the heat that the blacksmith said he could see all the way to the top of Conway's hill, where the rocks glowed like hot turf; then the light vanished—quenched as fast as you'd blow out a candle, the blacksmith said, and he threw himself flat on the road, which hissed from the heat, to ask God for forgiveness for all of his sins, the sins of his ancestors, the sins of every man, woman, and child living and dead in Kilroan; and he prayed for the repose of the soul of Albert Cagney, who he wrongly thought was either taken up body and soul into heaven or turned into a smoking pile of ashes.

—Only that that wasn't flesh and blood unlike yourselves standing there could have survived it, I tell you, said the blacksmith, who turned from the men and tightened the string of his eye patch, then sauntered off to the edge of the yard, where he pissed into the grass and the weeds underneath the sycamores. The men around the anvil didn't stir or utter a word, but stared at the ground at their feet. —And not a word of it is a lie, lads, I tell you, said the blacksmith, when he came back, tightening his belt beneath his leather apron. —However, lads, there's work to be done, so I must go on in, he said; and I felt a chill, as I watched him walk back into his forge, his sleeves rolled up to his powerful shoulders, his cap switched peak-side backwards, similar to how many of the farmers wore theirs on workdays, and the glorious autumn light filling the yard that would soon be covered with the yellowing sycamore leaves that fell steadily, the straight line of darkness the blacksmith crossed into at the forge door, where the fire blazed up before him; and in a few seconds, when the blacksmith was hammering away again, John Hogan, my father, Rome Kelly, and the other men raised their heads, smiled and winked at one another. Of course they would have had to listen to the blacksmith tell this many times over the years, so this evening's telling wasn't in any way new to them.

We then lived in our first house, what we would later call the old house. The year was 1968 or 1969, a few years before we got a black-

and-white television—at this time, only the schoolteacher and the parish priest had one, and a few of the farmers with more land. We listened to the news from Dublin on the wireless; there was only one channel. We all read *Ireland's Own,* and my father read the *Irish Independent,* which he brought with him from the creamery every morning. We ate kippers, fried in butter, on Fridays, knelt together and said the Rosary every night, drew buckets of water from a well down a stone path from our house, for the house itself, and to cool the milk my father took to the creamery, but we did have a second-hand Ford Anglia, with a lovely trophylike ornament on its hood. My brother, Dan, was the eldest; next was Kate, then Mary, and I was the youngest. Dan was my father's pet, and he was the one who asked our father to tell us a story this one night in spring. It was my mother who told my brother to go to the fire and ask our father; we had finished our schoolwork and were playing cards at the kitchen table, being too loud for my mother's liking, and it was still too early to make us go to bed. My father didn't say yes or no at first, but told Dan to turn the wheel of the blower for a few seconds, for the fire was dying out; then my father slid the newspaper underneath his seat, yawned, and carefully scratched his thick white-black hair, took his glasses off, leaned over and laid a few blocks onto the glowing turf; then he stood and lowered the kettle on the crane a few pegs, to heat water for the hot-water bottles, because that was an unnaturally cold night, and he stared at the kettle, hands on his hips and his bare feet in the warm ashes, and when the kettle began to whistle, he raised it up a couple of pegs, and then sat back into his seat and told Dan he could stop blowing the fire because it was now all right.

—Can't ye sit in at this fine fire, my father said. —Don't be letting it go to waste on a night like this. I will then tell ye a good one all right. I've been meaning to tell ye this one for a while.

Dan sat alongside my father. I sat by Mary and Kate. My mother, who was darning one of my father's socks, pulled her chair next to me. Before me, streams of rain were flowing gradually around the bumps on the firewall. I heard rain on the slates above my head, and rain striking the galvanized hay barn roof across the yard; my father turned his face from us to the firewall, where now the streams of rain ran faster, blackened and thickened by the chimney soot, falling heavily before his eyes until they hissed and died on the scorching blocks of wood.

—Albert was down below in the trenches in Verdun, was how he started it. —Faith, he was, with rats crawling all over him and soldiers dead and dying and screaming beside him in all the smoke and the blood and the corpses piling up, but Albert came back to us alive and in one piece but not too long after he was back he happened to be walking from Powers one night and the devil appeared to him in the shape of a ten-foot pig, stepped from behind a tree on Garvey's ditch on the hill road—Albert's father was Mr. Cagney the tailor; they lived down the path from us on Conway's hill. The tailor raised Albert all by himself. And only a young fella, Albert was, when he went to that war that killed and ruined so many, and then to come back safe and have the misfortune to run into the devil, when you think all the devils in the world were behind him and the devil says to him: *You my son have always been mine*—Albert told me every word of this himself the next morning in his own yard, his father asleep in the house behind him, told me that the devil had horns on him like a whitehead bull, Albert shaking in the yard like he was freezing but he did not look a bit like the young fella he once was, not one bit—he was that shook-looking, like he had aged fifty years overnight. His hair had turned to pure white, and he a very good-looking young fella once, but what I want to ask ye is is why the devil ever visited us here? Why, I ask you, of all the places in the world that he could go to, would he come here? We never done anything here but nothing—and didn't Albert himself have it hard enough, walking away from Conway's hill, out into the world and the trenches to a place called No-man's-land? The brave Albert, who was the devil's from the very beginning—*you my son have always been mine*. And, faith, Albert ended up in the home a few days after that night. They put him in there and he passed away a few weeks after, God rest him, talking and raving away to himself, saying prayers and reciting verses he'd learn off by heart from the Bible; such a dear friend of mine, the very best. A lad you'd think who had everything in the world anyone would want, a youngster who came home fine, and he posted letters during the war, writing about how he missed Mr. Cagney and me and all of us on Conway's hill, and how he missed watching the cows walk onto the hill after they were milked in the morning and in the evening; those chats Albert and me had back then, when we were all only young fellas, and you see Mr. Cagney could not read a word of those letters, so I was the one who had to read them, so Mr. Cagney crossed the ditch to the path and walked onto the hill in the evening when he saw me hunting out the cows, and he'd wave the letter over his head and he'd shout my name, and I'd run to him and stand before him like a schoolchild and read the letter out loud in the field, and after I read every letter he'd kneel down on the grass and he'd cry and say a Hail Mary to God to look after his child, aha, yes, my darling Albert, God rest him. His wretched and brave soul. His tormented and anxious soul that God put into him but the devil took away, but if only he had stayed at home, faith, stayed where he was safe, if only—and it wasn't like we didn't have our own troubles here at home. But off Albert went in the first place. Had to, it looked like. Wanting the adventure. But he saw too much. He saw the youngsters dying in the muck on their bellies with rats crawling all over them and bullets flying above them day and night that harsh winter in a country foreign to most of them in the last year of that awful war, and a soldier that you spoke to a second ago dead and bloody beside you, and all in a matter of seconds, it changed, Albert said, and they lay on their bellies in two feet of muck; you'd drown in the muck itself, he said, everyone's feet wet and perished, and your boots and your toes rotting off of you from the cold and the rain, Albert told us about the young men moaning and crying for their mother and for their God and home, and a grenade blowing up beside you and splashing you with muck and blood. And you wet yourself and soiled yourself and there wasn't a thing you could do about it, and in the end muck and blood and yourself was all the same thing, and you crawled along in the wet and the cold and it was never daytime but always night-time, Albert told me when all of us were young, thinking the world was right again, that nothing else could ever go wrong in it—but when I think about it now what anyone really knew was nothing, his mistake being that he was young and thought he knew everything. And then he thought he'd seen it all and the worst of life was behind him, that he had been down in hell and had the luck of God to come back up—

There my father stopped and took a deep breath. My mother laid the sock in her lap, and raised her head to the firewall; the streams of rain had stopped, leaving fading black tracks.

—Listen, Mike, you're only frightening them, she said. —Not one of them will be able to sleep a wink, and look at the state of that wall, me thinking the worst of the winter was behind us, but that'll need another whitewashing.

—I won't frighten them at all; my father spoke to the firewall, which he had not once taken his face from. —Words is all it is now, Nora, he added.

My mother picked up his sock. My father turned from the firewall; the shadows of the flames flickering on his long, red face. She had her head down; her needles were clicking. His eyes were filled with tears.

———

The tailor Mr. Cagney lived for thirty-five years after Albert's death; he was buried beside his son in Kilroan graveyard, and at this funeral my parents met for the first time. My mother told me about this in 1983, when she was in the Regional hospital, in Limerick City, where she was dying after her second bout with cancer in twelve years.

That graveyard in Kilroan is small. The older plots, where Albert and Mr. Cagney are buried, were at the back, sheltered by bushes, whose thick branches stretched out far overhead. The front of the graveyard had a low stone wall that ran parallel with the sloping village street. There were two or three whitewashed cottages directly across the street from the graveyard. The new church, where we went to second Mass on Sundays, was at the top of the street; it had seven or eight steps up on either side, a railing surrounding it, with statues of Saint Kevin and Saint Bridget on piers behind the railing. Below the steps was a tarmac car park, and across the street grew a long row of horse chestnut trees.

Next to the graveyard was Powers public house, which my father and Dan visited for an hour or two every Sunday after Mass. Powers was freshly painted blue and white. It had one large stained-glass window that faced the street, and a crack ran from one corner of the glass to the other; a strip of tape covered the crack inside. Every half-hour Leo Power ran out and swept the clean dust and the litter from the footpath into the channel. Next to Powers was a small grocery, with cracked and dirty white paint—a faded Bird's Custard sign over the door. This grocery went through different owners, and my father and mother didn't do business in there because one time my mother found mouse droppings in the rice my father had bought.

—I'm off, going down the street for a bit, Nora, are you right, Dan, said my father to my mother, as we made our way out of the church pew on Sundays.

—Try not to be too long, Mike. The children get hungry, she said, while smoothing her hand down the wrinkles on the tail of his Sunday coat.

My mother held my hand; I watched my father and Dan go with the crowd, into the church porch: the women wearing their Sunday coats, gloves, hats or head scarves, and the freshly shaven, red-faced men raising their Sunday caps to the women; all walked slowly, nodding their heads and smiling, shaking hands and touching hands, while leaning toward one another to inquire in lulled voices how everything was at home, how the cattle were, dipping their fingers one last time into the font, the holy water dripping from their fingertips and glistening on the tiled church porch, then out the front double doors to the churchyard.

Grand. Thank you. That sermon was a bit long. The same one, too, that he gave last Sunday, only a few different words, and the very same one he gave this Sunday last year, God bless him. But sure things don't change that much anyway and it won't do us a bit of harm to hear it again, I suppose. He is indeed up in years. We'll have a new one soon, or so I heard anyway from the housekeeper. Them children get lovelier every Sunday, Nora. Grow up another little bit every week, they do. And you turn them out so well. The lovely green jumpers and the white ankle socks and the grand sandals on them. Yes, indeed, that one's the spit of you, Jack. She looks more like her father's people every day. That one, Kate, yes, Nora. God knows who the little one looks like. Mary, oh, after her aunt, of course. I don't know one of those girls from the other. That indeed was an unusually cold night last week.

My father smiling, as he pulled his cap on in the churchyard, blinking in the sunlight, making his way to the steps, but obliged to stop and have a quick shake-hands with a neighbor, and my brother, who I couldn't see against the crowd, holding my father's hand.

That's the worst government we ever had. Hates the small farmer. They all do, those people in Dublin. Less said the better about all of them. What good will it do? Which one of them did you say now this was again, Nora?

My father and Dan vanishing down the steps.

In Powers they sat at the bar next to John Hogan and Rome Kelly, whose real name was Larry. Other men sat on the stools next to them, men from the village of Kilroan and from up around Conway's hill, which was at the opposite end of the parish from where we lived. The older men drank pints of Guinness; porter or stout, they called it, and, like my father, they smoked unfiltered Players Navy Cut and Sweet Afton. The younger men drank pints of Smidwicks and Harp and smoked filtered Major and Carroll's.

Dan sat on the barstool with the men, his long skinny legs dangling and swinging, far too short to reach the leg rest. The men joked with my brother about drinking and smoking; they made sly, but not vulgar, remarks about women, and when they had a few pints inside of them, they poked fun at Rome, who had never married; they told him he had no idea what he was missing, but in case he wanted to know again, it was what life was all about, even if half of the time it wasn't worth all the burdens, the misery that came along with it. Rome would turn his back on them; he'd lay his hand on Dan's head, ask him how school was going, if he had intentions of becoming a farmer like our father; and, if he did, to not worry about it, for there were many worse ways to make a living; he'd buy my brother a bottle of lemonade and a packet of Jacob's Marietta biscuits.

While my father and Dan were trying to escape the crowd in the churchyard, Aunt Mary, my father's sister (there were only the two of them) was walking through the crowd, in search of my mother. Aunt Mary always waited for my father to leave before appearing—the two of them had not spoken to each other for many years, but my mother and Aunt Mary were great friends and they chatted together after Mass every Sunday.

My aunt Mary had the reputation of being one of the best-dressed women at Mass.

—Jackie O. and Grace Kelly herself couldn't beat you, Mrs. Nash, the blacksmith's wife, used to say to her in the churchyard, and my aunt, turning from her, would reply impiously, Well, I try my best, and we all must try to do that much at least, May.

My mother greeted my aunt with a kiss on the cheek. They began their Sunday chat by saying a few words about the past week's weather, and when they started into what they called serious talk— the kind us children were not meant to hear—Kate, Mary, and I sneaked off to the graveyard.

—Say a prayer for the dead, you devils! Don't use bad language and don't behave like barbarians! Come home to me when I call ye!

These were the instructions my mother shouted after us, then immediately turned to my aunt and their conversation. We were down the steps by this time, having slipped easily through the thinning crowd, and we ran down the street, then over the graveyard wall, ran, cheering, through the uncut grass, around the old and new gravestones, to the bushes at the back, where we reached up and dragged the branches down, the teeming white petals on the blossoms falling around us, as the branches sprang back up—and, in autumn, we plucked bundles of haws from the same branches, shoved the haws into our mouths, then spit the stems and the stones out. The haws had a nutty, wild taste; their flesh tasted sweet and their red skin was tough to chew and sour on the tongue.

When we were done with the trees, we played hide-and-seek behind the gravestones, and when we tired of this, we ran through the graveyard and sat, breathless, on the stone wall, and watched down the street at the men going in and out of Powers and the women coming to and from the grocery. We waved at the passing cars and saluted the old men on their bicycles.

How're the lads. Tell your mother and father I was mad asking for them.

We gawked at the attached cottages across the street, with their lace-curtained windows and, outside on their windowsills, the blooming red geraniums growing out of brown pots, marveling at how strange it would be to live in one of those cottages, where people you didn't fully know walked past your window every day, drove cars and cycled bikes up and down the street, and to walk out of your front door and step onto a cement footpath, with the grocery, school, church, graveyard, and public house only a few steps from you. We were waiting for our mother to call us, and when she did, we jumped off the wall and ran screeching up the street.

By this time of the day, the churchyard was empty of people and cars.

My father used to park the Ford Anglia under the row of horse chestnut trees, the front facing down the street. The four of us sat into the back and waited for him and Dan. My mother did not speak then, but took off her scarf and slipped the hairpins from her black hair and put them back again in the same place; she put her scarf back on, knotted it tightly, raising her head high to watch the crest of the street through the front windshield. I sat next to her, against the door, the backs of my legs sticking to the shiny worn leather, where the white stuffing peeked through in places. Kate and Mary slept on the other side of her, their cheeks flushed from play and their black fringes falling thick and damp over their foreheads, their pink ribbons touching their eyebrows. My father cut their hair in a boyish fashion, much like the Beatles' haircuts in 1964.

Finally, we'd hear the laughter, the voices of the men swarming out of Powers. They said a few more words, then shook hands with one another and hurried off in different directions. I watched through the windshield, closing my right eye so that the ornament on the hood was at the center of my vision; and, to the left of the ornament, my father and brother would suddenly rise up at the crest of the street, my father holding Dan's right hand, the *Sunday Independent* sticking awkwardly out of my father's left coat pocket. Dan held a brown paper bag in his free hand, with a block of HB ice cream and wafers in it. They marched boldly toward us, the horse chestnut trees to their right, the church high up and to their left, the two of them dwarfed and darkened by the shapeless and tangled shadows—and my mother took her arm from around my shoulder, sat up and shook my sisters awake, while Dan opened the car door for my father.

—Hold on now, back there. Take it easy, my father would say, as he fumbled his way in. —I don't want to hear a word from any of you in the back.

I pressed my hands between my thighs and said good-bye to Saint Kevin and Saint Bridget, telling them I'd see them next Sunday, if this was God's will. Dan sat into the passenger seat, which fell backwards a little when he did. It took my father a few minutes to get the key in the ignition, adjust his seat, fix his cap in the mirror, tilting it down and to the left, bless himself and say a prayer, then look into the mirror again to eye the four of us in the back, a roguish smile on his face.

—Are you still alive back there or what?

—Fine, all alive here, Mike, thank God, my mother said. —We need to hurry on now or the ice cream will melt. Drive easy.

He drove us the winding, dipping road home, and my mother kept an eye on his every move. —Drive carefully, can't you, I tell you, we'll be home soon enough, Mike Carmody. She'd lean forward and tap Dan on the shoulder, —Are you watching your father and the road? She'd bless herself, her hand trembling as she lifted it to her forehead, and every Sunday, as we neared the Ryans' house, their hens ran along the road before and by the side of the car. My father pressed the brake and beeped the horn; the hens stumbled sideways and were swallowed by the long headland grass, and my father raised his cap and laughed, and we laughed along with him, but my mother never laughed; no, she frowned and warned my father to mind the road and be frightfully careful not to kill a neighbor's hen.

—Aha, it's only a cod, woman, for God's sake, said my father— and he raised his cap and laughed again. —Limerick and Tipp, Nora. Need to hurry on now, Missus, so I'll be in time for the start of the hurling match.

—Limerick and Tipp, Da, Dan laughed along with my father.

—Time enough for that old match of yours, said my mother. —There'll be another one next Sunday and the Sunday after. These children are hungry; they haven't had a bite to eat since early this morning.

My father gripped the steering wheel, one hand atop the other, at the twelve-o'clock position. I watched the back of his neck, red and furrowed from weather, and I smelled his safe and lovely Sunday smell of porter, cigarettes, Lifebuoy soap, and sweat.

We rounded Ahern's bend. The car slipped into the headland and the long grass whipped against the door of the car. The three of us giggled; then Kate hopped up and pulled at Dan's red curls. —I smell something, roll down your window, Dunce, will you.

But he never did, not even once.

—You be a good girl, Kate, you'll have your dinner soon. Your father needs to mind the road, my mother warned my sister.

Nearing Hanley's bend, my favorite part of the journey home, I sat up to watch the long line of rhododendrons that grew high up on the embankment; their petals shook like a long line of colorful flags. My father slowed the car and opened the window.

—This world, he sighed the Sunday after he told us about Albert Cagney. —This world, indeed. —Don't I well remember the day Albert come home from the war, nearly over fifty years ago now, didn't he come up to the rock field in Conway's hill where I was paling, and I only a young fella and Albert come through the fields and brung me an armful of rhododendrons that he pulled from right there, came to see me he did before Mr. Cagney even, brung them to me first.

My mother retied her scarf. —God rest that poor boy, she muttered.

—And how old did you say Albert was then, Da? said Dan.

—That boy was no more than twenty-one when he came home.

—And how old was you then, Da? Kate said.

—Aha, sixteen, I was, only a young fella, Katie.

—How long was he in the home, Da? Mary said.

—Well, now, child, there was a gun—

—A gun, Da, a gun! I sat up and shouted.

—A gun, what kind of gun, like the cowboys, Da? What kind! Kate swung on the back of Dan's seat, and Dan shouted at her to stop or he'd beat the living daylights out of her.

—Mike! For God's sake, Mike! My mother elbowed my sisters and me aside, and pushed her face and shoulders between my father and Dan. —Can't you watch the road, Michael Carmody, or you'll get all of us killed dead, and what in God's name are you thinking! Don't be telling the children such lies, frightening them, I tell you, and Dan and Mary after just coming down from Communion. Can't you leave well enough alone! Leave all that where it is!

Drops of her spittle landed low on the windshield and on the small Saint Christopher statue mounted on the dashboard between my father and my brother.

I bowed my head. All went quiet. The car engine droned. The exhaust rattled. My mother twisted her face away from us; she was squeezing her handbag; her knuckles were white.

—Aha, listen to your mother, and don't be listening to me at all, my father eventually spoke. —I'm only joking the lot of ye, lads. It's a great gas altogether, God forgive me. And when people start to reminisce, faith, what they do is start to make things up—but that blasted match must be on by now, it must be, God knows!

My father's shoulders shook with excitement; the car picked up speed.

—Drive on, Da, drive on, Dan laughed.

—Dan's a dunce, Kate sang.

—Dan's a dunce. Dan's a dunce, Mary and I sang.

—Tell them to stop their blaguarding, Nora, my father said.

—Stop the blaguarding, can't you, and listen to your father, she said. —Ye'd wear the patience of Job.

The car swayed over and back; then a few minutes later it turned right, onto the short potholed path, where our house was at the end.

—Thank God we're home, at last, my mother smiled down at us in the backseat. —And you lads in the front didn't miss too much of that match at all, she said cheerfully.

—Home at last, thank God. We are, another grand adventure, Nora, ha! said my father.

He began to whistle, and Kate, Mary, Dan, and I whistled along with him.

On the way home from Mass two Sundays later my mother said that when school was over she was sending me to Conway's hill to keep Aunt Mary company for a bit. My father began to hum "Sean South from Garryowen"; his head moved over and back and he held his hands steady and open a few inches above the steering wheel. Dan reached over and gripped the steering wheel.

—Send him off tomorrow, woman, sure there's no need to wait, my father said. —Send the whole lot of them off and give us a bit of peace. None of them learning much there at school by the looks of it, and it looks like with the mouths they have on them they won't be honoring us by being priests and nuns either.

—Hands back onto the steering, Da, Dan said.

My mother leaned forward and gently squeezed my brother's shoulder. —Enough of your talk now, Mike.

Kate, Mary, and I giggled and poked at each other behind our mother's back.

My father put his hands back on the wheel.

—Fine job, Dan. What would I do without you, said my mother, and sat back.

—This world. This world, my father repeated sadly. —I'd rather have been born in the desert myself; I'd have been an awful lot better off raised in a tent than under a thatch roof. The weather would have been a lot better, God knows, ha! Of course, you can't make much hay in the sand, Nora, but you yourself might be able to in an oasis.

—Aren't we blessed to be born where we are, my mother said.

—What's going to become of that young fella there beside you or any of the rest of them; you might be right in saying only God knows.

—Dan'll be a farmer, Kate said. —He can barely write his own name, Da.

—You're just jealous 'cause you can't sit up here, Dan said.

—These children are hungry is what it is, and that ice cream makes them mad. I'm at the end of my tether with all of you, my mother said.

We were passing the rhododendrons, and I sat up. My father slowed the car; he rolled his window down and inhaled deeply. The gorgeous smell of the flowers came into the car.

—Better this than you, Dunce, Kate sat up and laughed.

—God bless him, no matter what way he left us, no matter who or what owned him, and all he did—you couldn't keep him out of Heaven for too long, my father lifted his cap in a salute.

—Yes, said my mother shortly. —Jack will get to see now where that tragic boy lived, God rest him—hurry on now, Mike, before the ice cream melts.

—Was Albert a farmer, Da? Kate said.

—Not at all, Katie. Albert was a soldier and his father was a tailor.

—Did he fight the English? Mary said.

—Well, Mary, Albert had what you would call courage, but not too many around did agree with him going off to fight that war at all; listening to Redmond, they said he was, whose own brother died out there, but they would have been nice to Albert because of Mr. Cagney—I maintain that Albert was more brave than any of them begrudgers. And they did away with all the leaders of the Rising and then they tried to conscript the whole lot of us, God's sake—

—Keep straight, Da, keep straight, Dan said.

—We'd be dead in the ditch years ago, young fella, like so many were, only for yourself, my father said.

—Dan's going to be a farmer and marry a nun, Kate sang.

—There you are now, Katie. To think at my age I could have brought such a clever one as yourself into the world. You have grand talk for a girl. You didn't pick it up from your mother, that's for sure.

Kate laughed and pushed her face into my father's neck and my father tilted his head back to her.

—I'm going to marry Rome Kelly, Da, she said.

My mother reached out and pulled my sister back into the seat.
—Oh, for God's sake, Katie, shut your trap, can't you—

—You'd be marrying the very best, Katie, my father said. —The best friend I ever had, met him the first day of school. I know Rome better than I know myself.

—Auntie Mary said Rome is an Italian, Mary said.

—No, she said Rome's a Jew, Kate said.

—Did not say that, Mary said.

—He's not the pope, Kate said.

—The pope can't get married. Ye don't even know that much, Dan said.

—I'd have married a good few years earlier I could have had another few bright sparks like these ones, Nora O'Neill.

—I can't believe it. Where do the lot of ye find such talk, my weary mother said.

—I'll marry a nun, too, I raised my voice.

—You shut your mouth, or you won't be going anyplace, my mother scowled and slapped me on the shoulder. —You're as bad as the rest of them.

—You'll find a nun on Conway's hill. I heard one's been living up there for ages, my father threw his head back and laughed; his seat shook.

—It's the same thing every Sunday, my mother said.

—And I thought I was improving, mind you, Nora, my father said, —and 'twas the world that was getting worse.

—Go on with you, and your devilment, my mother said.

—Dunce, Mary said.

—Dunce, Kate said.

—Dunce. Dunce. Dunce, Kate, Mary, and I sang.

—Jealous. Jealous. Jealous 'cause you can't sit up here, Dan turned around in the seat and waved the brown paper bag before us.

—They're very clever, Nora, all right, the lovely vocabulary and the grand manners they all have.

—Thank God I only have to hear it from you on a Sunday, my mother said.

═══

—I'll get to walk down the boreen and see where Albert and Mr. Cagney lived. I can't wait to see it, I said with great excitement, sitting across from my mother at the kitchen table.

—Oh, there's probably not a thing of that old place left, Jack. But you'll have a grand time. Your aunt Mary is flesh and blood, no matter what your father does or does not say to her, but he knows that himself. That's just the way his people are.

It was an hour after dinner, which on Sundays we ate after Mass. My father was snoring in his bus seat. His hair was flattened down by the shape of his cap, his head dropped into his chest. The wireless was turned down low, but I could still hear Michael O'Heir's thrilling voice, the recurring cheers of the crowd at the hurling match. Kate, Mary, and Dan were shouting in the meadow beyond the barn; they were playing cowboys and Indians.

My mother folded her arms across her breasts, and watched through the door the swallows and the jackdaws flying down. —I'll miss your help, Jack, she sniffled, her eyes filling with tears. —I'll miss your company terribly when you go away.

Her tears baffled me, and I told her I was only going to be gone for two weeks.

—Oh, I know it only too well, Jack—but you don't be listening to your father and his talk about Albert going away. That upset your aunt today when I told her he'd told ye about him, but this will be the first time any of you have left me, she said, her tears falling into her apron. —Oh, what's wrong with me. I shouldn't be talking to a boy of your age like this. You not knowing a thing about it.

She pressed a corner of the apron to her eyes, and turned her head from me. —Too young you are, Jack, too young to know what's been going on in the world since Adam, but you will one day leave here, too, and you won't come back either. You can go places, you can, Jack.

The tears on her cheeks made me want to go around the table to her, but she seemed too far away from me; it was the way she had spoken those words.

—I don't want to go away anyplace, I told her earnestly.

—But you will, son. I know well that you will, she said, and picked up the corner of the apron again. —But we don't have to worry about any of it now, Jack. There'll be time enough to worry about it when the time comes.

My father muttered something in his sleep, and we immediately turned our attention to him. My mother rose and turned off the radio. —Jack, she said, her voice normal again, will you look at the state of that fire. Go out and bring in a few blocks, and before you go out to the meadow to the lads make sure that the cattle are all right.

———————

That September, when the hay was home in the barn, and the after-grass was thickening in the meadows, they took her into the hospital; this was the first time. The ambulance arrived in the yard and two men in blue uniforms and a nurse in white stepped out. Limerick City people, smiling as best they could, bashful around country people, like we were with them, only worse. They inquired how all of us were keeping and told us how lucky we were to live in so much quietness, and our mother would be back home soon and be far better off into the bargain. My father stood between the two front pillars of the hay barn; a cigarette hung from the corner of his mouth, his head down and his hands pushed deep into his pockets. My mother and he had been together in the room for an hour before this, with the door closed. I had sneaked up to the door and heard their whispering, then her sobs, and when I heard that sound from her, I turned from the door and ran into the yard, where the swallows and the hens went mad, through the barn and out to the meadow. Dan leaned against the pillar, to my father's right, where the pony was tied. Kate wept and held my mother's right hand. Mary wept and held her left. My mother stopped at the back door of the ambulance. She fixed her hands on their shoulders, and slowly took the three steps up. She wore her navy blue Sunday coat, her black scarf, and her black Sunday shoes. I had polished her shoes the night before and I stood in the doorway of our house and watched them crossing the yard to the ambulance. I was upset about them becoming dirty.

The ambulance sped out the path. It swayed from side to side, because of the potholes, and its roof broke the lower branches of the bushes. The broken leaves spinning in the cloud of dust and exhaust fumes, in the rays of brilliant sunlight through the bushes. I sat in the path, in the quiet evening, and I called and called her name. I promised her that all of us would be better behaved, no more bad talk in the car on Sunday, making a joke of one another and of the neighbors.

In October and November the blocks groaned beneath the flames in the hearth. There was a small pile of dirty socks, underpants, and shirts under the window of Dan's and my bedroom. Frost hardened on the panes. I could not see out. The birds went quiet.

When I was alone in the house, I sneaked into their room and pulled open the door of their wardrobe to see once again that all of her clothes were gone, except on one wooden hanger, the light blue summer dress with prints of small white and red flowers. My aunt had given the dress to her, but my mother had never worn it, maybe because my father didn't like it: *You couldn't wear a thing like that around here. In London or New York, you could get away with it. Why did she waste her money on them things?* The dress smelled of dampness and mothballs. It had a wide V-neck collar, a visible bust, and a line of four tiny, round cloth-covered buttons, with matching cloth hooks that ran from the neck down to a tightening waist. I bit down on the buttons and pressed the collar to my mouth and nose. I took off my jumper and shirt and ran the dress along my chest and belly and under my armpits. I dropped my trousers to my ankles, and shoved my underpants down, and I pushed the dress between my legs, across my backside, up and down over my hard mickey till I came. Then I pressed the dress to my eyes, and my tears soaked into it and the flowers turned brighter—clear, like they were floating in water. I went to their dust-covered back window, next to their bed, the blankets my father had not turned back in months, the shape of a head crushing one pillow only; beyond the window, the bare alder branches hardened against the icy breeze; and I wiped the dust from the pane with my fingers and held the wet and stained dress up against the gray light, watching through it, into that strange world.

In December, above the hay barn, the sharp and naked poplar branches stung. A Christmas went by. I pressed my body to the damp wall. Dan slept. He seemed all right. They all did. It was only me; it was the wintertime—a lack, a want.

My sisters must have done the housework. They must have washed the clothes in the tub in the yard and draped them along the crane over the fire at night and hung them on the line behind the house, when the day was dry. They fed me and my father and brother. They boiled the kettle over the fire and filled the hot-water bottles, when it was close to bedtime. My father and brother milked and fed the winter cows; they fed the cows in calf and cleaned out their house; morning and evening, in the dark, they walked into the top fields with a flash lamp to fodder the cattle. I followed them into the field. The beam from my father's flashlight swam back and forth along the hard and barren ground. I wanted to hear him breathing, and I wanted to hear Dan and he talk about which one of the cows would calve first, whether it would be a bull or a heifer, hear them go on about the future. My father took the milk to the creamery in the pony and common car; he brought the paper home, read it for hours, without saying a word, sitting in his bus seat, at the hearth. We all fed the hens and the sow. I helped them. They made you keep going. You had to do your jobs.

The ambulance brought her home in late February; on its way in the path, its wheels smashed the ice in the potholes, and the trapped water slopped out, then trickled back in. She sat at the table, and did not take her blue coat off. I sat in the chair next to hers, watching up at her. She did not once look down at me, or say my name. Her knuckles were too white when she reached her shaking fingers out for the cup of tea, which she held to her mouth but did not drink, even though she complained more than once to my aunt about how watery the tea was in the hospital ward. She did not eat the slice of Madeira cake on the plate before her. Mrs. Ryan and her husband were sitting there; Mrs. Ryan had baked the Madeira cake; it was a lovely cake. Rome and John Hogan and my father drank mugs of tea. They smoked and laughed, and their smoke drifted forever across the sun-lit table, out the front door to the yard, where the sparrows and the swallows and jackdaws swooped down and picked at the hens' feed. Kate sat on Rome's lap; Mary sat on John Hogan's; Tommy was outside with the cattle. My father said to John Hogan that things were never better; he couldn't ask for more. My aunt talked quietly to the Ryans. John Hogan told us all to pay attention to him, and he told the joke Paddy Crosbie told one Sunday on the radio.

The horse fell down into a hole and broke his leg, said the boy.

And what'd they do about that? said the man.

They'd to shoot him, what else could they do but put him down, said the boy.

They'd to shoot him in the hole, I suppose? said the man.

Not at all, they shot him in the head, said the boy.

John Hogan jumped out of his chair and ran laughing, around the table, his huge and hairy arms, like they were wings, gathering Kate, Mary, and me together. Everyone was laughing. My father said to give that man more tea and cake so that we might hear another good one from him. Rome was smiling when he turned to my mother to tell her that she looked grand and the worst was over, and God was good and the winter was nearly behind us, and the spring would ar-rive soon, and we'd all hear the cuckoo again, and the ground would soften and the new calves would be born and the birds would sing, the bluebells and buttercups and daffodils grow out of the meadows and fields, the leaves come back—hide us all from the world, thank God. She did her best to smile at Rome, but her mouth and eyes kept slipping sideways. She was too thin. The shoulders of her coat sagged. I remember thinking that it was the two ambulance men and the nurse who took her left breast away.

Those Sundays years ago in the graveyard, when I broke the blossoms and ate the haws with my sisters, I don't ever remember us searching for Albert's and Mr. Cagney's graves; nor do I recollect ever seeing the gravestone of my father's parents, and not for one second did it cross my mind that my own father and mother and Aunt Mary would in time be buried there, shaded in this world by the bushes, along with the rest of the Carmodys, next to the tailor Mr. Cagney and his son, Albert.

The older gravestones then were already worn thin and smooth, and many of the names had eroded from them. Some of the stones were covered in white-gray flakes that had the brittleness of cobwebs, and Kate, Mary, and I tore the flakes away, and sometimes we'd pull the ivy from a gravestone, but we were not looking for anything. We were only country children, playing in a village graveyard, waiting for our mother to call us, and we did not connect those worn and forgotten stones to the men laughing and talking in the public house, to the women who talked in the churchyard, the grocery, and the street. The name Cagney would not have meant anything to us, and if we did find the name Carmody on a stone, we would not have taken any great notice of it. There were a couple of families of Carmodys around Kilroan, and we all were related in some way, which, in itself, was no great consequence. It might very well have been one of the three of us who wiped the names of Cagney and Carmody from one of those stones; innocently we might have, before we sat on the wall to watch the whitewashed cottages and wave to the people in the street, before our mother called us.

—Children, she'd shout from the crest of the street. —Children, will you please hurry on. The day's not getting any younger and I have a million things to do before dark.

I was twenty years old when she died in the Regional hospital, in Limerick City. (My father died two years before, Aunt Mary six months after him.) I had been working for three years as an apprentice barman in Dublin City; in one more year I would become a professional, and my wages and pension went up then. I had procured what my parents and the grown-ups called a job for life, and to them, nothing surpassed a job for life. These were the nineteen eighties; it was hard to find work, and young men and women were immigrating again. Every day the Troubles was grim news: Prisoners in the H Block were smearing their own shit on their cell walls, starving themselves to death, and we said our prayers, read the papers, called names, took sides, but life went on, went backwards and forwards like it always does—

Save for a car, Jack. Put a bit aside for a house, Jack. Find a nice girl to marry, Jack. These were their mandates, and to say to them I was not content with what I was doing, what I had, would mean I was selfish and ungrateful, and I didn't want to be seen as or feel like that kind of a person. So I kept my mouth shut. I was never the sort to upset anyone.

Dan was living at home. He continued farming, which had changed from dairy to the raising of dry cattle, all to do with the E.E.C., which we once called the Common Market. Dan had inherited the farm and Conway's hill. He had built a new house and leveled the house we grew up in; the new house was a bungalow, with large windows and a stained-glass front door; it had a Stanley range, an electric cooker, a fridge, carpets, a color TV, a large toilet and bathroom, the telephone; a *modern* house, was what my mother and the older people called it. My brother had married a local girl, Helen

Ahern, who had brought some land with her. Mary and Kate were nurses, working in different hospitals in London.

On weekends in July and August I'd take the train from Dublin to Limerick City and spend the afternoons at the hospital with my mother. Dan and his wife visited during the week. My mother wore the faded pink nightgown that had the embroidered primroses and buttercups around the collar. The nightgown looked very out of place in the sterile bright light of the hospital ward. For most of my life, I had seen it draped across the headboard of the bed in the old house, in that room where the leaves of the alder tree, in spring and summer, swept over and back across the windowpane.

It was a fine summer, and I used to wheel my mother outside, to a quiet place underneath the trees, at the back of the hospital lawn, where we'd talk and watch the people walk in and out of the hospital. I crossed my legs on the grass, next to her chair, and I smoked and crushed the butts into the ground.

—Jack, do you think my garden is all right? she asked.

—Dan and the Missus are taking good care of it, Ma, don't be worrying about it, you'll be back in it soon enough, I said.

—I will, of course—there's so many have had it harder than we do, Jack, and you see it here before you and you don't have to travel too far from here to find more of it, and here am I only worrying about my garden.

—You're grand, Ma.

—You're saying your prayers for all of them, you are, Jack.

I didn't say anything. I watched the hospital doors opening and closing; and after a while, I turned to watch her, but who am I fooling, for on those Saturday afternoons I wondered at her, as if she were an apparition, and when she spoke, I tried to remember her every word, for I thought then I could, and I watched her hollow chest rise and fall and I watched for a flicker in her eyes, listened to her breath, and I wanted to ask her, but I never did: Are you afraid? I used to repeat those three words to myself coming down on the train, when I was made happy, seduced by the lovely afternoon countryside beyond the window, the voices and the laughter of those in the seats around me, but when I sat on the darkened train going away from her, I cried, cried then, when no one could see me, and when I sat down on the grass beside her, my eyes saw the long bony fingers clutching the rosary beads, the Padre Pio scapulars, the Saint Martin De Poores medal, and the medal from Knock hanging on a chain around her neck; Christ, but she was a fortress, every corner you can think of covered—

I stood and arranged the blanket around her shoulders. I pulled the wheelchair back a few inches when the sunlight was too direct— it's not as though she would ever complain, or even mention it. She shivered, though, when I touched her, or when I moved the chair. She was in great pain, which the nurses told me was from the chemo, but she'd never say to me she was in pain: I saw it in her withered face, her darkened, sunken eyes, in her fleshless arms, the cautious footsteps, and the breathless and faltering voice. She'd just look down at me and smile, as though it were an ordinary day, then raise her face to the July sunlight, and proclaim, This day, I'm cured, Jack. I'm new again. I'm finally over it. I'm beyond all of this at last.

She'd gag and spit up whatever was inside of her, into a plastic cup.

—That's the last of it, Jack. It's all up now, thank God and his blessed mother. There's not a thing of it left, but let me tell you this, before you have to leave me.

Her father's name was Jack, and I'm named after him. He owned a grocery in the next parish, at a desolate crossroads, about five miles on the other side of Kilroan village, right on the Tipperary border. He had traveled to the funeral with my mother that day in a pony and trap car. My mother had heard my father's name mentioned before this day, but she had never seen him, and in spite of the fact that he was more than twenty years older than she, she instantly found him handsome. The best-looking man at Mr. Cagney's funeral, she told me. My father was tall and slim; his red hair was oiled and parted at the side; his shoulders were broad. A strong man, from working all those years on the land, and he would remain like that. This afternoon my father wore the suit Mr. Cagney had made for him years back.

Five years before Mr. Cagney's death, my father had left Conway's hill after his own mother had died. He was hired on to milk cows and do farm work for a farmer with many acres, outside the village of Oola. It was at the time of his mother's death and his going away that Aunt Mary came back from Dublin to be with their father, who eventually sold off six of the family's twelve acres, and split the money equally between my father and Aunt Mary. My grandfather then willed the remaining six acres and the cottage they lived in to Aunt Mary.

That afternoon of Mr. Cagney's funeral my father had cycled the eight miles from Oola to the funeral. His and Aunt Mary's father had died the year before. Aunt Mary lived alone on Conway's hill, never having married.

My father happened to be standing a few feet away from my mother, near the gate to the graveyard. Down the street, John Hogan and Rome Kelly stood amongst a crowd of men, who were waiting for Leo Power's father, Stephen, to open up for business. My father had not seen his friends in a long time, and they were excited to be together again, were in a hurry to duck into Powers and have a chat, smoke a few cigarettes and drink a few pints before milking time. My mother was waiting for her own father. Their horse and trap car was tied under the horse chestnut trees up in front of the old church. (The church I went to as a boy was built the year I was born.) Many horse and trap cars were tied there, and the horses stretched their necks out, as far as their tethers would allow, and ripped at the coarse grass that grew unchecked around the trees.

My father gripped his cap, and took those few careful steps toward her, telling her that Mr. Cagney was a fine God-fearing man, the best tailor God ever put breath in, and his son was his boyhood friend and neighbor, but he died all of a sudden years and years ago. My mother said she had heard Mr. Cagney was indeed a skilled tailor, but she had never heard mention of his son. She was wearing her long green woolen coat, knotted at the waist with a wide belt. She was shorter than he was; she was thick in the hips and chest. The O'Neills had a few acres behind the grocery, where they kept a few cows, and it was my mother who milked them, while her father managed the counter. She wore a dark headscarf and gloves that afternoon. All the women at the funeral did.

—Beg your pardon, Miss, my father said to her, —who would you be now?

The weather was mild. The bushes the men gathered underneath at the back of the graveyard were abundant with leaves.

—That's my father over there. My mother nodded at my grandfather, who was standing under the bushes, talking with the men, smoking his pipe, and having a mouthful of whiskey along with the rest of them.

—That's Jack O'Neill the grocer, said my father.

—Yes, that's my father, my mother spoke shyly, glancing up at my father. She thought his slicked wavy red hair was brilliant.

Jack O'Neill always wore a wide-brimmed felt hat. He was tall and thin, stylish in his suit behind the grocery counter. Rejoiced in it, was what my mother told me one Saturday. He had attended Mr. Cagney's funeral because down through the years Mr. Cagney had made all of his black suits, the only suit color he ever wore at Mass and behind the grocery counter, with a white, collarless shirt underneath. He was a widower with many years. My mother was his only child. His wife died giving birth to her.

Jack O'Neill and the men under the trees that afternoon agreed that the tailor was gone straight to Heaven, where he rightly belonged, for he was an honest man who had used his talents well, and although he was inclined to overcharge at times, he did also suffer much on earth, and they laughed and said that he and Albert were at last together again and the two of them could sew and mend all the clothes they wanted for all the people in the village of Kilroan who had gone there, and down through the years many had gone there, they would have said, watching John Joe Dillon shovel the clay back into the grave, and it would have been repeated later by them, when they stood at the bar and sat at the back tables in Powers.

My aunt Mary was at the funeral of her neighbor, too. She never told me this, nor did my mother, but she was definitely there. She would have stood in the street, talking to the people she knew all her life in the village. Her neighbors Ned Franklin and Mick Russell from Conway's hill would have stood with the men who were waiting for Powers to open. After the funeral, my aunt would have wandered over under the trees to kneel at her own parents' grave.

My father had saved the money from the six acres his own father sold on Conway's hill. He wanted to leave the farmer in Oola, who was overworking him and not paying him enough for it, but what my father really wanted was to get his own piece of land, to marry and start into his own life. He and my mother did not court for long. I don't believe people did back then. If you started courting, the chances were that you would marry that person, when land came available, or you might emigrate, and many did; they didn't have any other option. My father knew how the land, the cows, and the weather worked. He missed the neighborhood and friends he knew on Conway's hill. He was over fifty the spring Mr. Cagney died. My mother was in her mid to late twenties. Above all else, they valued their duty to God, to church and country, which was that they marry and bring Catholic children into the world.

It was Jack O'Neill, who died when I was four or five, who helped my father buy the small farm where my brother and sisters and I were raised, two miles from the village of Kilroan. I was born into an old white stone house, with a gray-slated roof. Every house then had an open fire and a blower. This was how the houses were heated and the baking was done. In our house, there were two rooms off the kitchen. Dan and I slept together in one room, Kate and Mary in the other. There was another bigger room behind the fire; this was my parents' bedroom. The thirteen acres surrounding the house were wet in spring and winter, but in summer the meadows gave good return with hay, and in August, following harvest, the after-grass was plentiful and delicious, and this was the time of year the cows were happiest and gave the most milk.

That land was better than the few rocky acres my father and Aunt Mary were born into on Conway's hill. So out of place it was for my grandfather to will the few acres left on Conway's hill to my aunt, so peculiar to put the girl before the boy in matters of land, or in any matter, but my grandfather wanted his daughter to come home from Dublin, where she had lived for many years, working as a secretary. She had left home because of Albert Cagney. They had courted, and she was mad about him and he was mad about her; madness, in love and rage, is the only word I'll ever know how to describe it.

The June morning I went to visit Aunt Mary, I had a paper bag under my arm, with a change of clothes that my mother had washed and ironed. I first walked through our two bottom fields, crossed the dyke, then over the ditch into Tommy Ryan's top fields. I walked quietly around his herd of grazing cows and into the Ryans' yard, which disturbed their sheepdog, Rex, who started barking, though he knew me well and ended up following me to the border of Ryans' land. After Ryans' there were two very large meadows, which were blocked off for hay. Next to them were more fields with herds of grazing cows. Well-worn paths crossed each field, and the paths led to gates I climbed over, or I crawled up and down through the higher parts in the ditches that had been cleared of briars, furze, and fencing, due to people crossing over in the same place year in and year out. As I got closer to Conway's hill, the fields were steeper, smaller, and rockier, the grass coarse and less abundant.

As the crow flies was what the old people called traveling through the fields, because the crow flew in a straight line, and across the fields was the more direct, the shortest route. I could have walked the winding road to Conway's hill, a roundabout way that would have taken over two hours. My father had told me that the steep boreen that started on the hill road and ended in my aunt's yard was nearly a mile long.

How happy I was that morning—a boy alone, walking past the grazing cows and the few horses, the grass thick with clover and daisies, bluebells and buttercups; insects buzzing around me, birds singing and calling to each other from every bush, the heat of the sun warming the back of my neck. I was delighted Kate and Mary, my father and Dan, were not with me, glad to be freed for a few weeks from their talk and the farm jobs that were never done; let Dan and Kate cheat and fight at rummy, was what I was thinking, when I stood tall on the ditch, saw and smelled the smoke from my aunt's chimney rise up in a straight line above the evergreen trees; let them cheat till the cows come home, thinking of all the times Mary and I implored upon them to stop and not to ruin another game, my father eventually having to raise his head from the paper and tell us harshly to quieten down or he'd put us outside for the night, my mother sitting across the fire from him, sewing, and not lifting her head to any of it.

Oh, the joyful look on my aunt's face the moment I saw her standing in her doorway. My mother and she had planned my visit in the churchyard the Sunday before, and my aunt had been watching out for me. She shaded her eyes and waved when she saw me walking through the evergreen trees; she cried out, —Is that yourself, Jack. You brought the fine day with you.

I came out of the trees and ran across her yard to her. She scratched my head, and pulled her fingers through my hair; then she gripped my shoulders, stroked my cheek, and I put my arms around her, pressed myself to her, then closed my eyes to the fragrant heat of her body. She had powdered her face, like she did on Sundays. Her eyes were bright blue, the same color as my father's, and she wore a youthful, crimson summer dress, though she was anything but a young woman at this time. Her short graying hair was neatly combed in the middle and cut high across her forehead. Her full lips shone with red lipstick.

She had an immense passion for brightly colored clothes: the long, pink overcoat, the white one, too, that she often wore to Mass, no matter the weather, as if to defy the muck and the rain and the dampness; a bright blue hat with plastic red roses; many corsets, jumpers, and blouses of all colors, which she never wore. Clothes patiently waiting for carefree times that did not then and never did exist. She had brought them back in chests from Dublin when she had returned after my grandmother's death years ago, and she kept those clothes in immaculate condition. More than once I'd heard my mother say in the cow house to my father that Aunt Mary took better care of her clothes than most people around here did of their children. My mother's voice was severe then, as she sat down to milk another cow. My father raised his head and began to whistle.

That evening, while my aunt boiled potatoes, cabbage, and bacon, she asked me to walk out and bring in two buckets of water from the pump at the base of the hill. Large and small white limestone rocks swelled out of the ground along the hill. Clumps of grass and moss grew along the rocks, and around them. I opened the gate in her yard, an enamel bucket in each hand, and I followed the path through the evergreen trees that surrounded her cottage. Beyond the trees, the path was dry and cracked from the sun. It led to the pump and then into Garvey's fields and in some roundabout way it led to the boreen that went down to the hill road. The Garveys did not live on Conway's hill anymore. They had left years before, but those fields would forever be known as Garvey's fields. One of the Garveys had married well. More than once, I heard my father talk about this to my mother at milking time, but I also overheard it from my aunt, my mother, and other women, in the churchyard after Mass.

There were a few cows and calves and two goats grazing not far from the pump. The animals were not my aunt's, but Ned Franklin's, one of the few people who still lived on the hill and my aunt's closest neighbor, an elderly man who gave her a few pounds every year and milk every day for letting him graze his cows and goats.

When I hung the first bucket on the spout of the pump and

pressed the creaking handle, I put my ear to the cold green metal and with each thrust of the handle I listened to the water rising from deep inside the rocky ground, icy water aching in the hollow tunnel as it surged upwards and then splashed with such force into the bucket that my boots and trousers were drenched. I let the handle go and took a few steps back and laughed and my laughter resonated along the rocks, and the goats and the cows and calves raised their heads and swung their tails briskly a few times before returning to their grazing. I had to walk slowly in with the full buckets, and some of the water splashed onto the path underneath the trees. A single pink rosebush grew from between the flagstones and clung to the whitewashed gable end wall. My aunt was singing inside. It was a song I had heard my mother sing, when she milked.

> I WISH I WAS IN SWEET DUNLOE
> AND SEATED ON THE GRASS
> AND BY MY SIDE A BOTTLE OF WINE
> AND ON MY KNEE A LASS.

I had never heard my aunt sing before and was surprised she had such a fine voice. The bacon smelled smoky and delicious.

—Come on in here, Jack, she called, when she heard me put the buckets down at the gable end. —Come in here and eat your dinner before it gets cold, and don't be killing yourself with work. I want to show you your bed. I put nice clean sheets down that I've had for years and years and never once had the chance to use them till this very day, but thank God I have them. I knew in the first place that he gave them to me for some reason.

I slept underneath the window, in a small room next to the kitchen, which was the room where my father and aunt slept when they were children. It was a cool, shaded room that the sun could not reach fully into, because of the evergreen trees across the yard. The wallpaper was a dull cream color and the floor was covered in red linoleum. Old photographs in elegant dusty frames hung along the wall, above an unused fireplace. A photograph of my parents' wedding hung there, the same one that was on the kitchen wall in my own home, next to the Sacred Heart and John F. Kennedy. There was an old table, covered with a fine layer of dust, in the middle of the room. An empty white egg bowl, on a doily, sat in the middle of the table.

I woke the next morning to the sound of my aunt and Ned Franklin's distant laughter, beyond the shut door. Rays of sunshine shone through the small window above me and the shadow of the evergreens stirred inside the window's shadow on the linoleum.

I sat naked on the edge of the bed, and cautiously held my toes above the linoleum, where the evergreen trees shifted and glimmered, like there was a pool below me. I wriggled my toes, watching across the room at an old dresser, pushed into the corner, with a stained oval mirror overhead, where my father would have combed his hair and fixed his tie, when he was my age, on his way out to school and to Mass, and the times the grandparents I never knew walked in and out of this room; the fire was lit back then in winter. Albert and Mr. Cagney ate in this room; many times, they did, on summer evenings they walked in from the path and sat at the table and drank tea and ate boiled eggs, with a sprinkling of salt and a lump of butter, and they ate my grandmother's bread, also smothered in butter, for there was no woman down at their place, and Mr. Cagney told stories about the ups and downs of people on the hill and in the village of Kilroan, and he never ceased complaining about the English, then the Black and Tans; he couldn't, till the day he died, understand them at all; such savages, thieves, and murderers, they all were, and the tailor never neglected to mention whose clothes he was mending, and he told them exactly where the holes were, made jokes about how those holes came about, also saying he had patched the garment so many times that at this stage it was all his, and he'd tell them who he had just measured for a suit this past week, and if he hadn't measured anyone, he complained that he and Albert were about to go hungry, but he often repeated that since our real father and mother, Adam and Eve, were sent out of the Garden of Eden, which was our real home, all of their descendants needed clothes, so thank God Eve had the courage to defy the man above and eat his apple. No life otherwise—in any case, when I came out of the room this first morning, Ned Franklin and my aunt were sitting opposite each other at the hearth, just as my mother and father did. My aunt sat on the right side, where the blower was. She had raked a nest of hot coals out of the fire, and laid the teapot on them. She and Ned Franklin drank mugs of tea; they chatted away, as though they had not seen each other in years, although they sat for hours there every day. My aunt had boiled him an egg in an old blackened saucepan that was now sitting at the edge of the fire, and she asked me if I wanted one. I had pulled a chair out from the kitchen table, and was lacing my boots. I thanked her, but said I'd wait until later to eat, that I had something on my mind.

—Is that so, Jack, said she in a rather surprised way.

—And how's young Carmody? Ned Franklin smiled at me.

—Fine, thanks, Mr. Franklin.

Ned Franklin was small, balding, and thin. He had a very red, weather-beaten face, and his eyes constantly wept. He wore a cap, like all the older men, and he had taken it off, just as they all did— took them off and said God bless, when they crossed the threshold of their own or a neighbor's house.

—Shake hands, young fella, Ned Franklin grinned, holding his hand out. I walked over and shook his hand. He held my hand, watched me up and down; then he gently dropped my hand, saying to my aunt I was a fine, healthy young fella, and he turned to me to ask how my father was keeping, for he hadn't seen him in a dog's age.

—He's fine, thank you, Mr. Franklin, I said.

—If you go down to Powers after second Mass, Ned, you'll see him all you like, with them other two, said my aunt.

They both laughed, my aunt smoothing out her freshly ironed apron.

—And what did you say was so pressing on your mind, Jack, she asked.

—I'm going to go for a walk down the boreen to see Albert's cottage.

—What business have you going down there for?

She spoke so crossly that I took a few steps back from the hearth, and Ned Franklin crossed his legs and leaned across the fire, toward my aunt. —Albert Cagney, ha! His anniversary must be around now, Mary, God rest him. I haven't thought about Albert since God knows how long. Sure he and Mike were the best of pals all them years back.

My aunt turned to me. —Jack, for God's sake. There's no cottage there anymore, and you'll only cut yourself on the stones and there are all them thistles and nettles and docleaves. Go for a walk out on the hill, if you're so mad for a walk, and see that Ned's cows and calves are fine. There should be the six of them and the three calves, and take an empty bucket from the gable end with you and bring in another bucket of water while you're at it.

She lifted the tea mug to her mouth and eyed Ned Franklin. He jerked his head toward the firewall, and I could not see his face. —Let him off down there, for God's sake, Mary, he's a fine strong young fella for his age and it's only natural for a young fella of his age to be curious.

My aunt took a deep breath. She laid her mug down in the hearth and picked up the tongs and began to gently poke the coals.

—But there's them thistles and nettles, and God knows what else, Ned, she said timidly, raising her face from the fire, laying the poker against the wall. —And how could I face the child's mother if he got hurt in any way. They'd never forgive me for that. Crucify me the two of them would, himself enjoy it very much.

—Aha, he's old enough, Mary, don't be worrying about him. Not a bit of harm will come of him, a fine strong young fella, as I said, and sure as you say yourself, all that's left of that place is weeds and a few stones.

My aunt was looking down at her apron, picking at threads I could not see.

—I don't know, Ned, she said. —I'd rather for him to go for a walk on the hill, where he'd be much safer, and I wouldn't have to be worrying about what might befall him if he goes off down there.

Ned Franklin didn't pay much attention to what my aunt had said, but turned to me, his eyes swelling with tears. —Gwan down there with you, young Carmody. Gwan with you. What's left of that place is at the gap in the ditch, after them blackberry bushes.

His sad green and crying eyes, tears falling for nothing onto the hearth that morning. He turned to my aunt, —The young fella's more like the other side. He's the dead spit of his mother, isn't he now, Mary.

My aunt smiled proudly at me, said I most certainly was. She nodded toward the door, and before I was out the door, Ned Franklin was telling her that his she-goat did not look the best on his way in this morning.

—Is that so, Ned, I heard her say.

The air trembled with the sounds of insects, the bees floated in and out, the thrushes and blackbirds sang in the briars, as I sauntered down the path in search of Albert and Mr. Cagney's cottage. It was the time of morning when my father would have arrived home from the creamery and was reading the paper and drinking a mug of tea by the fire, while my mother silently swept the floor around him, and my brother and sisters ran laughing through the poplars, where the exposed knotty roots resembled starved limbs elbowing their way out of the ground, forty minutes before my father finished reading the newspaper and told my brother and sisters on what jobs had to be done for the day; but they should, as usual, begin by bringing a few buckets of water from the well.

After the blackberry bushes, I stood at an opening in the ditch, where a few feet back from the path was a small mound covered with clumps of hardy nettles, thistles, and docleaves. Small stones and broken bricks pushed against the clay, as if they were growing out of there, too, along with the weeds. Behind the mound was a small meadow where the grass had not been cut in years. The tops of the weeds stirred in a wind I only felt then—there was no shelter here; the hill opened out, and I raised my eyes to look beyond the mound and the meadow, down across the small steep fields and blocked meadows, the tiny houses here and there, the trees and ditches and stone fences and gaps, hay barns, reeks and cows, to the hill road in the distance, twisting its way toward the village of Kilroan, which I could not see against the trees there, only the spire of the church rising into the sky—so excited, I was, like another world I had been imagining my whole life was, at last, real before me, but my eyes kept landing on the weeds, the bricks, and the stones in front of me; and this part of it I couldn't understand; I had dreamed the cottage would be standing, as it was over fifty years ago; I had imagined myself walking up an overgrown path, pushing the tall weeds out of my way, careful of the nettles and thistles, then going around the back and wiping the dust from a windowpane, to see a sewing machine in a room, with a measuring tape dangling across it. Silent rooms and hollow wardrobes with empty coat hangers.

Nothing before me even hinted a home ever existed, that Albert and Mr. Cagney lived and died in a cottage here once upon a time; to even think that for years in time this piece of the earth was ever theirs was unfathomable, and I kept staring at it, blinking, deluding myself that I'd open my eyes and it would have changed into the place that lived in my mind, and what was really before me was only another one of their jokes on a young fella, because they owned it and changed it to their liking as time passed, then handed it down as gospel—I nearly fainted when someone growled, —What in God's name are you looking at there, young fella. I know well who you are by the look of you.

I began to back up the path. My first thought was that the man walking toward me was a ghost, but he more resembled a tramp you'd see walking the road, and I had been warned many times to be careful of tramps, to make a run for it when you come across them. The sleeves of his coat were frayed; the pockets were in tatters the way you'd expect a tramp's to be. His eyes and ears were large, his face was flushed and long, and his hair, which looked like a crow's nest, stuck up in black and gray clumps and waved sideways in the breeze.

—Albert's cottage, I managed to say, and I would have run back up the path from him, but my trembling legs wouldn't let me.

—Where are you from at all, you young scut you. You're a good many years too late. And what would you know about Albert Cagney? You weren't even a bad thought in your old fella's head when that boy was alive.

He had stopped walking, was standing in the path, his feet apart. —By the way, how's young Mary Carmody doing?

—Fine, thanks.

—Tell that lovely looking girl Mick Russell is still living on his own down the boreen and he was mad asking for her. Only codding you, young fella, but I must make the effort and go up and visit her soon. I don't have the time to go to Mass nowadays, so I haven't seen her in God knows how long.

He cleared his throat and spat. —Your father and myself walked to school together, we did in rain and snow and none of us able to afford a coat and the teacher beating the shite out of us for nothing 'cause they could. Do they still bate you, them dirty bastards?

—They do, I told him.

—Is it a he or a she or what kind of animal do you have to put up with?

—Mrs. Grady, I told him.

—Aha, them Gradys. I heard that she was a bitch, all right. That whole family was that. Don't I see her driving around in that new car. I'm glad we have such a fine government and a fine clergy that pay people like her for terrorizing children, but we all had to put up with them at one time, your father and your aunt and myself and many more of us drudging down this fucking hill and walking the hill road to school, over and back every day. For what, I still don't know that, to learn Irish and Catechism. All the bloody good that ever did any of us. What did they think was going to become of us? By the way now, you never did tell me which one of the two Carmody lads you are.

—Jack, I said.

—Aha, after your grandfather, the mother's child. I heard back at the creamery that the other one is the farmer, all right, but tell me now young fella, is your old fella still in the land of the living is what I want to know? That fucker must be well over a hundred if he is alive.

—Who?

—Your father, who else do you think I'm talking about, is he still in the world or has he left us? Sure he's even older than dirt, ha!

—He's fine!

—And the mother, he said, stepping closer, and the very mention of her sent scalding tears to my eyes, but I rapidly wiped my tears with my sleeve, bowed my head and sulked.

—Aha, what's wrong with you? I'm only codding you—by the way, you wouldn't have a smoke on you, would you?

He was going through his coat pockets, and dragging out the ripped lining.

—Your father wouldn't have a coat for me, too, would he now? He might have been lucky enough and found one somewhere, but sure where he's living now is not much better than here, only a few less rocks. If Mr. Cagney was still alive, I'd have all the coats I want. He'd make me one in a week, stay up all night and sew the fucking thing. The old bastard give me one for my Confirmation, but that was your friend Albert's coat.

He turned from me, mumbling to himself, and he walked off down the path, his long arms swinging wildly with each step; his body shone, when he walked into the shafts of sunlight piercing the thick bushes. I stood and watched him, wiped my eyes with my sleeve again, trying as best as I could to imagine he and my father when they were boys my own age, before their first horn, before they even had hair down there, a few years before I did, the two of them passing under the bushes that they never took much notice of, in the same way they wouldn't take notice of a cow grazing in a field, but the thickness of the bushes and the rays of sunlight would have then been exactly the same, the living smell of mold and dampness and the coolness that shrank your balls, the hardness of small stones pressing against the soles of your boots, and the mud squishing; but what was going through their heads, precisely what was bothering them and what they wanted was what I was after, and will be till the day I die; but walking through it and putting up with it, not think-ing too much about it and not resting your eyes for too long on mis-fortune, doing your best to keep going, when it happened, praying and believing that each misfortune you saw and felt was the last one, though you had to be forever ready for the dead worst at all times; that's what they would say: my father, Rome, John Hogan, the whole lot of them, and when I could not see Mick Russell anymore, I turned to look once more at the weeds and all I saw through my tears were weeds, and I turned from them and started back up the path, but I did turn around more than once to make sure no one was after me.

While my aunt and I were eating supper that evening—fried po-tatoes and onions, rashers and fried eggs, and her homemade soda bread—she inquired if I had found Albert and Mr. Cagney's cottage to my liking. I said lackadaisically that there was nothing there any-more but weeds and a handful of stones, exactly as she herself and Ned Franklin and my own mother had told me. I didn't say a word about Mick Russell. I knew if I told her how he had frightened me and told her what he had said about herself she wouldn't let me walk out on my own again.

—I walk past that place on my way to Mass, Jack, and the village, and I never think to look at it, God rest them all.

She had cut four roses from the bush and placed them in a vase on the table. She was again wearing the crimson dress. Tiny earrings I had never seen her wear before sparkled in the window light.

—Your mother is too busy to explain to you these things, she said, showing me the right way to use a knife and fork. —But you need to know them before you go out into the world. You don't ever want strangers to be laughing at you, because laugh at you strangers will.

For dessert, she had made bread pudding and custard. My mother must have told her I liked it. My aunt winked as she poured the hot custard into my bowl.

—When we're done with this, Jack, and you put in the hens for the night, we'll have to celebrate your visit. We'll have a drop of whiskey. I have a bit of a cold in my chest and the drop is the very thing that'll cure it, so we'll kill two birds with the one stone.

I went out into the yard and fed the hens and then hunted them in and bolted their door. I went to the gable end and brought in a bucket of water; she had already swept the floor and boiled a kettle of water, and was washing the dishes in the white enamel basin. I went over and she smiled down at me and passed the dishes to me and I dried them. Drops of water ran off the dishes and dripped onto the stone floor that the sun dried in minutes; all this time she hummed the song.

—Are them pullets fine, Jack?

—They're grand, Aunt.

—I have to keep an eye on them because of the bloody fox.

—We have to do the same thing at home, I said.

—So delighted you are here with me, Jack. This was a great idea of your mother's. And I'm very thankful to her.

She put the dishes away in the cupboard, hung the basin up on the nail, and went to the window and fixed her hair. I walked after her to the window, and I stood next to her and watched her reflection; the daylight was beginning to leave the yard, but I could see the blue of her eyes. We went to her bedroom and sat in the green armchairs that faced the window. This was once my grandparents' bedroom. My aunt had painted the walls yellow, and the ceiling and the trim white. A wardrobe, with a full-length mirror, stood in the corner by the window, which had a fine lace curtain. The linoleum was the same kind that was on the floor of the room I slept in. Above my aunt's bed hung a small painting of a blurred and barefoot couple sitting on a seat; a dark river flowed before them and a path separated them from the river. A wine bottle and two glasses lay at their feet and the shadow of the wine bottle was a long red smear on the path. The trees behind the seat bled into a white-blue sky. It was the only picture on her wall.

She went over to the wardrobe and brought out two small glasses and a half-bottle of Paddy whiskey.

—Just a little drop, Jack, she said, —all the way from Cork, and there's no need to say a word to anyone at home, your mother included, that we had a drop of spirits. That's our business.

She sent me to get a jug of water from the bucket in the kitchen. When I came back, she was sitting in her armchair, watching through the opened window, where the tops of the evergreens moved. Like they forever will, as long as they exist. She poured a good drop of whiskey into her own glass, but only two corkfuls into mine. She insisted that I add an equal amount of water to my own, but she said hers was fine the way it was. I didn't add as much water as she had told me to.

—You're comfortable in that chair, you are, Jack.

—I'm grand, thanks very much, Auntie.

—They came here on a train from Dublin years ago, if you can imagine it. Ned Franklin brought them from the Junction up the boreen in his horse and cart. Mick Russell down the boreen helped him. I had warned the two of them beforehand to cover them and make sure they did not get dirty or wet.

I took a sip, and held it in my mouth. I let it down slowly, but still it burned. She asked if I had put enough water in it.

—It's grand, I told her, and covered the top of the glass with my hand. I had seen the older people do this.

—Your mother and I were close from the first time I met her a week or so after the tailor's funeral. I always thought your father was very lucky to get her.

I put my hand on the armrest and she laid her hand on top of mine. Outside it had turned a shade darker, but I could still make out the treetops from the sky. A wind blew at the curtain.

—You knew Albert well, Aunty.

—Albert Cagney, she said. —Your father and him were the best of friends all them years ago, like Ned said this morning, Jack.

She began to tap nervously on the back of my hand. I closed my eyes to the thistles and nettles; the big docleaves swaying in the wind, drenched by rain on an autumn day.

—Nothing but weeds. That's just it, I said.

Her fingers stopped tapping, but she left her hand there. —What's that you're going on about, Jack?

—Nothing but weeds left down at the tailor's place, I said.

—Oh, he was a fine lad, all right, a soldier, Jack, the tailor's son was, went off to the war like Redmond told him, the only one on the hill to go, he was, though many others across the country went.

She took her hand away and picked up the bottle, and added whiskey to her own glass. She said I had enough, but she herself needed one more drop for her cold, but then she added two corkfuls to my glass. She laid the bottle at her feet. —Albert was a holy terror for the girls and the gambling after coming back, Jack, every tramp on the hill and in the village wanting him, and there was always a few obliging tramps around then, like Ann Leary was one. May Purcell, too, who wound up marrying Saint Nash, who was then and still is completely off his rocker, if you ask—

—Didn't I hear him myself talking back at the forge about Albert and the thing he saw in the sky—

—Well, Jack, they say that was all from the poteen. You see he was a bit too fond of what he himself made in a secret room, so they say, that no one has ever seen under the trees at the side of the forge. He's a bit of a cod more than anything else is what he is, though a very good blacksmith, so give him that, but a wife was what he was after, and when he became a saint, he asked all the girls around to marry him, told them they'd be marrying a saint, that the man above had shown himself to him. He asked me to marry him, Jack. One Sunday, he cycled back the road after me, he did, when I was walking home from Mass, but I would not have a thing to do with him, not that your grandfather would let me, even if I wanted to, forge or no forge. But May Purcell was lucky to get him. She was lucky to get anything, but she still believes she's the bee's knees for getting Saint Nash—

—So that's all that was ever about—

—Well, we have to be saying something, Jack—

—By the looks of it there was only the few rooms, I'd say, Mary, in the tailor's cottage down below, I said.

She moved to the edge of the cushion, and raised her head high, like she was giving a speech. —There was only the three, Jack. I sat at that table many times when I was a girl, helping with piking hay or when they killed a pig, and they came up here and helped us, too. They kept turkeys one year but it nearly broke Mr. Cagney's heart. He got too fond of them to kill them in the end; they said he sat out in the yard talking to them, and he couldn't stop crying the night the man of the Ryans came to kill them turkeys around Christmas—I was very fond of my father and he very fond of me. There was only me and your own father, but times were hard and your grandfather was terribly hard on your father, but men are most of the time like that, as you will see one day for yourself, Jack. Sure look at your own, who've been killed and killing since Adam, and if you ask me, if it isn't land and religion they're at each other's throats over they'd find another thing, because they're not happy unless they're at it over something, but they wouldn't have the liberty for such devilment if there wasn't young men like Albert Cagney out there to do their fighting for them, and sure there's not a blade of good grass on the hill outside and never was. Grass don't grow on rocks. You yourself must have at least learned that much in school.

—Did Albert help out with the hay, too?

—He did, indeed, every summer, and the first time I saw him was the week after he came back from the Great War, as they call it, was in the meadow behind the cottage and Ned was there. Your father and Rome Kelly was there and John Hogan was.

—My father told us about the devil, I leaned toward her and whispered. —He said Albert met the devil on the road at Garvey's bend.

—Men and their devils. I don't have a clue what you're talking about—they're the devils, is the problem, she said hastily.

—Eggs, I giggled.

—Eggs—my talking and me. What's that now, Jack Carmody?

—The walls, I nodded. —There're the very same color as eggs.

—Ha, eggs, all right. I never noticed that before, Jack, mind you. You're a very smart young fella. Well then, here's to eggs, hens and pullets and bantams, she laughed, and raised her glass high.

She had kept the light in the room off, and I turned now to see the sharp outline of her large nose, her lips filled out in the light that shone from the kitchen through the open door. Her earrings glittered.

—You see my father told us not too long ago that Albert was coming from Powers and he met the devil on the hill road.

—Aha, Jack, you've no idea what happened back then, but I wanted to marry Albert Cagney and go away with him. He and me had that planned and then he ran away—that good for nothing did.

—Ran away where—

—Yes, Jack, she leaned over and whispered. —He ran away for a whole five months, and don't you ever mention to your mother or father that I was talking to you about any of this, not a word, but Albert won money in a card game back in Powers, so off he went, and he didn't take me with him. He didn't even tell me or anyone else he was going—

—Poker, it was, I bet.

—Rummy I think they played then, poker—I don't know what the difference is between their games, Jack Carmody. The thing is is that he won money from John Hogan who had sold cattle that day at the Fair and they had a few jars taken and John Hogan the fool lost money to Albert Cagney.

She tapped the back of my hand. —One more drop now for me and a corkful for you and you'll sleep like a log, Jack.

A few drops of whiskey fell onto the back of my hand.

—We play rummy with my father, and Kate wins nearly every time. Dan never.

—Well, your father wasn't much of a card player either.

She took a few quick sips. She went quiet. I watched out the window; the yard was fully dark. I could not see the trees, but I heard them.

Then her voice, suddenly strange and weary. —Aha, I've turned into an old woman, Jack. That's what happened to me.

She squeezed my hand tightly. I leaned over and whispered, —You're grand, Aunt.

—I'm not a bit of it, Jack. I'm just an old woman, with a wardrobe full of old stupid clothes, and not a man would even look at me anymore, living here in this old place that will be the very same as Cagney's cottage down the boreen in a few years.

—My mother always says your clothes are lovely, I lied.

A vixen howled on the hill, and Ned Franklin's sheepdog barked a few times.

—What's the use, Jack. What's the use, it's all over with for me now but you are young.

The vixen howled again; I shuddered and slumped deeper into the armchair.

—You'll have to go out into the world. There's not a thing here for a young fella like yourself. You know Dan will get that farm and the girls will have to move, too. I often curse the day my own father wrote to me in Dublin and pleaded of me to come back here. It was a few weeks after your grandmother's funeral and your father left to work for that farmer in Oola. He was not able to put up with your grandfather anymore, but your grandfather wrote a letter to me and I did always miss my father and the hill and was lonesome without all of them, and I wanted to be with my own people, because you always miss your own, but if only I never come back, if I had stayed where I was, Jack. Maybe them useless clothes behind you could have been of some use—aha, but I remember it like yesterday the day I saw Albert Cagney in the meadow after he came home from the war like there was no war going on at home, Jack, if he was so mad for the fighting, like we didn't have our troubles here in our native land till the end of time it looks like. I'd say myself that's one of the reasons why he went so mad. Fighting the wrong people, going by what Redmond told him to do, although he thought he did the right thing by going over there.

She stopped talking and chuckled. —Albert, he was that fine-looking, all right, better-looking to me than Rome Kelly even, who they say was a Jew, I remember your grandfather telling me one time that Rome came from a place in Dublin as a baby and was raised down in the village of Pallas with the Kelly woman, but she died of the flu one winter when Larry was a three-year-old and he was brought up to those few acres where one of the McGraths lived, who's dead long ago, God rest her, and now Larry lives in that place. You see, Mrs. McGrath never had a child herself. Her husband disappeared not too long after they married and she was related to the Kelly woman through marriage and the McGrath woman went down to Pallas and lifted Rome out of the pram the very day the Kelly woman died, brought him up to Kilroan, she did. Your father and Rome were the best of friends from the first day they met at National school—but I was only sixteen, Jack, and I went down to

Cagney's meadow to help the men with the hay and I took down a gallon of tea and a plate of sandwiches that your grandmother, God rest her, and me had made for them.

—That bad wild-looking meadow I saw behind where the cottage was today.

—The very one right behind the house that I said earlier, she said.

—The grass hasn't been cut there in ages.

—Well, that's the way it is now, but it was a fine meadow at one time, Jack. They always had to put manure on it and grazed it, and they got a good few wines of hay out of it in summer, mind you there was a lot of thistles in it, and I remember well tidying the wines there—well, Jack, I put the tea and sandwiches down under the ash trees in the corner, by the stream that there was never a drop of water in in the summer, and I called them over and they stuck their forks in the ground and walked over, walked over so slowly that I can still close my eyes and see them as clear as yesterday, son, and I had spread a towel out on the ground to lay out the sandwiches. I remember well, him walking toward me with his sleeves rolled all the way up, and me a child up to that day and I could not take my eyes from him but I was trying very hard to—

—And was my father there—

—Indeed, he was. Wasn't he, along with the rest of them, with his nice and tidy red hair, red like my mother's, God rest her, trying to get a rise out of Albert about the girls and the war; they were all laughing and they sat down and I was pouring the tea into the mugs and my hand was shaking at the very sight of him and didn't the brave Albert see that.

She looked up toward the picture above the bed, the outline of which we could only see. —The picture of them two up there. He brought it from Dublin or wherever he was when he came back, appeared outside in the yard dressed like a king, he was; they say it was Dublin, but you'd never know with him, but I nearly killed him, king or no king. Your father tried to stop me and your grandfather did, but fondness will do that to you, I'm telling you now, Jack, and I couldn't show myself to anyone on the hill or the village afterwards.

—You're codding me, Mary, I said.

She rose up from the chair, took those few steps out of the light from the kitchen, to the window, the back of her dress wrinkled around her backside. She stood so still there at the window, took a sip from the glass, watching into the night.

—I'm not codding you at all, not one bit, Jack Carmody, she spoke, as though all of it had only happened yesterday. —The awful disgrace, so as I told you my father sent me off to Dublin. I got a job in an office in the city. I always had good manners and knew how to turn myself out. Like you, I was good in school—but that first day in the meadow I looked up and he was smiling and looking down into my eyes and he put his hand over mine to steady it, smiling like the rogue he truly was. It happened that moment, his fine dark hair and green eyes and the very next day I was hunting the cows onto the hill after milking and he crossed the ditch from the path to me and my heart came alive in my chest. For the first time I felt it, beating like it was trapped all that time and that day we sat behind the ditch eating blackberries and we could hear Mr. Cagney's sewing machine going hell for leather inside, and we were laughing in the ditch and we started courting. But if there ever was a devil he was one.

She hung her head down, and turned from the window; the left side of her fringe had fallen over her forehead. She sat into the seat, while pushing her fringe back, holding her head high.

—An old woman, Jack, she sighed, and laid the glass at her feet. —Listening only to the trees whispering now at night, that's all I am, an old woman whose not much longer for this world, not much at all, Jack, and I would not do that with him, Jack, no matter who or what he was. I was not that kind of a girl ever to do such a thing before they put a ring on my finger, but you don't fully know what I mean.

She was looking toward the picture again, which we could not see anymore. —Me and my tales to tell a boy, she said softly, I should be ashamed of myself, but I've no one else to tell it to, and the problem is I have to tell you. I have to because he's near to me still, Jack, and I go through the days here, talking to him by the fire in the evening. Are you all right there, Albert? The war is never over. Never better now, Mary Cagney. It's an awful thing to die, Jack, but more awful if you are only young.

—Oh, Jack, she said with great torment. —That I might have been born someone else, hoping someone else would see something in me what I couldn't see in myself, like I was Mary Magdalene waiting for Jesus himself to walk up the hill road, faith, that it had all worked out and we had fine children like yourself, and I had the courage to pardon him, like any decent human being would, but they'd cart me off to Saint Joseph's if they heard me talking like this now, but that fondness, when you feel it, and you will, because every human being does, well they do if they're human at all—as you saw yourself down the boreen today, everything else is stones and weeds.

She reached her hand over and touched my fringe. Her sweet breath, then her lips touching my cheek.

—You're a grand young fellow all right, Jack, to come up this lonely and forsaken hill to visit me, put up with an old woman like myself, a fine young fella, you are, and you should go on into your bed now or you can lie down there in that bed if you like. It's a fine comfortable bed.

She was nodding at the bed, but she did not herself get out of the seat, but settled in. Her hand reached over on top of mine, and I closed my eyes. She snored lightly. Stones and weeds, my mind drifting—ha, young fella, I heard my father say, and I saw him, as he looked now, walking up the boreen in broad daylight, hearing his whistle, as he walked under the trees; then there was the warm summer days in July, turning the hay with my brother and sisters, piking it after the cows were milked, in the dusk as the moon rose above the hay barn and the poplar trees. All that was soon. The pony hitched to the float, standing motionless in the meadow. The smell of new hay and the pony's sweat. My father's cigarette glowing in the dark. Smoke drifting under my nose. Kate picking on Dan. Mary saying she was hungry. Laughter in the dark. My father warning us that it was all right to laugh, but to keep going with the work. My father, who all his life worried about rain, especially when the sun was shining—

The vixen howled again, and I opened my eyes to the darkened room.

—Don't worry, Jack. It's her young, my aunt said sleepily. —That's what's up with her. Ned Franklin killed her cubs this evening in the furs. He kills them every year at this time, because they'd kill all the hens and the bantams, and for God's sake go on into bed like a good boy, can't you.

—I will. I will. I'll go into it in a minute, Mary, I said, and shut my eyes, wanting to drift back to where I was before I first heard the vixen's lonely howl, before the stones and weeds. —I'm on holidays now, Mary. There's no hurry. I'm fine sitting here where I am. I've never been happier in my life.

———

Once upon a time, the tailor Mr. Cagney and his son Albert lived in the middle cottage along the boreen that led to my father and my aunt's cottage on Conway's hill. The path sloped up and around the hill, and when it rained, mud and pebbles, leaves and twigs were washed along the path and down to the hill road. Even on bright summer days the sunlight could not penetrate through the trees, for the branches were so tightly lashed together overhead, and the trapped heat created a damp and rotting smell in the path. With a fair bit of effort a horse and cart traveled up the path, all the way to my aunt's cottage; and years later, without any effort at all, a tractor could.

My grandparents, Dan and Joan Carmody, and my father, Mike, and my aunt, Mary, lived at the top of the hill. The Russells and their ten children—Mick, the youngest, had lived alone for twenty years the summer I met him—lived in a house back in the trees where the boreen was steepest, next to the hill road. Many other families lived on the hill years back, but all had left, died, or emigrated. They lived on small farms and milked cows, at one time made their own butter, kept a horse to plow the fields, take their people to Mass, and bring the milk to the cheese factory or, later, the creamery. They raised a pig and killed the pig in autumn, gave some of the fresh meat to the neighbors they were closest to, made black puddings from the guts and cut the meat into slabs and salted it in a barrel—a stan, they called it. They grew potatoes and cabbage, carrots, onions, parsnips, turnips, beets, rhubarb, and strawberries. They baked their own bread and kept hens and ducks for eggs and meat. They believed that they should suffer, but that God looked upon them with an endless amount of grace, love, and mercy, and all of their anguishes in this world would be repaid with glorious happiness after death.

When the Great War came, Albert joined up.

—Albert posted those letters to Mr. Cagney. Did I tell you that part of it already, Jack. That your father had to read them letters, my aunt said on another evening, when we sat at her table, drinking tea and eating biscuits.

—You didn't, I said, —but my father told us that.

—Well, it's a wonder he remembers that much; he's good at making things up, as you yourself well know; the tailor, mind you, was a very smart man, Jack, very well respected—a bit of a clown, too, but also a bit like an old prophet in the Bible, and the strangest things came out of him, most of them back at Powers after a few jars, it was said. He was such a fine tailor; he had the most perfect stitch and could sew better than any woman I ever came across. He'd look at a man's body and know exactly what kind of suit would suit him, its size and the material, everything; they said there never lived a more skilled tailor and he mended and made clothes for half the country, and he was rewarded at the end by the biggest funeral I've ever seen in Kilroan, God rest the poor tailor.

Then the war was over and Albert Cagney took the train from Dublin to Limerick Junction one fine afternoon in May. He stepped off the train and walked the road to New Pallas, up through Old Pallas, then a few more smaller roads; a handsome man, four years older, the happiest time of his life, like he had risen up from the dead, the worst of life behind him, he thought, and he still a young man, as he marched proudly past cows, who grazed peacefully in the fields beyond the ditches, the clean and smokeless air, the only sound was the thrilling birds, marching down the dusty hill road till he stopped at the mouth of the boreen, where he threw his bag down, for he saw the four younger children of the Russells playing on the flagstones, and they, too, saw him and they screamed with delight, pulling at their mother's apron and pointing at Albert. Mrs. Russell was sweeping the flagstones, and had her back turned to the boreen.

—There's Albert, Mama, there's Albert, he's home, Mama, was what the children cried, still clutching her apron, and Mrs. Russell dropped the broom and spun around, running like mad along the flagstones, her eyes large and swelled out from her face, waving her arms, crying that all was well above on the hill and in the village and the world was right again now that Albert Cagney had survived the awful heathens and come home to us. She threw her arms around the soldier's neck and he lifted her once off the ground, her children still clutching her apron, laughing and happy as they ever were or would be again on the day of Albert's return.

And my father was above on the hill fencing—Garvey's cows had ripped up the pailing posts the night before. He had his back to the hill, a staple tight between his teeth as he malleted in a pailing post, the sound of his mallet echoing up along the hill and through the fields to the hill road, and Albert left the Russells behind and sprinted up the path, for he knew that sound coming from Carmody's rock field was my father's, and Albert hid his bag in the briars in the boreen and crossed the ditch, ran a few miles through the fields until he came to Hanley's bend, where he crossed the ditch there and slid down into the dusty road, making sure first there was no one on the road because he did not want to encounter anyone he'd have to stop and talk to. He ran along the road until he came upon the rhododendrons, crawled up this ditch, crawled up it, maybe, the same way he did out of the mucky trenches in France, only the grass on this ditch was fine and dry after weeks of good weather, and when he was on top of the ditch he took a penknife from his back pocket and cut the rhododendrons, and as he was slipping down the ditch with the flowers he heard my father's mallet again, ringing in the air like a dulled bell: Whap! Whap! Whap!

And there was my father kneeling on one knee, a new staple clenched between his teeth, and he heard his name being called: Mike! Mike! But he did not turn, believing the voice to be his sister calling him in for tea and he wanted to finish the fencing first; then, the voice was closer and he heard human breath behind him, the cows snorting and running, and he turned, the staple still tight between his teeth, to see Albert Cagney running through the parting cows with the bundle of rhododendrons in his arms, and my father's eyes and mouth opened wide, and the staple fell from his mouth, Albert running and laughing toward him, as though they were lovers, and my father shouts, Did you do away with all the heathens for us? Are they all gone forever? There's more at home to be done away with now, and Albert flung the flowers upwards, into the warm air above my father, and the flowers dropped onto my father's shoulders and face, and they tumbled and bounced onto the barbed wire and the grass, as Albert grabbed my father and threw him onto the ground, the two of them laughing and rolling along the grass and the fallen flowers, I'm home and I'm free forever, thank God, Mike Carmody! laughed Albert, as they held one another, Albert telling my father to finish the cursed fence till they go on and go to Powers to see Rome and John, but that he must get his bag out of the briars and go over and see Mr. Cagney first. And my father scrambled along the ground, away from his friend, both of them crying and laughing with joy, my father castigating Albert, because that was his last staple, and what in the name of God was he going to do now to finish the fence. He delicately fingered the coarse grass around the fence post aside, eyeing the ground as though it were gold itself he had lost, at the same time warning Albert to watch out that he not ruin his boots or his grand uniform, for Albert was standing deadly close to a large pool of fresh cow manure, and Albert said, I've seen an awful lot worse than cow manure, Mike, I tell you, never seen anything like it, cow manure is gold and heaven compared to what I've seen.

And in June and July, Rome Kelly, John Hogan, my father, and Albert were saving hay, and at night, over the weekend, they went for a few pints to Powers. They sat at the bar, and Albert told them his stories about the fine-looking girls in Paris, who would give a man whatever he wanted, and toward the end of the night the men sat back at the tables, and a few of the Russell brothers, and Ned Franklin, James Nash, too, joined them in games of rummy or poker, depending on the mood they were in, and they thanked God that Albert was home and they thanked God for the good weather, and their cigarette smoke circled to the roof and clouded the one window in Powers, and Stephen Power leaned on the bar, watching the young men sideways to make sure there were no indiscretions. He read the paper.

And as my aunt told me the night she and I had the few drinks, Albert saw her when they were saving hay in Cagney's small meadow and they started meeting in the boreen and on the hill road in the evenings, which made my grandparents, Mr. Cagney, and my father very happy, that Albert Cagney and Mary Carmody might settle and save for their own few acres, the two of them begin a life together. But as the months went on Albert changed. Back at Powers, after a few pints, he cried about all the dead soldiers in the trenches who were never buried, and all men deserved that much at least, saying those soldiers came to him at night, woke him up and sat there crying and bleeding on his bed; some were headless; others were without arms and legs; all were wrapped in unraveling and bloody bandages, and their blood soaked into the bedsheets and dripped onto the floor, and they cried and pleaded with Albert to not forget them, for no one else cared a damn about them, and their souls would never get to heaven, and when Albert spoke like this, the people at the bar turned from him and shook their heads in dismay, and Mr. Cagney walked up the path and sat at the hearth and told my grandparents that the war had upset his young fella beyond belief, for Albert was shouting and screaming at night that it was his duty to change the way things were in the world, calling, also, for the mother he never knew, and Mr. Cagney had to go in in the middle of the night and sleep in the bed beside him, hold him and rock him in his arms, as though Albert were a baby again, boil his son hot milk and bread and sugar and spoon-feed it to him, in an attempt to bring him back to where he was and not where he thought he was, and all my grandparents were able to do was give the tailor strong mugs of tea and some of my grandmother's bread, encourage him to eat a boiled egg, and nod their heads and listen.

The summer got older and Albert went to Powers early in the day and stayed out at night and the girls in the village like Ann Leary and May Purcell, and girls in the next village, too—none of them girls, Jack, my aunt told me about them again, but tramps, calling him their soldier boy, taunting him back in the street, nodding at him to go back the road with them or into the graveyard, that they had exactly what would save any soldier.

And many a drunken afternoon Albert did take a girl into the back of the graveyard, where the bushes grew over the graves, and one of those girls was Ann Leary. Albert and Ann Leary made love, Albert not even shoving his trousers down, but only unbuckling his belt and unbuttoning his trousers, then dragging Ann Leary's knickers down to her ankles, the two of them fumbling and grunting under the trees, going at it for a minute or two only, Albert rolling off her after he came, crying, Christ what have I done to Mary Carmody, Christ forgive me, Albert's big wet mickey so foolishly exposed and shamefully shrinking back to nothing outside his trousers.

My aunt was pleading with Albert to go away with her, that they could begin a new life in Dublin or England and if they saved enough they would take the boat to America or Australia, where things could only get better, but Albert continued to spend his days at Powers, and Mr. Cagney sat at the hearth in Conway's hill, with his head in his hands, telling my grandparents that he was having a hard time sewing, for his eyes kept filling with tears, and Albert rarely came home at night anymore, but slept in the ditches in the boreen or along the hill road, and Mr. Cagney was worried as to who would go to him and comfort him when he raved and became frightened in the dark.

And my grandfather warned my aunt to be careful. Grandfather was hearing bad things about Albert and girls; he warned his daughter to tell Albert Cagney that he needed to think about Mr. Cagney and he did not need to be messing with his own family either; this was the rock Albert Cagney would perish on, soldier or no soldier, neighbor or no neighbor. Then Ann Leary ran into my aunt in the village and she cried to my aunt, said she was frightfully sorry, but she had gone into the graveyard with Albert and he would not now talk to her, and she knew she had a child in her, and when her father finds out what man put it there he would kill him and herself, and she was going to have to run away to England, and my aunt cried all the way home, walked into the house and threw herself on my grandfather and grandmother's bed and my grandfather sat by her and held her and told her that Albert was nothing but a rogue and a fool, and my grandmother got cross and told my aunt to come out of the room immediately: There was milking to be done and hens to be fed, but my grandfather held my aunt in his arms and shouted at my grandmother and my father, who at this moment walked into the kitchen, to get the hell out of his house, for he must comfort his daughter, she being the only gift God gave him. He left my aunt grieving on the bed and stood in the room doorway; he roared at my father that the fence he had mended was broken already and without a doubt Garvey's cows would break in again, saying, too, for my father to make sure the buckets of water were full when he brought them from the pump, screaming at my father that he was a lazy lump and a worthless son, and my grandfather then picked up a chair and threw it across the kitchen at my father, while my grandmother pleaded with her husband to leave their boy alone, because all he ever did was work hard on the farm, and how could he treat his only son in such a manner—I could not do anything, Jack, my aunt told me, not a thing, though that dislike my father had for your father separated me from your father all our life—and my grandfather shouted that Albert was a good-for-nothing soldier, a fool for John Redmond, fighting for others and not his own, thinking he's too good to fight for his own, that his own aren't good enough to fight for, the chair only having grazed my father's shoulder, my grandfather shaking and red with rage, his fists clenched, telling my father, who himself shook with fear, that he was wasting his life with them young fools back in Powers, and if he met the cowardly traitor, Albert Cagney, in the fields or the path or on the hill road or the village he'd break every bone in his worthless body; he'll let him know rightly what it's like to be in the war; at the same time, my grandmother begged my father to not listen to his father, who was only having a fit, and for my father to turn as quickly as his legs could carry him and leave the Godforsaken house. —Run outside before he kills you! She pushed my father out of the kitchen doorway to the yard. My father ran crying down the path, hearing my grandmother wailing behind him, again asking my grandfather the forever impossible question, as to why in the name of God any man would treat his own flesh and blood like that.

My father ran across the fields to Powers. He guessed Albert would be there; he was, sitting at the bar, cigarette butts circling his barstool like spent bullets, when my father strode breathlessly up to him and told him what had befallen his sister and that my grandfather would kill him stone dead when he sees him, because Albert had done the very worst thing any human being or animal could do to my grandfather: He had hurt my aunt Mary Carmody.

Fearless Albert shrugged his shoulders.

—I've seen worse than him—you'll have one with me, Mike, he nodded and raised his hand to Stephen Power, who started over, but my father told the publican he was grand. Stephen Power nodded and turned back. He had taken the bottles from their shelves and was busy polishing them with wet newspaper at the other end of the bar.

—I need to go back and finish this fencing. The cows have to be milked soon, and you need to go away somewhere for a long while, my father said. Albert raised his face and looked into my father's eyes. His hand shook when he brought the lit cigarette to his mouth. —You have to stop it for a bit, Albert. It'll ruin you, take the pledge, for God's sake, go on up and see the priest—but if I was you now, what I'd do is run away. There's not anything you can do to fix anything unless you're Christ himself.

—I keep praying and praying for them, Albert said, —but they'll never leave me alone. I should have helped here at home, Mike, is what I should have done. I'm a traitor after all that; that's how most of them see me, a traitor—but if I had went to Dublin it would be all different, but one war is more than enough for any man.

He reached his shaking hand out, and grabbed my father's wrist.

—Enough of it. Stop it, Albert, my father said, —I don't want to hear another word about it from you. There's not a thing you or I can do about that now. The last thing you want, I tell you, is my father's wrath upon you. You'd nearly be safer back in a trench or in a post office in Dublin.

As my father was leaving Powers a few minutes later, he ran into John Hogan in the doorway. It was a Friday afternoon and John Hogan had been at the Fair and had sold a few bullocks. He shook hands with my father and told him he wanted to buy him a few pints, but my father said he needed to get the paling done. Rome

Kelly was with John Hogan. So were Mick Russell and a few others. All were cheerful, coming from the Fair.

My aunt told me that Ned Franklin was not in Powers at all this evening. She also told me one day that John Hogan was an only child; his father died when he was a child, and John lived alone with his mother, so from a young age John was doing a man's work, which is why it was he who was selling at the Fair.

An hour or so later, the young men sat at the tables and Albert Cagney dealt the cards. Rome Kelly and Mick Russell were out in less than an hour. By eight o'clock it was down to Albert and John Hogan. A large share of Hogan's money was already spent on buying drinks for the house and Albert had the upper hand in the games. The men circling the table were silent; they smoked and sighed as each hand was shown, and by ten o'clock the card game was over and Albert Cagney had won twenty pounds, which was a substantial amount of money then, or any other time on Conway's hill. John Hogan stood quickly and lifted the table with his left hand, the cards and the ashtray and the glasses of porter and whiskey flying in all directions.

—In the name of God, what am I going to tell my mother, John Hogan cried. —How in God's name can I face her! You dirty rotten soldier that you didn't stay and die in your fucking trenches.

The men stepped back from John Hogan. The chair he sat in had fallen behind him. Stephen Power was pushing his way through the crowd; John Hogan was lurching forward, trying to reach Albert's neck, but Albert flung himself at him, elbowing him sharply beneath the ribs, which sent John Hogan flying, and he landed, firm, against Powers' window.

—Yes, Jack, that crack is from that day, my aunt told me one afternoon we were walking on the hill. —But when the men at Powers heard the loud noise, it was said they thought it was a bone in John Hogan's body, but then they saw the crack spreading out like the branch of a tree across the pane of glass. John Hogan was tough, though, Jack—it would be hard for any man to best him. Being an only child you had to be.

Stephen Power, having finally got through the crowd, was furious, and he stood over John Hogan, who was facedown on the floor.

—You'll lose more money now, Hogan, paying for that pane of glass. Do you or your likes have any idea what a pane of glass like that costs! And your mother will know every word of this, and where the hell were you anyway when that brave young fella was lying in the muck in France, only lying at home in bed, waiting for your mother to bring you in a mug of tea in the morning! The only muck you ever saw was in a gap—yes, you wait till I see your mother in the street tomorrow, that fine, brave young fella, who did what no one around here did.

John Hogan sat up and rubbed his sore head. —I'm sorry, Mr. Power. Very, very sorry, I am—but Albert, oh, Albert, what have I done—you can have all the money you want. It's my mother I'm afraid of, Albert, my dear.

It was only then that they all noticed Albert was missing. He had picked up his winnings and, in all the commotion, he'd slipped out of the bar.

My aunt said John Hogan never did pay for the window, because Stephen Power did not push it in the end: John Hogan, being an only boy and the son of a widow, would be forgiven bad conduct that other men his age wouldn't. Stephen Power stuck tape over the crack and when he died, his son Leo did it, and every spring the dirty and worn strip was dragged off and a new strip was stuck on, like that crack was forever a fresh and bloody cut.

—That cursed morning he came back from Dublin, Jack, I was sleeping in the room you're sleeping in now and I was woken by a slight knocking on the window, although I wasn't sure at first that it was knocking; the first thing that came into my mind was that it was a cow who had gotten out, or a fox had strayed into the yard and the hens had heard him sniffing around their door. Anyway, I looked at your father sleeping in his bed along the opposite wall, but as you know yourself he's a powerful sleeper and a bomb itself wouldn't wake him.

—And it was Albert, after five months, I said.

—Indeed, it was, Jack, and it was very cold. It was April but it felt like a few months earlier.

She sunk back into the armchair and waited a few minutes before speaking again.

—And not a word from him since the night they say he took the train from the Junction after winning that money from John Hogan.

A very low whisper she heard, was how she put it to me. She sat up in bed and wiped the sleep from her eyes. She turned to the window: *Mary, Mary, Mary.* The raps getting a bit louder and longer. Then she saw knuckles smudging the frost, but it was the shadow of his head upon the pane she recognized, the way he combed his hair up high over his forehead. His knuckles becoming fully visible, where he'd worn the frost away. And the whispering, *Mary, Mary, Mary.* She carefully got out of the bed. Put her feet down onto the cold floor. She shivered in her petticoat, glancing once at the clock over the fire that had burned out hours ago. It was six o'clock. She slipped on her boots and quickly went to the window and whispered for him to hold on a second, to on no account wake anyone in the house, for there would be trouble if he did. She glanced once across the room at the thin bundle that was my father, and before she left that room she would, without a doubt, have looked into the mirror to straighten her brown hair, which would have tossed overnight: All her life she was the kind of woman who would not have presented herself to anyone without first taking a look in a mirror.

She opened and closed the bedroom door slowly. The door to the yard was to her right and next to the door were the old everyday coats hanging on nails. She slipped her own coat on, her breath clouding about her face. She had her hand on the doorknob, ready to open it and step onto the yard, into Albert Cagney's arms.

—I paused then, Jack—

She paused, blinking in the dazzling morning light that shone through the cracks between the boards, distracted, too, by my grandfather's snoring; their door was ajar, and she turned to watch a beam of light along their floor, her grandmother's feet propped up beneath the blanket, my grandparents' worn-out wellingtons that lay neatly against the wall outside their door. A mouse scurried across the kitchen table, his tail wriggling around the egg bowl. She watched and waited for the mouse to appear again. He did not. She took the few careful steps to the kitchen table and looked in at the bowl that was nearly full of unwashed eggs. She tucked the bowl under her arm and went back to the door and stood in the light beams for a few seconds. She told me that what she should have done was say a prayer for guidance; but, instead, she slowly opened the creaking door and stepped onto the cold and glistening flagstones, as though she were stepping onto a battlefield.

I have often wondered what it must have been like for her to see Albert again. His eyes shifting from the smudged windowpane to her. Who knows what he had done or gone through those five months they all said he spent in Dublin. Who knows, even, whether he was in Dublin. He might even have gone to Liverpool to visit Ann Leary, but that probably never happened. I imagine that she wasn't on his mind at all.

The evergreen trees unwavering, stiffened with frost, behind him. Across his shoulders lay a purple shawl with embroidered flowers. He wore white shoes, and a bright blue suit, the likes of which my aunt had never seen in her life—in fact, so unbelievable did what he was wearing look to her, she told me, that she thought what was before her was a ghost—but those were Albert's bleary and reddened eyes shining at her, the neatly combed hair, but the suit and shawl crumpled and stained. Under his arm was a parcel wrapped in newspaper. He did not take a step toward her; he held the parcel out: the trembling and cold hands that could barely hold it.

—Mary, he croaked, —I wanted to bring you back something

nice, his stammering voice rising; and he stumbled—lost his footing for a moment on the slippery flagstones, which might very well have been from the look in her eyes.

She dipped her hand into the bowl and let the first egg fly, which exploded on his handsome face, the yolk sliding slowly down the purple shawl and splattering on the flagstones.

—Take that. Chalk that one down, Albert Cagney, she screeched, reaching again into the bowl. This egg broke on his chest.

But he didn't move, didn't even blink. —I'm sorry, Mary, he joined his hands. —I'm frightfully sorry for all I have done. But I come back to you. We can go away, we can. Blessed are the peacemakers—

She didn't let him finish that; instead, with remarkable speed, she dipped into the bowl and cast one egg after the other at him. —How could you do that to me, she was crying. —Go away and everyone in the street looking at me after Mass, knowing what you did to Ann Leary. And probably to that worthless bitch of a May Purcell, too. You can go to hell. That's what you can do. You can go straight down to hell!

The cock crowed; the hens started up a clamor, which woke my father, who must have wondered at the odd thud of breaking eggs outside the room window, and, even stranger than that, his sister screaming. He ran through the kitchen doorway and out to the yard. He jumped on my aunt's back and wrapped his legs across her stomach. He pressed his mouth to her ear and whispered loudly, —What in the name of God are you doing. Is it to get him killed you want! Is that what it is!

He dragged her to the ground and the bowl fell from underneath her arm, though it did not break obviously (for this was the bowl that sat on the doily in the middle of the table). My father saying, —Do you want to get him killed stone dead by the old fella, do you want to get the whole lot of us killed dead!

Albert joined his hands and bowed his head, then raised his head and smiled calmly at the two of them. Albert in a different world, gone from this one for good—my father could probably see this, because of the clothes his friend was wearing, and not to mention the queer look in Albert's eyes—the yokes and whites of eggs now dripped down his shawl, to the flagstones; bits of eggshells stuck to his suit and trousers and the white shoes. Eggshells scattered around his feet—my father and my aunt rolled about on the flagstones; my father clasped his hand over my aunt's mouth and, like a madwoman, she bit into his fingers.

—Albert Cagney and Ann Leary can go to hell and you can go to hell with them!

—Please be quiet, Mary, my father pleaded. —For the love of God, please.

My aunt pulled at the front of my father's nightshirt. The buttons flew across the flagstones. My father wound my aunt's hair around his hand, and my aunt cried out, —You care about him more than you do me! You care about everyone else in the world more than you do me! And I'm your own flesh and blood! But flesh and blood isn't anything to you!

Then my grandfather was in the yard, with my grandmother behind him, who had wrapped a shawl around her shoulders against the frosty air. The first thing they noticed were the eggs broken along the yard and the empty unbroken bowl (which was a gift to the family from my grandmother's family). Such sinful waste that was, to break all of those eggs, they would have thought—and what was there to eat for breakfast that morning and for the next few days? And my grandfather, who like my father was only wearing his drawers and nightshirt, went and stood over his son and daughter, my father flat against the freezing flagstones, my aunt lying, face toward the sky, on top of him. She wept and clutched her nightgown at the neck, her hair concealing my father's head and face entirely. My grandfather stood over them, gritting his teeth, telling my father to loosen his hand from his daughter's hair or he'd pay dearly, while my grandmother ran to Albert Cagney, ushering him out of her yard and warning him to never return again, for he had brought nothing but misery and unhappiness to her family, and she couldn't take any more of it, because when it came to misery, her own plate was full. She gently turned him around and led him to the gate like you would a blind man, Albert smiling, and peacefully whispering: Blessed are they which are persecuted for righteousness' sake: for theirs is the kingdom of heaven.

There he was, the day before he died, wandering in the world that didn't touch him anymore; my grandfather had pulled his children up from the yard, and the four of them stood and gazed at Albert Cagney, who now walked through the rays of morning sunlight, which pierced the evergreen trees, his shawl rippling around him, my grandparents, my aunt, and my father gone silent, as the soldier disappeared down the path.

My aunt ran across the yard and picked up the parcel and held it tightly to her breasts, crying out to God to comfort her, as she ran into the house; and grandfather, instead of giving my father a good slap across the face, raised his face to the sky and began to laugh; then he walked into the house, went back to bed, and laughed himself back to sleep. My grandmother and my father started the day's work. My aunt locked herself in the bedroom, which she did not unlock for two days, and for those two nights my father had to sleep on the floor of the kitchen, next to the hearth.

—That we could still go away, aha, yes—I'll tell you this now, Jack, that the only good thing about being fond of someone is that you do in time get over it and after that you have some semblance of your own life left, but it's not the life you had before, but you can't have that anymore; that's gone forever—oh, but he was cracked, Jack, and I didn't see that then. No one wanted to see it, and I just saw it all the way I wanted, said my aunt, with such torment and sadness in her words, the two of us sitting in the armchairs, sipping from our mugs before the darkened window, and the forlorn wail of the vixen outside on the hill, crying for what was forever vanished, in the room where my grandparents once slept, next to me the bed where my own father was conceived—where my grandfather held my aunt the afternoon she had the bad luck to run into Ann Leary on the village street. I often think maybe it would have all been different, that it might not have been so bad, if she had never run into her.

The day before I went home I was walking down the path and Mick Russell was walking up the path. I had run into him a few times over the two weeks, when my aunt had let me walk out on my own. Mick and I had chatted, and he gave me cigarettes—Player's Navy Cut, the very kind my father and his friends smoked.

—How're you keeping today, young Jack? he said.

—Fine, thank you, Mick, I said.

—You're leaving us tomorrow.

—I am, I said.

We shook hands and lit up. He then walked off, into Cagney's meadow, telling me to follow him.

—I might as well tell you this now for nothing, he said, as we were walking through the meadow, me having to walk fast to keep up with him. —We all wanted your aunt back then, young Carmody. All the young fellas around did, every man with a decent pair of legs on him, but your miserable grandfather thought no one was good enough for her and a Russell from down the path wasn't for sure, but your grandmother would have given your aunt away to the tinkers if she could get rid of her at all. She thought your grandmother was no more than a troublemaker, but that was because your grandfather was too fond of her, but Albert Cagney was good enough for her in the beginning, when he was all right in the head. They all had great respect for the tailor, and the son was a soldier, and there wasn't many of them around, and the kind that was wasn't the kind we liked.

We were standing underneath the trees, both of us watching the mound of weeds.

—So my aunt said, Mick, that it was the war and not the devil at all, I said, taking a long drag from the cigarette like he did.

—Well, I wouldn't know a thing about the devil at all myself, he said, walking away from the trees, going toward the ditch, where he stopped. I stood next to him, and we watched down across the hill. A car glinted in the sunshine on the hill road. Mick Russell squinted, pointing at a gap in the trees where the car had just passed.

—'Twas a tree right down there, he said, poking once at my shoulder. —An elm tree there that got blown down after, into Garvey's big field in a storm a long time ago, and Garvey himself was afraid to cut it up and burn it, because of all the talk that was going around from the fool of a blacksmith and the others like him. The reason the whole Garvey family left the hill was because they thought that bloody tree was bringing them bad luck. What bad luck! They had the most and the best land on the hill, bought it up for nothing as the people left. Said, too, that they paid certain people in the Land Commission off to get it, and the devil didn't have a thing to do with that, lazy as sin is what the Garveys fecking was. They drove your old fella mad, their bloody cows breaking in morning, noon, and night. Anyway, a tree is a fecking tree and that's all it is. Albert Cagney was gone in the head. Everyone knew it, including your own father, but no one wanted to admit it. No one wanted to hurt the tailor. You know the soldier turned a gun on himself back there under the trees where we were just standing, and he killed the two of his father's goats before himself, he did, too. That happened the day after the so-called devil appeared to him, as your old fella likes to tell it.

I felt his eyes on me. I didn't look up. I watched the hill road.

—My father said something about a gun, but then he said he was just codding with us, 'cause my mother told him to—

He spat into the grass. —Your old fella is a good one for the codding all right, him and the Jew is and that good-for-nothing of a Hogan is. Those boyos have been at that with years, living like kings down there in the lowlands, but your aunt above don't know a thing about it, and you see they wouldn't be able to bury him back in the graveyard, so they had to hide it, but they didn't want it to be known by the tailor, even. Your grandfather was the boss of all of them, but as I was saying it was myself who found him, and it's long ago and none of it makes an iota of difference anymore.

I took a deep breath. I watched four cows grazing in the shadow of the far-off ditch. The tree and the cottage and the truth; all of it was gone forever.

Mick Russell lit two cigarettes and handed me one.

—All them old people were tough as nails, Jack Carmody, and your grandfather from up that hill was certainly a tough one, but look what's about you here.

A sudden gust of wind lifted his hair and pushed it over his forehead. He put his hand up and pressed his hair down; he kept his hand there. There was a frightened look in his eyes. —Found him right over there underneath them trees where we just was, he pointed with his free hand. —I have the gun down in the house below.

—You're codding me, I said, and his fierce, watery eyes were upon me. I took a step back. The blood was gone from his face, but the tiny red veins there bloomed.

—I found him, all right. Do you think I'm lying to you, is that what you think? He cleared his throat and spat, mumbled something about the young people these days, and set off toward the trees.

I went after him, telling him I was sorry, and that I didn't think he was lying to me at all. He turned around and stared down at me. —You might have to see something like it someday, young fella, and I'll tell you now that it's not a good thing for anyone to see, because you never stop seeing it is the problem, but the soldier would have seen an awful lot of it in the war and all, and you don't see much carry-on like that around here and when it does come about everyone's glad to have something to talk about, but there's always scuts like yourself who'll go on about it. Young scuts having nothing better to do these days. Ye didn't have to put up with the things that we had to, and it's people like us made it all an awful lot easier for you, fought for scuts like yourself, we all did, and for what, for what, I ask you. I'll tell you for what, so that you all could go away and leave us, cross the pond or go to the big smoke and make yer money and we'd never hear another word from any of you, but we're as well off to be rid of the whole lot of ye.

He spit into the grass, and walked off toward the trees, where he stood with his back to them; he was staring over at the mound of weeds, and I stopped walking a few feet from him. He took four attentive steps to the left, three steps forward, and two steps to the right.

—'Tisn't dancing I'm doing here, young fella. Now come over here to me, he motioned. I walked over and stood by him. We were in the shadows of the tops of the dark trees.

—Right here. Right there, he pointed at the ground, the cigarette smoke wafting around his long yellow, trembling fingers. —This is not the first time I done this, in case you want to know. In fact, I come here often to this very spot and kneel and say a prayer for Albert.

—What, I said, looking down at a patch of grass.

—That. That there, he said, shutting his right eye, holding his hand straight and steady in front of him, his open eye on the mound; then he let his hand fall. —Yes, right here on this very spot was where I found him. I heard what was the shots earlier but it was not what you think shots would sound like, so I didn't pay a bit of attention to them at all. I thought that sound came from Saint Nash's, but I heard another sound and was fully sure I was coming across a litter of pups that some bitch had pupped. That's the kind of sound I believed it was—

I interrupted him to ask if Albert was wearing a shawl, a suit, and a pair of white shoes. He made a face at me and rolled his eyes like I was completely off my head, so I said no more about it. He then said he had stood there for a long time listening to the sound before he eventually walked over to where the two of us now stood, and there was Albert, his body having flattened the long grass where he lay, his uniform coat fully open and the tail of his shirt dragged out over his trousers, the shirt unbuttoned from the bottom to halfway up his body, his naked belly exposed, the belly moving up and down the way alive bellies do. He could not see Albert's eyes, which were smothered in blood, and his hair was matted and stuck to his forehead from the blood. His feet were jerking up and down, like he was having a fit, his arms stiff by his side and his fingers trembling, his nails clawing into the flesh of his already ripped and bleeding palms. Mick Russell looked up to see the two dead goats a few feet from the dying soldier, the tailor's nanny and puck goat, their heads blown utterly away, bits of flesh all over the grass, an animal or human eye watching up at him. Bits of bone scattered along the grass. Drops of blood dripping thick and slow from the long and tilted blades of grass, like someone mad had swung a wet paintbrush. Mick Russell did not at once connect the bits of flesh and bone and the blood to either Albert or the goats. He was too young; he'd never been to war, where you come to know too soon that bodies turn into that, and although he'd seen pigs and birds slaughtered all of his life, chickens' heads lopped off with a butcher's knife; pigs hung up and stretched on ladders, then split down the middle with hatchets, their steaming insides tumbling out in one firm heap; seen his mother shove her hand into the slit holes of chickens and turkeys, but he turned feeble at this smell of human blood, bone, and flesh, the stench of human shit and piss, this not being a new smell to him, either, when you take into account that he was raised in a small house with eight or nine brothers and sisters, with no taps indoors, and Mick Russell turned from Albert, joined his hands, then rolled his eyes up toward the quiet sky, and he screamed like it was him who was going out of breath forever; he screamed for God, and when nothing happened there, there was no one left to scream for but the tailor.

—And where in the name of God would he have got the gun? I said.

—He was a soldier, wasn't he, Mick Russell scolded me. —What the hell do you think soldiers do young fella, only kill fucking Indians!—listen to me now, the soldier had spent that night before in Powers. He stood on a table, telling them all he had come home to save them and free them. 'Twas even said he was going to go down and walk on the Main Trench and part the waters in the bog and free them all from the English like Moses did and they were all laughing at him. Stephen Power didn't know what to do. Nor did the tailor know what to do. They say he just stayed at home, praying to God for the son to come home safe to him. They tell us that God works in strange ways but God hasn't done a day's work since he hunted us all out of his garden—but I wasn't back at Powers that night, and neither was your old fella or the Jew or Hogan, none of that crowd was. Their mothers and fathers wouldn't let them go back there, and without a doubt your grandfather wouldn't let your own father even leave the house, but they would have been all too upset, too. No one knew what to do with the brave soldier anymore, and what else can you do with mad people, only lock them up and say a few prayers for them and hope for the best.

In the end, Mick Russell found strength enough to run around the tailor's cottage, and in the front door. There was only the sound of the clock that ticked on the wall opposite him, when he stood breathless, squinting into the darkness in the tailor's doorway. Mr. Cagney was snoring by the hearth. A coat he was mending lay across his knees, with pins dotting the lapels. Mick, crying like a child, ran to the tailor, shaking him, then pulling him up out of the chair.

—Come out, Mr. Cagney, for the love of God come out, can't you, he cried, but the tailor resisted, saying he had a bit of sewing to fin-ish, but Mick finally managed to pull him up, and he dragged the old man by the hand, out the door and around the cottage to the meadow, the tailor asking him if he was in a dream now or if it all was real, because he hadn't slept in weeks, and that he needed to put on a few spuds for Albert, who would be back from the war soon and would be ravenous with the hunger, those French people eating nothing but frogs and snails.

Mick Russell didn't drop the tailor's hand until they both stood over the body of Albert, who was now dead.

—Look, for God's sake, look down, can't you; can't you look down at the poor misfortune, Mick Russell cried, covering his eyes with his hands, stepping back from the tailor and the body.

The old tailor stood over the body of his dead son, while Mick, in stepping backwards, trod upon something hard, which he thought must be a stone, but he knelt and dug his fingers into the long grass and picked up a gun, and slipped it underneath his coat, while the old tailor knelt, one stiff knee after the other, by his boy, asking God as to why he let this happen, and who, in God's name, did this to his brave boy; and he placed one hand on his son's chest and his other hand on his son's belly, and the tailor raised his hands up high, then bowed his head, dropped his hands and gathered his son's bloody and torn head to him, and he kissed his son's bloody forehead and lips, cradled his son's head to his chest, and he looked up to the quiet sky, at the drifting and meaningless clouds, and he gently squeezed his son's head, licking his son's blood from his own lips, and he cursed God for letting this happen to his son, that he would damn God till the day he died, right down into hell, where God's son really belonged, for what grief he had brought upon all of us, what an untold amount of anguish he had brought with him into his world; and, for as long as he lived, he was going to search for the man who did this to his boy, find the bastard and make him suffer like no man or woman on earth had ever suffered; and, without a doubt, it was one of the Tans who did it; those bloody bastards, jealous because his son was a real soldier who fought and died for something, but they were only savages, who terrorized for nothing and nobody.

—Those barbarian savages, the weeping tailor repeated, as he rocked his dead son in his arms, rocked him in death, as he did when Albert was a motherless child in nappies, crying by the hearth in the cottage beyond.

And when the dark had arrived that evening, Mick Russell blundered through my aunt's open doorway. She and Ned Franklin were having a cup of tea at the hearth; Ned said he had come up to wish me good-bye, although he sat opposite my aunt at the fire and only talked to her. He was clean-shaven; he wore his white Sunday shirt, and a brown sports jacket, which, he told us, the tailor had made for his father years and years ago, and when Ned had walked in, my aunt looked upon him with great interest, telling him how grand he looked in the jacket, and why had he waited till now to wear it—regardless of all that, I was sitting on the floor at my aunt's feet, and the three of us turned to see Mick Russell, looming, unsteadily coming toward the hearth, his hair more tossed than I'd ever seen it, his shapeless mouth, and that mad look in his eyes. Ned Franklin was up out of his seat like a light, inquiring severely as to where the Russell manners had gone to, for what an awful cheek it was to walk into a neighbor's house without a knock on the door or a God bless. My aunt was standing, too, and I stood and gripped her dress, half hiding behind her, a weakness coming over me, knowing whatever was about to happen was partly my fault.

—You're welcome, Mick, my aunt said kindly, —will you have a cup of tea? Then to Ned Franklin, —Careful there now, Ned. It looks like he has a few jars on him, and she stepped directly between Ned Franklin and Mick Russell.

—No thank you, young Mary, Mick Russell snorted, winking madly at my aunt.

—Get out of this house you drunken scut! said Ned Franklin.

I wound my aunt's dress around my fist. Again she spoke, calmly, calling Mick by name, saying that there was a fresh pot of tea on the hob, and would he sit down for the love of God, for haven't they been neighbors who have got on so well, known each other for years and years.

—Get out you pup, to behave like this in a neighbor's house. Ned Franklin's face was so red that it had turned a shade of black; a huge tear hung from the end of his nose.

—What the hell's wrong with you, Franklin? Have you not asked her yet? Does she not want to go down the hill and live in your auld place?—God, but don't you look like the bee's knees this evening. Is this the evening to ask? How strange it is the very evening I myself came to visit. But didn't you not give up that game a long time ago or have your tears blinded you too much to notice that the young woman is not so young anymore?

Mick Russell laughed; he took a few steps back from us and shadowboxed before the table; the handles on the two buckets of water by the door rattled; then he came forward, his long hands stretched out in front of him, reaching for Ned Franklin's neck. My aunt spread her legs and raised her hands up high between the two of them.

—Oh, what am I going to do now, she shrieked, —with Mike's young boy hearing this; please, Mick, can't you behave yourself and be quiet, with Mike's son here; and my aunt was now pressed between the two men, me pressed between her and Ned Franklin, whose rough trousers was scraping the back of my leg. —Please, for God's sake, she pleaded, Mike's boy is here, please, this will bring the wrath of God down upon us. There's not a day's luck in this behavior.

—Aha, yes, the boy himself, Mick Russell winked down at me, I trying to hide from him, but at the same time peeking out to see his huge eyes glowing like the hot coals themselves, his white teeth shining. —The boy, he said, —a priest is what that boy is, but now that I think about it, he'd only be a great one to hear the confessions; then Mick took a step back again; the three of us didn't budge, as he reached into his coat pocket and pulled out a pistol, a small one, the likes of which I had never before seen, but I had only seen one in the comics.

—The God's honest truth, ha, at last, as they say, and he raised the pistol up the way a drunken cowboy outside of a rowdy saloon would, his finger pressed against the trigger. —Do you know how many years I have the truth, boys. He did away with himself, God bless him, Mary, Mick Russell laughed. —And I was there to see it all. Right there, near the trees, I was! I saw every bit of it and I have to see it every night of my life. The bloody Tans had nothing to do with it. There wasn't even a sign of them anywhere.

He pulled the trigger. The gun clicked. The three of us jumped with fright, not Mick, though, who only hollered.

—There's not a thing in it, don't worry, he said, pointing the gun at the three of us, lowering it to his waist, gripping the gun now with two hands, keeping it pointed. —Don't worry. Whatever was in it was used on the goats and himself, Mary, and I lied to that old tailor. I lied to him and he give me a fucking free coat for my Confirmation and who else would have done that around here and there was my thanks—I lied to him! They all told me to not say a word, your own father being the king of all of them. Had always to do what old Jack Carmody says. Everyone had to. The king of the Conway's hill. *Don't say a word now, Mick. Not to your own father and mother or no one else. Whatever you do don't say a word about anything. Don't ever ever tell a soul*—Mick Russell said in a mocking, childish voice. —Well now, I can tell all I like, where's the harm in it now. No harm left at all.

—Aha, for God's sake, Russell! Behind me, Ned Franklin raised his voice. —What good would it do, Russell! What good would it do his poor father to know, you dirty scut you! That there wouldn't be a bullet in that gun you'd have put into yourself a long time ago. Wandering around the roads like the tinker that you are. A shame you are to the father and mother that raised you. You ass you, and God blast you, to come up here in that state, terrorizing your neighbors in their own homes like the foe did years back, and where's the good in it for the poor tailor to know any of it, I ask you, you dirty fool! Where's the good!

—I'll die, I'll die, my aunt was wailing, but she didn't move. Mick Russell stuck the gun back in his coat pocket, came toward the three of us again, and while Ned Franklin pushed against my aunt's shoulders, Mick Russell tried to get to me, saying, —Let's hear what young Carmody has to say about all this, he being the one going to school, where they tell you everything, so they say, and, again, my aunt pleading, —He's Mike's son, for God's sake, he's only a boy, and don't bring talk like that into this house.

Mick Russell only laughed and drew the gun out of his pocket again, and now held it before Ned Franklin's face, directly above my aunt's head.

—What good is it, right enough, Franklin, Mick gritted his teeth. —But you yourself didn't have to see it or watch his poor father see the son. You wouldn't say what good is it if you did, you being such a brave fella yourself, but have you asked her yet, Franklin? Did you ever even have the backbone to even do that much, ask her and then tell her that poor Albert did it to himself, and there wasn't a sign of a Tan about—

—She knows that with years, you galoot! Ned shouted. —She knows with a lifetime. What in the name of God do you think we've talked about all these times! Cows and goats! Is that all you think we're ever able to talk about!

Mick didn't seem to hear that, or if he did, he didn't take any notice of it.

—And you know what else he said; Mick stepped back, and cocked the gun at my aunt. —You want to know what else Albert said, Mary. *She won't forgive me,* was what that poor boy said, *she'll never forgive me,* the poor soldier cried, so put that in your pipes and smoke it so that I don't have to carry it around with me anymore. Not anymore! Sure you have the young fella there to thank for all that—

—Help me here, Jack, before someone gets killed dead, and my aunt and I pushed Mick Russell, I pushing against her backside, and Ned Franklin pushed my aunt's shoulders, all of us pushing him toward the door, where he all of a sudden broke free from us, roaring like a savage, as he jumped into the dark yard. I fell down on the floor and my aunt immediately went and sat in her seat by the hearth, her head pressed into her hands. There was one last yell from him in the yard: —Have you asked her yet! Have you! It's time you did, if you haven't!

Ned Franklin leaned his hands upon his knees, then lifted his right hand and gripped my shoulder and shook me. —Don't be listening to him. No one knew then and no one will ever know and it doesn't matter one bit, and if you want to know, they were more than a few around who thought that Albert brought the devil home inside of him, that he had brought a curse home with him, and every calf that died in springtime and every cow and pig that got sick they blamed Albert Cagney over it, and that, my boy, is the last of it, and you should not ask another word about it. Are you listening to me now, Jack Carmody.

He waved his finger before my face. I shamefully bowed my head, watched the tear-wet floor, thinking what a curse it must be to have to cry all the time.

I thrust my hands into my pockets. —I promise I won't ever again mention another word about it. I won't ask or look, Mr. Franklin.

—Good boy, he said. —That's exactly what I want to hear from you, God help us, if your mother only knew half of the trouble you've caused, you wouldn't be let leave the house again till you're my age.

He went and stood next my aunt.

—I'm frightfully sorry for everything, Ned, she cried into her hands, —I didn't have much say in any of it, I was only a girl, and that's all I ever was in my father's eyes, and you know yourself what a tyrant he was, God rest him.

Ned's tears now fell at her feet; he wiped at a few stray tears from her shoulder, and rested his fingers there.

—Don't I know that only too well, Mary, he said. —Those days are all done with, thank God, and I'm glad they are, and we're fine now.

He lifted his hand and gently stroked her gray head, fixing the strands of hair that had fallen from around her ear.

She sobbed louder. —Oh, I'm so sorry, Ned. I'm so sorry for every bit of it. I could never get Albert out of my mind. If he'd lived, it would have all been different. He would have become like everyone else, an ordinary, everyday person, but I couldn't see beyond him for years and when I was in time able to, it was too late for all of us.

—You're grand, Mary. Not a bother, Mary, Ned was petting the top of her head. —You're fine this moment, and that is the most important thing of all to me—

My aunt suddenly raised her head. Ned's hand fell away. He cleared his throat. His face turned a shade redder. He bowed his head, went and sat on the other side of the fire.

The look of terror on my aunt's face would make you think the house was on fire. —Jesus God, is Jack Carmody all right; I completely forgot about him—

—I'm fine, I said. I was sitting in the middle of the floor, enjoying very much watching the two of them.

My aunt's eyes narrowed and darkened. —You never told me you met Mick Russell. You never said a word to me about him, Jack Carmody—

—I'm sorry, Auntie, I said.

—Did that fecker give you cigarettes?

—Only the one or two—

—Aha now, Mary, the one or two won't do him a bit of harm, Ned Franklin was leaning over the fire, turning the coals with the tongs. —Did that madman give you any drink, young Jack? he held the tongs up and squeezed the handle.

My aunt made a face at me and winked. —Not a drop, Ned, I said.

—Sure, there's nothing to worry about then, Ned said, —as long as he didn't give him the drink.

He put the tongs aside, and sat into his seat. He straightened the collar of his coat and shirt, then crossed his legs and folded his hands across his lap. —That was a good bit of excitement, sure enough, he sighed. —That's about enough for the next twenty years or so, Mary.

—What we need now more than anything else is a mug of tea, my aunt said.

Ned Franklin immediately crossed the hearth and picked up the teapot at my aunt's feet; he filled the mugs, and handed me mine.

—You know you can't tell them a word of this at home, Jack, said my aunt. —They'd go stone mad, Jack.

Ned sat into his seat. He took a drink, then rested the mug on his knee.

—That young fella won't say a word. Don't be worrying at all, Mary.

—Not a word will I say, I looked at my aunt, who hadn't taken her eyes from me. —They'd blame me for it, anyway. They'd say I was poking my nose into places where I shouldn't, I told them, believing and knowing this to be the truth.

Ned Franklin grinned. —Well, they'd be more than right there, but you're a good boy, too, I do declare.

—Jack's the very best in the world, my aunt smiled. —You had a grand holiday, you did, Jack.

—The best I ever had.

—I'm very fond of you, Jack.

—Don't I know that, I said, and drank my tea.

—We're as grand as we've ever been, maybe even more fit for it than we were before, Mary, Ned Franklin said.

—We are, Ned, she said; then she turned to me, asked in a puzzled voice, —But why, in the name of God, Jack, are you so interested in Albert Cagney anyway?

—Well, as my father said, he had the courage, I said, though I had no clue what I was talking about, so I asked, —What is courage exactly?

—You should know that yourself. You're the one who's going to school; Ned Franklin smiled contentedly at my aunt. —The young people these days. Don't know a thing, do they now, Mary, he added.

—Yes, indeed, Ned, said my aunt. —You often have to wonder what they spend all their time doing up there in that place at all.

───

—But why were you so mad to know about him? my mother said to me on the hospital lawn, on a Saturday evening in July, all those years later.

—I'm not sure of it, to be honest, Ma, I said to her. —Maybe it's because I thought all the excitement happened before I was born, and Albert went away and had these adventures—

—Adventures that killed him, or if they didn't, they drove him mad, she said, as though it were a warning to me. —And you wouldn't be so fond of those times if you had to live through them. You'd want to put those events out of your head as quick as you could and go on—

I interrupted her. —I suppose Mick Russell was the one who was right, though, about what happened to Albert in the end.

—I have to say, Jack, you know more about it than I do. Your father and I didn't have much to say about those things at all—

—But the two of them didn't make it up, I said. —Aunt Mary and my father—

—Oh, you're dead wrong there, Jack, said she. —They did make it up, but they went on behaving their usual way after Mass, behave like children, the two of them always did, although as you yourself know, they slept in the same room when they were children, but they made it up the summer you went off to work in Dublin, about two weeks after you left. We all missed you very much, and your aunt Mary especially—she used to go on about you after Mass, but your father, God rest him, says to me one morning, I need to go up there, and I asked him what was he talking about, and he said I need to go back up home and see her. That was the first time I had ever heard him call that place home, so I was pure delighted, of course I was. It must have been your going away that caused it to happen, after Kate and Mary, but later that morning, Dan drove him around to the boreen, and the first person he ran into was your old friend Mick Russell, and he had to go in there and have a jar, but I'm sure that helped him, gave him a bit of courage to walk on up that long boreen and face her. He ended up spending all day up there, and when he came back, he was in very good form—had a few with his sister, he did. Your aunt was known to be fond of a drop on the quiet, when she got into one of her states—

—I had no idea, Ma—

—Well, Jack, your poor father didn't live long after—

I quickly said, —Ma, I ran into Rome, by the way. Back at Powers, two weeks ago, I was in there with Dan on a Saturday night. He was with John Hogan and the son Marty. John and Rome were mad asking for you, asking when were you coming home. Rome said he'd come in to see you but it's hard for him to get around now, he's such a fine age—

—Larry Kelly, my mother watched the hospital doors. —Rome Kelly. I was always very close to Larry and he was very kind to me, never married himself, Jack, a bit too old, Larry was, though he never did look a day of it, she said sadly.

She never did discuss my father's age with me, and I never brought it up.

—Dan still laughs about how they all used to make fun of each other in Powers, on a Sunday after Mass—

—I'd believe every word of it, she said. —Oh, I'm so excited, though, Jack, Mary and Kate, back home next week. It'll be grand, all of us together.

She coughed into the cup, and twirled the cup in her lap; she sighed, —There's something I have to tell you about, Jack.

—Go on, Ma. She had a grave look on her face, and I was certain she was, at last, going to admit to me foreboding news I already knew about her illness.

—Dan is going to sell Conway's hill, she said. —He asked me would I tell you, and I said I would. He thought it was best that I be the one to tell you.

—That's fine, Ma, I said, taken aback for an instant. —My father gave it to him, I stuttered. —It's his land now to do whatever he likes to with it.

I had spoken without remorse. It's not as though I wanted to come home from the life I was making in the city and live on Conway's hill, or any other place around where I grew up. None of that seemed possible then or ever.

—Your aunt Mary's cottage didn't survive the past winter, my mother said, —and it's so far in from the road and sure the land is worthless. It's all rocks, but you know how tourists would give anything to own that, the loneliest and most miserable place in the world, but those people can turn misery into luxury with their money, she said bitterly.

—It seems our only choice is to go with the times, Ma, I lit a cigarette and said.

—It's all God's will, I suppose it is, in the end, Jack. That's all I ever understand.

She held her hand out; and I held and kissed the back of her frail hand.

—I'm getting better, Jack, I feel a thousand times better than yesterday. She spit into the cup.

—I should wheel you in and head for the station. It's nearly evening; and I stood and wiped the grass from the seat of my pants. I tightened the blanket around her shoulders, and undid the lock on the wheelchair.

—Larry, handsome Larry, my mother said, as I wheeled her down the path, away from the trees, toward the hospital doors. —I remember seeing him for the first time stand outside Powers at Mr. Cagney's funeral, and I remember seeing him standing at the bar after, talking to your father. I was thinking who is that dark foreign-looking fella. Of course I didn't know any of those people back then. Oh, Jack, I have to admit to you that I have wished here at night, wished it as I listened to the dreadful sound of the city, wished the world hadn't found us and didn't take the things I love away, but I should be ashamed of such thinking, because I got my children, and what more could I ask for. They were my great blessings. They were my life, and I wouldn't have wanted it any other way.

All the things they don't tell you, and then the things they do. Her last few days. The hospital doors split open. I wheeled her through the vestibule, past the reception desk, where the nurses waved and said, Hello Mrs. Carmody, Hello there, Jack. One dark-haired nurse, with bangs and shining green eyes, leaned over the desk and told my mother that it looked as though the fresh air was doing her the world of good. The nurse's breasts swelled up beautifully against her uniform. My mother waved and smiled at the nurse. I did, too; then I bent over and kissed my mother on the head.

—When I'm well, Jack, we'll have a dinner at home in Dan's new house. They have everything in it. Sure your father and me had nothing when you were babies. But we'll have a big dinner and invite Larry over. He was a fine singer, too, you know, very fond of me—

—Didn't he sing in Powers when I was in there with Dan, I told her, —and as usual everyone stopped talking and listened to him.

We were in her room by then. I pushed the wheelchair up to the window, where she could look down on the street, or out over Limerick City, though she did neither, but sat in the chair, with her hands joined on her lap, her head lowered. Cities near or far were of no interest to her. She wanted the country always; she longed for the air, the fields, and the great silence.

—"I'm at Home in Any Tipperary Town," he used to sing that one, she said.

—Well, there you go, Ma, I said, —that's the very one he sang.

I was standing behind her chair, watching the sky; a far-off tattered rain cloud moved slowly across the window. My mother was humming the chorus of the song.

LEAVE ME ON THE ROAD TO NEANAGH
HEAR THE RIPPLING SHANNON CALL

WHERE THE ARRAGH MOUNTAINS JOIN THE SILVERMINES
I'LL BE HAPPY TOO IN CAHIR, WHERE THE GALTEE
SHADOWS FALL
I'M AT HOME IN ANY TIPPERARY TOWN.

She stopped humming. —You were born in this city, Jack, not in Tipperary town like your brother and sisters. I told you that one before, didn't I?

She hadn't, and I told her.

—You were, indeed, not too far down the road from here, it was, I think. Rome came in to see me that evening, a few hours before you were born. I had no idea when you were going to arrive, Jack Carmody.

She gave a strained and hearty laugh; and, in a peculiar burst of energy, she began to arrange the dressing gown around her knees. I emptied her cup down the sink. I turned the tap on and rinsed the cup out, dried it off, came back and put it into her hand. I knelt next to her chair, and held her bony wrist.

—He wanted to marry me, Jack, years ago, Larry did. But I was fond of your father. I knew from the moment I saw him at the tailor's funeral I'd spend the rest of my life with him and that, Jack, was God's will, and there's no more to say about it, and you don't be asking me anything, she warned in that voice of hers.

—But did Rome say to you that he wanted to marry you? I asked in amazement, though my words didn't sound it, but this one I wanted settled there and then.

She laid her right hand, flat, upon her empty chest. —Well, Jack, the week before I married your father he came up to the grocery, codding me in some way, he was, knowing nothing could change, but he picked me up in his arms the day he visited me here, with you inside of me, a few hours before you were born. He picked me up in his arms and his lovely black eyes crying and he took me up the stairs. The steps were wet and shining from mopping, but I felt very safe in his arms. I didn't think I could fall or anything.

She joined her hands at her chest, and began to cough, a forlorn, hollow, and blasted sound—I got up quickly and stood behind her, rubbing gently between her shoulder blades. Her bones were sharp against my fingertips; I told her to hold on for a second, as I dashed to the sink and filled a half-glass of water and brought it to her. She took one sip and retched, then held the shaking glass sideways to me, and the water splashed onto the floor. I took the glass from her, put it down on the floor. I dragged a paper hankie from my arse pocket, and wiped the water up.

—He cried to me then, Jack, she composed herself. I flung the hankie across the floor, into the rubbish bin, and I looked up at her. —He cried and said he lived with a great fondness for me, and that I was beautiful to him. He said it was all very hard for him at times, having to live with it. How I have not forgotten his words, in all these years. Your father knew Rome had a bit of a grá for me. But I never told your father he visited me in here the time you were born, and you can be dead sure Rome never said a word about it to your father.

—Should I brush your hair, Ma, I didn't want to hear anymore of it—I was going to be late for my train.

—Not at all, my hair is fine, Jack, you can brush it next week, when you come down. Oh, I'm going to miss you so much till then, Jack. I enjoy the chat so much, but I'm very tired now, but Mary and Kate will be here next week. Say your prayers, Jack, won't you.

—I will, Ma, I will—you have clean handkerchiefs?

—I do, I've too many. I'm fine, Jack, she said. —Please, you don't ever have to worry about me; in a few more weeks, I'll be right as rain. I'm a million times better than I was last week, that's for sure. Go on now and get the train. Get that train and don't be late for work in the morning. Mind your job always. That's all you have now, Jack.

—Right so, Ma, I got up from my knees. —I'll head off then. You're grand, you are.

—Never better, Jack, she glanced up, smiling as best she could.

—I'll see you next week, Ma, God bless, I held her hand; I bent to kiss her cheek.

She squeezed my hand. —They have a fine big kitchen, they do, Jack. Dan and his wife Helen do, but that would be a fine dinner for all of us, Kate and Mary, you, all of us again, and we'll invite Rome Kelly over. He'd come, too, sure Rome's on his own all the time. I often think in here how lonely he must be. Dan could drive over and bring him. It'd be lovely, Jack, like the old days again.

━━━━━━

So Rome was fond of her. She was fond of Rome. No, it couldn't be, she made it all up, a few days before she died, when she could say whatever it was that entered her head, not having to worry about what they call the future, anymore. The pain, it was; she was out of her head. But did Rome have a fondness for her? I couldn't stop thinking about it: Rome hunted his cows in and out morning and evening, milked them, talked and laughed with John Hogan, and my father, when he was alive; Rome leaned over his gate, watched his cows stroll through the field, into the shadows of the bushes, wanked like a bachelor, walked up the street in Kilroan, all dressed up on a Sunday morning, before he became old and his hair changed to white, before he got shook-looking; back then his coal black hair oiled and shining, the thick, stiff strands parted at the side, the perfect knot of his red Sunday tie, snug against the collar of his flawlessly ironed shirt, his round eyes and his clean-shaven face and his big awkward nose, his heavy bottom lip, which he bit down upon, showing his two front teeth, when he was talking to you in a serious way, Rome singing "I'm at Home in Any Tipperary Town" in Powers, shaking hands and chatting away with people about the weather after Mass, living with that want for years and years. He did have a want for her; of course he did; so then, if he did, he held her in his arms, carried her up the steps of the shining, menacing stairs, with me turning toward the world, that he didn't slip and fall on the fucking stairs, save me from all of them!—no, no, he did not. Pure madness. They all had it in them. Just making your life up on the spot. I wouldn't put anything past either of them. But it could have been the mind going, too; and, when that goes, you're completely fucked; I heard that said for the first time back at the forge. Rome himself might have been the one who said it. A life before me I didn't know a thing about and a life behind me I didn't know a thing about.

She died the Tuesday after that Saturday. I took the evening train from Dublin to Limerick Junction and Dan drove over and picked me up. Kate and Mary flew into Shannon on Wednesday morning, with their English husbands, whose four parents were born in the west of Ireland. We waked her at home, in the back bedroom, with the thin lace curtain on the window, which she had brought from her and my father's room in the old house, which she cared for, like others would family jewels; the curtain had originally come from her own father's house. Kate, Mary, and Helen boiled kettles of water on the range to brew pots of tea. Plates of sandwiches to be made. Loaves of Kiely's sliced bread, on the kitchen table. Sagging brown paper bags of summer tomatoes. Blocks of Galtee cheese. Heads of lettuce, with clay stuck to their roots, brought in from the haggart. A bowl of hard-boiled eggs. Pounds of butter left out to soften. Two boxes of salt. Pounds of sliced ham, wrapped in wax paper. Bottles of Powers and Paddy whiskey and crates of beer, which Dan and myself went to Powers to buy, brought them home in the boot of the car. The sisters' husbands helped. Like family now. The four of us had a pint each in the bar, smoking and silently watching the racing on the television, while Leo Power and his son, Jim, got it all together. Had one more pint each then, which Leo stood to us. Leo said, —Your father's people I knew well, lads, a course, my own father, God rest him, knew them a lot better. Ye're sitting in their places right where ye are—but sorry for yer troubles now about the mother. I heard she had a long battle with it.

The neighbors starting to trickle in, in the early afternoon. Men and women in their Sunday clothes.

Have to go to that wake at Carmodys. Have to go to that funeral tomorrow, too, God knows. Sure don't I know them Carmodys my whole life. And I know the O'Neills from way back. Have to go so. Their father not dead a long time. Afraid so. Can't miss that one. The children are all away except for the one at home.

The men and women filling up the kitchen: The men opening the top buttons of the shirts, dragging the ties loose, sighing with relief. Putting the glasses and the plates on the floor and on the edge of the table and the top of the television. The sweating women, at the end having to unbutton their coats, unknot their headscarves and shove them into their coat pockets. The women's red lipstick shining. The men had to shave in the middle of the week. Save them from doing it though on a Saturday night for a Sunday morning—a fine day in early August. The cars were parked on both sides of the road and in along the path, the cars driven up and tilting sideways on the headland. Dan had to stand outside and direct the cars.

How're you, Dan? How're you keeping, son? Sorry for your troubles now, Dan. Are they all back from abroad, they are? I wasn't at the mart at all last week. I might go a Friday of next week, Dan, if I can get the second-cut of silage done. If the weather will hold up. Sure you couldn't expect her to survive too long after himself. Yerra, sure she's much better off where she is now, that much I can tell you myself, Dan.

Heads bowed, taking their caps off at the hall door, then down to the room, kneeling on one knee, putting their cap underneath the knee. Then a rapid sign of the cross, out of the room and down to the kitchen, as fast as a light.

She looks grand. She does. God bless her. Her hair does look grand. All dolled up. The girls did a flaking job. A cup of tea, I will. Fair enough. I'll start with that. May God rest her. May God have mercy on her soul. She's gone straight up to heaven, where all her

people are, and himself is; a course he is. I have the very man here for
you. Not tea at all. But get that into you and when you're done with
that one I have another one for you. And thank you very much for
coming. Sure don't I know your people my whole life. And I'm very
sorry for your troubles. I knew your father well. And that was years
ago. Living on Conway's hill. He was then. With his sister. Never
knew your grandfather but he was a bit of a hard one. So I heard
from my own father. Sure living in that place would turn Janey Man
himself into the devil. And your aunt. She was great gas. An indi-
vidual is what the people on the TV would call her.

Cousins from afar who I'd never met before, though Kate and Mary
knew them. Went to the Secondary school in the village of Hospital
with them, to the Nuns and the Christian Brothers. One in the Civil
Service now, the other working in the bank in Tipperary town.

Fine jobs. Jobs that will last you a lifetime. It would be great if you
could just hand them on to your own. Hand them down like the
Royal family has the right to do. Right to do whatever they want.
Royal my arse. Now, now, on a day like this. But, sure, we have to
laugh, too, Janey Man, ha! Your poor mother wouldn't mind it one
bit. I will so just have the one more. Then I'm off. I'll get out of yer
way now girls and let ye work. You will not you'll sit down there and
I'll make you another sandwich. Sure she was as well off. Yes. She
had a massive battle with it, all right. The patience, she had, with the
man above. Very devout. Yes. It was hard on all of ye. The going and
the coming. The coming and going. The going back and forth. And
now all that's over with. Have to milk the cows. That's the only other
thing in life you can't escape. A drop of whiskey or a bottle of stout.
The whiskey will do fine. God but England is suiting the two of you.
And this is the husband. And that's the other one over there. I was
wondering who those two tall lads are. I knew I'd never seen any of
them around before. Grand to meet you, all right. You're very welcome. A pity it's under such circumstances mind you. Is the craic still
good in Cricklewood? Ha! That's enough now. That's too much. I'll
drink it anyway. It might even do me some good. The hay and silage

would kill any man stone dead. The young fella does the milking now. All they have to do is turn on the machine. Press a button in the milking parlor and it's all over with. That's if they're milking cows at all. They're paying us now not to milk them. Sure we'll take it. Take all we can get from them. It's not better or worse than the old days it's only different. What's the use. Too much time on their hands is what's wrong with the young people nowadays. Bating up the old people. Stealing their few pennies. Afraid to do a decent day's work is what's wrong with them. They should be ashamed of themselves. Take everything they can from the government for nothing. And they give it away to them, too. Don't appreciate all they have is the thing. But sure, too, you'd have to know the other side of it to appreciate it. What's the use in talking about it. Grand house, mind you, it is. Far better than the old one. And the lovely garden she grew outside there. Fine view from the window. See all the way to the end of the world. And the range. The Stanley was certainly a miraculous invention, whoever did it. It must have been an Englishman who did it. Not the same one who went up the Congo after your man, I'd say. But they might be related. A course they might.

The smell of farts and face powder, the air in the kitchen thickened with cigarette smoke. Sweating faces and patches of sweat under the arms. The smell of Lifebuoy and Lux soap and Ponds cold cream. The men began to move out the door, to the yard. The women stayed in the kitchen, sipping their tea, sipping their sherry. The women able to chat with one another now.

Dan and Jack, will ye take a few chairs out for Rome and John to sit in. They're in the front room. There's coats on top of them but just put them on the floor. Barely able to stand, those two boyos are. And that's not from the age. Forgive me for laughing now on a day like this, but I must. Strange, isn't it. But I'm handling it.

That's grand, Dan. Move it over here a bit so that I can watch your mother's flowers. Your grand mother. God bless her. I'll take that one, Jack. Turn it that way. Keep the light out of my eyes. How're you, Jack? How're you keeping? There you are, young Jack.

Another bit the other way. A fine-looking man, you are. It's a lovely day, after all. Rain threatened this morning that never came. And how're things up in the Big Smoke, Jack? Looks like it's doing you the world of good. Making the money, I hope. Send some down our way, ha. The pension wouldn't feed a hen. But what else can you expect from the government. I will have another sandwich. Don't want to put you out now. Come over here to me, Jack. I will have one then, while you're at it. Come back here to us, Jack. Come here, young fella. The girls will do all that. Saw your bare arse in nappies in that old house. Saw your small mickey. Just slagging you, Jack. Shake hands with me, Jack. You have to have the laugh. Put it there. Right there. I knew your father all my life, God have mercy on his soul. But you know that only too well. He's up there now with the blacksmith, God help the two of them. Tormenting each other. Like the man having to push the stone up the hill that rolls back down for all time. Come here to me, Jack. Come back here, son. Very sorry, Jack. Very sorry I am to hear about your mother. A grand lady she was; indeed, she was, Jack. One of the best that God ever put breath in. Can't see a thing 'cause the sun's strong. But glad to get it. Don't need the sun for the silage like it used to be long ago with the hay. You remember piking the hay, of course, Jack. You weren't too bad in a meadow. Not as good as your brother, mind you. She grew grand flowers all right.

Will you have a cup of tea, Rome? A cup of tea, John? Not at all. Grand. Grand. I will. I will then. What's that shrub called, Dan? You don't know, you wouldn't. Weren't very good in school. That's a lovely shrub, mind you. Never seen the likes of it around here before. What's that shrub called, Jack? A foreign name, ha! Latin, that is. Everything these days is turning foreign. The foreigners have been coming to these shores since the Vikings. A long time before them even, I do suppose. The Vikings were marauders. Got the bejasus bate out of them in Clontarf in the end. Brian Boru was the one who bested them. Put an end to them. Bate them out of the country. But then Brian Boru was killed himself after the battle. Killed dead on his knees praying in his tent by the head Viking. Cut him open with his hatchet. Can't think of that fella's name that killed him. Not for the life of me. Can't think of it. So you're saying that Brian Boru won and lost at the same time. You could put it that way. And sure that's the way it is with all of your history. And sure after that they became like the rest of us. Like so many did. Became more like us than we are like ourselves. And what's that about? That's about nothing is what that's about. Jack! Jack! You ever go out there as far as Clontarf! Did you, Jack? The Vikings dragged them boats up onto the strand. I've never been as far as the sea, myself. How could we go to the sea when the cows had to be milked and the hay to be saved and 'twould freeze the arse off you to go there in the wintertime. Not much good in that. The salt in the wind would burn the eyes out of your head. Or so I heard. Very very sorry to hear it, Jack.

And a cool breeze came from out of the fields. The smell of the bog with it. A hint of autumn in the breeze. The sun skimming the trees and the sunlight slanting along the yard, through the tops of her flowers and shrubs. Crows cawing, then lifting out of the poplar trees, in the paddock beyond. I turned from the men to watch them. Dark rags in the sky. Never saw them like that before. Will, till I die, see them this way.

Not a bad life, at all, Nora Carmody had. Sure, she'll be with everyone she knows now. Could be an awful lot worse. The people starving in Africa. They have too much of the sun and we don't have half enough of it. It's never just right, it looks like. The young ones are good all right with their Trocaire boxes. I see them putting the pennies in. You have to hand it to them there. That's the truth. He was certainly well up in years when he met her. A lucky man he was to meet her. Here's the parish priest himself. Have to stand up out of the chair now. Have to get up out of it for him. How're you, Father? That's a grand new car you're driving, Father! And you didn't ever wear down the tires on the last one. You might as well, if you can, Father, ha! How're them racehorses keeping at all, Father? God bless every last one of them.

I went down into the room later. They would not wander in here anymore. They had done this part of it. In a few hours they'd put her in the coffin and take it to the church. Tomorrow, after the Mass, Dan and me and Rome and John would shoulder the coffin, lower it into a hole in the ground underneath the trees. Down there, with the rest of them, where their flesh was changed to clay, which nourished the roots and the white blossoms, made the thick skin of the haws red. Her curtain before me filled out like a sail. The candle on the night table next to her bed was almost burned out. I pinched the wick between my fingers. Her body was lean, tidy beneath the dark quilt. Kate had powdered her face and dabbed rouge on her cheeks. Mary had balled up paper hankies and stuffed them inside, to fill her cheeks out. A box of matches that Dan had tucked underneath her chin, concealed with the quilt, to hold her chin up, so that her face was toward the ceiling. The crucifix on the wall above her, the scapulars and the medals still around her neck, the rosary beads like a crown in her joined hands. Ma, I whispered, sitting on the edge of the bed, watching down at her face; Ma, I said loudly, and my own voice came back to me. I wanted to kiss her face, stoop and kiss it. But I couldn't, although I had a glass of whiskey in me. She was gone. Her blood was. And all this pageantry. To have to endure it. Just so that others can have a bit of a get-together. Celebrate the life of the dead you or they don't know a thing about. Their poor mother. Not long after their father. Oh, to be alone! To be alone and far from all of them! Back in my flat in Dublin and dancing on a Saturday night after work, pissed and holding a girl against a wall to the pounding music, my mickey filled with warm blood. My posters of Bob Dylan and The Smiths above my single bed. Listening to my records. Reading sentences from my books. My shirts hanging in the wardrobe. My clean underwear and socks in the top drawer. My worn pair of shoes, inside the door, next to the meter I fed the fifty pences into, so that there was light and heat. The door of the 16 bus hissing when it stopped at the bus stop on Drumcondra Road, then revving up, dragging a plume of black smoke after it, whose smell re-

mained in the air above the Tolka River for hours, drifting through
my window; that was all I wanted—the sun was fully sunk and the
light was going out of the fields, the curtain still swollen. The blue
walls. The body. The insufferable present. Give me anything but
now. A car on the path taking off. Off home to milk the cows. The
gravel spitting up underneath the car. I got up from the bed and
went to the window and pulled the curtain back along the rail. My
sisters crying, saying good-bye to a neighbor, in the hall. I opened
the window out and took a smoke from my shirt pocket and lit it up,
leaning my elbows upon the windowsill. The edge of the sky above
the trees streaked bluish and gray. The cows and the calves lying
down for the night, following routine. Life would be tolerable if you
were one of them. Their pain was in a moment, then forgotten. She
was gone and the world was changed. If I only had the balls there
and then to go into the toilet, take the blade from Dan's razor and
make one orderly cut on each one of my wrists. In the kitchen, in a
day or two, they'd have another get-together. All those delicious
sandwiches made and eaten in my honor. Bottles drained and cups
of tea drank. That wouldn't land me up above with them. I'd be sent
down below. Albert was there. The balls that Albert had. My first
hero. The one who went away and came back home and then fell to
pieces. The one who was the devil's. The one they couldn't kill, who
had to kill himself—but it was probably the coming back home that
killed him more than that war that made their next war and their one
after that one materialize. No end to it ever, it looks like, Jack, as
Rome Kelly would say—and all Albert was now was clay, as my father and my aunt were clay, and soon my mother. For there was no
down below or up above. There was only the clay; that's all we all are.
I raised my hand and waved good-bye to the cows. I then said good-
bye to the fields and the trees. This was Nora Carmody's world. She
and Mike Carmody made it. Adam and Eve Carmody. The Easter
Rising. The Civil war. The six counties. The Irish Republic. The
Troubles. The small farmer. Put up the ditches and made the gaps
and plowed the fields, milked the cows and had their children, lis-

tened to the priests and DeValera and those who came after him, praying like they were the chosen ones. I flicked the ashes out the window. For her, it had always been about the other side. For to suffer meant he had picked you out. The man above had. One of his personal favorites. Hail queen of Heaven. The patience of Job. Go on back with you so; go on; go on back to where I hope you'll find him and every single one of them. Rome should be up there with you before long. Here was nothing. Here was clay and cancer. Blood and a very big mess. People blowing each other to bits till the end of time. Stupid shite. A waste of time, pestering myself. Back and forth and over and back. Bollox. And where will any of it lead you to, Jack Carmody? No place. Mind your job always.

———

Three days later I was on the night train from Limerick Junction to Dublin. I sat in the smoking carriage; the lights were off, and the moonlight shone on the meadows, the fields and haycocks, the houses and the gardens, ponds and trees. The country accents; the laughing and joking of the heavy porter when the train stopped at Thurles; the smell of pig manure. The carriage doors opening and shutting, the laughter and the shouts of strangers and the sweet harvest air briefly drifting in. Letting people in. Letting people out.

What's going to become of him? So many times my father said those words, when I was small, and I never understood them, but on the train that night began the long and strange journey away from my mother; her death had freed me, and I could wander far away and be alone, with no one to watch me, no one to answer to, and no one anymore to need. I saw myself wandering down a street in London and a street in New York, staring at things and the people going by. I wasn't thinking about Dan selling Conway's hill, or that my aunt's cottage had fallen to ruin, as she had predicted and, like Albert and Mr. Cagney's cottage, that it would become a mound of stones and weeds. I thought about my sisters, in an airplane over the Irish Sea, my brother walking, alone, through a field behind our house, and I saw clearly the petals on the rhododendrons flickering like flames in the bright sunshine of a spring Sunday morning, feeling safe then, with my mother's warm body beside me, as we made our way home, and I heard my aunt singing: How lucky I was that day I walked through the evergreen trees, to have heard her voice; the single pink rosebush growing through the flagstones and clinging to the gable end of the whitewashed cottage; the land my father was born and raised on.

Her Black Mantilla

DAVIE CONDON WAS ON HIS WAY HOME FROM THE CREAM-
ery one morning in May when he saw the girl on the road ahead,
walking in the headland beneath the blossoming hawthorn trees. He
drew up next to her, stalled his horse and cart, and pulled the peak of
his cap over his eyes, while his horse, in stretching its neck to the
headland grass, wrenched the cart toward the headland and blocked
the girl's path. She stood motionless and silent as a statue, her head
level with the cart wheel, holding a small red suitcase to her chest.
Her long black mackintosh was buttoned to the throat, and she wore
a black mantilla that covered her head and the back of her neck.

Davie asked if he could give her a lift someplace, and in a low and
childlike voice she said she was looking for the Tarpeys' place.

—The Tarpeys. That's not so far down the road at all, he said,
gazing at the dusty road before him, the undamaged hoofprints, and
the tracks his cart had made a few hours earlier, the hawthorn blossoms drifting aimlessly along the road.

—Yes, sir, that's the name of them, sir.

He told her to sit up on the back corner of his cart, that he'd be
passing the Tarpeys' place, and without a word she lifted the red suitcase onto the back corner of the cart, which creaked when she sat up.
He waited until he did not hear her breath before he shook the reins,
told the horse to Git up, and the horse swung away from the ditch,
dragging a clump of grass in his mouth.

—It's a long walk from the station, Miss. He glanced sideways, guessing the station was where she had come from. He heard a faint reply, though he could not make out a word of it against the sound of the creaking wheels, the horse hooves striking the road, and the clinking traces. Then he slowed the horse, and glanced around to see the lower part of her round, pale face, her thick blood-red lips. The mantilla hid her forehead and eyes. Her legs hung over the edge of the cart, and he noticed she wore new shoes that were coated with fine dust from the roads. He pulled the reins to him and told the horse to stop. —Take them shoes off if you want to. Your feet must be sore, and we have a good ten minutes to go yet.

The girl leaned forward and unlaced the plain, black shoes, which she then held tenderly in her lap. She was wearing no stockings, and as Davie shook the reins and the horse began to move, she lifted her legs out before her, and the mackintosh parted to the knees. He drew his legs together, faced the road, and lashed the horse's rump with the end of the reins. The startled horse snorted, raised his tail, and broke into a brisk trot.

At the crossroads, Davie pointed to the farmhouse, in a paddock sloping upward, where four cows and a pony grazed. The girl put one foot on a spoke and stepped down, then reached up for her shoes and suitcase; she turned her back on him and stared at the farmhouse, her shoes in one hand and the suitcase in the other.

—Thank you, sir, she said, watching the cottage, but not taking a step toward it.

—You're welcome, he said, —and you don't have to call me sir, either. There aren't any of them around here.

He watched her put the suitcase and shoes down on the road; then she opened her mantilla, her hands rapidly fixing it around the top of her head and neck, and then arranging it around her face. He bashfully looked away from her, to the sagging thatched roof of the Tarpeys' cottage, part of which was obscured by elm trees growing far into their paddock. He bid her a good day; she kept staring and said nothing, as he led his horse and cart through the crossroads, went on down the road, but as he approached the first bend he told the horse to hold up, and he turned, because he felt she was still standing there, and now watching him, but behind him the crossroads were empty, only for a sudden and ghostly breeze he did not feel that shook the long and wild grass on the tall ditch.

Twenty-eight years ago, a shorthorn bull Davie's father owned crippled the Tarpey brother, James, who was then thirty. The brother had borrowed the bull and was leading it through the crossroads when the bull turned on him. It was talk for a long time about what bad luck had befallen the young man, who had been planning to marry a local girl, and never again did James Tarpey appear in public. He was bedridden all these years, cared for by his sister, Lena.

Davie had stopped again, to watch his cows grazing in his big field that went all the way to the crossroads. Then he was passing the Coughlins' house, which was down a short boreen. Mrs. Coughlin was carrying a bucket to the dairy; she did not see him, but if she did, she would have walked down to the roadside for a chat, although Davie was happy enough that she did not see him, for he avoided her if he could at all, like he did everyone else. Davie and Mrs. Coughlins' two boys—Brendan and Michael—had gone to National school together nearly thirty-five years ago. Michael had emigrated in his early twenties; Brendan lived at home and, like Davie, was unmarried. That morning, on his way out of the creamery store, he had run into Brendan, who told Davie about an upcoming dance in the parish hall, inquiring if he had any interest in going; a few of the lads were meeting beforehand in Powers.

—The winter put years on me, Brendan, he told his neighbor. —Anyway, I'm way too old at forty to be going to dances. I'd be far happier sitting at home reading the paper.

—There'll be loads of time left for you to sit reading newspapers, Brendan Coughlin laughed and slapped his neighbor on the shoulder.

Davie's horse and cart were traveling down the short boreen to his house. On both sides of the path, the poplars had filled out, the sunlight glinting on their silvery leaves. Davie felt the blood rising to his face; he squeezed the reins, shut his eyes to the irritating light, but only to see again the strange girl slipping her black shoes off, her pale ankles and the coat falling away, while the hawthorn blossoms floated above the road behind the cart—the horse had stalled on the flagstones before Condon's house, whose front door was shut. Davie threw the reins over the horse's back and hopped down. The noisy chickens gathered at his feet; he told them to hold on, he'd feed them in a minute; he was unhooking the traces when he noticed, out of the corner of his eye, his mother and sister walking through the big field beyond the house, on their daily journey to his father's grave, which had begun twenty-two years ago.

Alice Gilmartin was sixteen, an orphan sent out to the Tarpeys by the nuns and the help of a local parish priest, to work the small farm and help old Lena Tarpey with her bedridden brother. Lena Tarpey put Alice in the one room upstairs. It was small and rectangular, with a slanting ceiling, and one single bed below a small window. There was one homemade chair next to the bed, and an old wardrobe in the corner of the room. Alice put her shoes and the suitcase on the floor of the wardrobe, and hung her coat and Mass clothes on the hooks.

Lena Tarpey's bedroom was underneath the stairs, to the right of her brother's, whose solid brown door, with a rattling white doorknob, stayed closed until she had to empty his chamber pot, take in his food, the pan of warm water every Saturday afternoon to wash him, and she then only opened the door enough to slip in and quietly shut it behind her.

Lena Tarpey was thin and stooped; her face was brown and wrinkled. On weekdays, she wore a blue, faded scarf, and on Saturday night, when Alice went upstairs to bed, the old woman boiled two kettles of water over the fire and washed her hair with Lifebouy soap, in a basin at the kitchen table; after, she washed her scarf in the same water, rinsed it out and draped the scarf along the crane, where it dried overnight in the dying heat from the turf.

Alice was not a stranger to farm work: She had been sent out to help on farms before, so she brought the Tarpeys' four cows morning and evening, milked them, and hunted them out through the trees, into the paddock. She tackled the pony, hitched him to the cart, and took the milk to the creamery. Every Tuesday and Friday she brought a shopping basket and went into the creamery store to get a pound of butter, tea, sugar, or flour, whatever the old woman had ordered. What the Tarpeys owed was written down and deducted from their milk money at the end of the month.

When Alice returned from the creamery, she untackled the pony and went inside for breakfast. After she ate, she fed the hens, gathered the eggs, forked out the cow house, and wheeled the manure to the dung heap, in the wheelbarrow. Her last job of the day was to sweep the flagstones before the Tarpeys' door. The old woman came out of the house then and walked to the edge of the yard, where she stared into the elms, her arms folded, her back turned to Alice.

—You're worse than James ever was, she turned from the trees and remarked to Alice one evening. —Mad for work like yourself, he was, too, when he was able to do it. But come on inside now and eat the supper before it gets cold. That very same dust will be back again tomorrow.

The kitchen table was covered with a cracked, faded white-and-red oilcloth. A milk jug, butter dish, and chipped sugar bowl were in the center of the table. For supper, Alice and the old woman ate fried eggs and soda bread that the old woman had baked over the fire in the afternoon, while Alice worked outside. Alice's favorite part of the day was suppertime; she felt relieved and hungry, her body light and weary after the day's work, as she watched through the window the sky above the elms. Lena Tarpey sat across the table from her. She told Alice that James used to sit exactly where Alice was sitting, and he couldn't keep his eyes from the window, either. When she mentioned her brother, Alice was reminded that another human being lived under the roof, and when the old woman was not in the kitchen, Alice had gone to his door a few times, straining to hear a breath or a creaking bedspring, but she never heard a thing; and when she worked outside, she noticed his window was so soiled that no shaft of light could possibly get in.

One Monday evening, not long after Alice arrived, she was on her hands and knees searching for a hen's nest in the ivy and the long grass that covered the ground underneath the elm trees. She knew a hen was hatching, because she did not come in at night when Alice called. Alice was startled by a shadow falling over her, and she turned to see the old woman holding a bundle out.

—It belonged to James, when he was your age. I washed it this week.

She handed Alice a neatly folded gabardine, similar to the one the old woman herself wore.

—Thank you, Mam. Alice stood quickly, and bowed graciously.

—I want you to get the flour tomorrow, but be watchful of that fella, said the old woman.

—Beg pardon, Mam, said Alice.

—That grocer, keep an eye on him. He's the very kind to take advantage of a stranger.

—Oh, yes, of course, Mam.

—Watch the way he weighs it.

—I will so, Mam.

—I suppose them men in the store make a cod of you.

—They do, Mam, but mostly only one of them.

The old woman folded her arms and stared through the trees. —Don't worry about them at all, she assured her. —They cod everyone, and you're only a girl, anyway.

—They don't concern me, Alice bowed her head. —The nuns warned me, she whispered.

—You're a good girl then, said the old woman. —That's a grand sky up there tonight, thank God.

—Yes, Mam, it is, said Alice.

—It'll be a grand summer for all of us, God willing.

—Yes, please God, Mam.

—We don't bother with saving the hay anymore, with only the few cows left, the old woman said. —We'll buy a reek later in the year.

—All right, Mam.

—If it's that hen you're looking for she hatches over there every year, the old woman pointed to a clump of tall grass at the edge of the paddock.

When the old woman went in, Alice walked over and found the nest, which was where the old woman said it would be. Alice knelt beside it and gently stole her hand underneath the warm hen, and one by one her fingers touched the eight warm eggs. She stood and ran to the dairy and brought out a cup of meal, and she carefully lifted the hen from the nest and sat there guarding the eggs and watching the hen eat.

The next morning, Alice tied the pony and cart to the railing outside the creamery store, where the other ponies and horses were tied. She tugged the mantilla around her face, pulled the peak down over her forehead, and then tightened the clumsy gabardine around her waist. She walked across the gravel, the wicker shopping basket swinging on the crook of her arm; she opened the door to the smell of cigarette and pipe smoke, sour milk, and cow manure, and she stood there for a moment, waiting for her eyes to adjust to the dusky light from the one window to the right of the door. She was aware that a few men leaned against stacked bags of grain there, though she had never directly looked at them. They talked and read the paper, but now Alice felt their eyes following her, as she made her way, head bowed, to the counter. She peeked behind the counter at the two dusty shelves, stacked carelessly with mouse poison, packets of sugar, rice, jelly, oat flakes, tins of meat and fish, cans of peas, and custard, many of whose labels had faded out. She stood at the counter in front of the weighing scale. Flour, tea leaves, and grains of rice were scattered along the countertop.

Gerald Clohessy, the grocer, was stout and bald, only for the few wisps of white hair above his ears; he wore a white shop coat. A gray mustache hid his upper lip. He smiled and nodded, saying God bless to Alice, bending toward her, in an effort to see beneath the mantilla. Alice bowed her head, whispering that Miss Tarpey needed three pounds of flour and the usual pound of butter, if you please, sir.

Brendan Coughlin, who was tall and wiry, with tangled red hair, stepped up next to Alice; he was one of the three or four men who stood at the end of the counter. —It must be a Tuesday or it's a Friday already, and I didn't even know it, but whatever day it is isn't it time you took that veil off, so we all can have a good look at you. It's not in mourning you are, or is it? A young one your age shouldn't be acting so shook. Believe you me the time goes by more quicker than you think.

He had leaned his elbow on the counter, also trying to see beneath the mantilla; the men at the end of the counter were laughing. Alice pulled at the corner of the mantilla, but she did not budge an inch. She was watching the grocer scoop flour into the metal dish, his stomach shifting against the edge of the counter, and she watched the needle on the scale darting back and forth. The grocer lifted the dish of flour, emptied it into a small bag and shoved the bag toward Alice.

—There you are, he said. —Don't forget to tell Lena and the brother now that Gerald was asking for them.

—That's a grand dress you're wearing today, Brendan Coughlin said, and they laughed. —It must be very hard to come across one that nice. You must have gone to town to buy it, he added.

—Put more flour in, sir, if you please, sir, Alice said firmly.

—What is it I'm hearing you saying, the grocer spat on the floor at his feet. —What did you have the cheek to say to me! You, you nobody, a stranger and a girl to walk in here and talk to me that way!

Brendan Coughlin stepped back down the counter. —She's putting you in your place, all right, Clohessy, that's the best one I ever heard around here, he smirked.

—You didn't put enough in, sir.

—You dirty forward bitch, said the grocer, as he snatched up the bag, tore the neck open and heaped more flour in; he then plopped the bag back on the counter before Alice. —Take that, and get yourself away from here as quick as lightning. You don't belong here, and your likes never will.

The men at the counter sniggered like schoolboys, and through the settling cloud of flour dust, Alice saw the spittle shining on the grocer's twitching mustache, as she reached out to pick up the bag of flour and the pound of butter, and drop them into her basket. She went quickly to the door, and when she was almost there, a hand reached down and shoved it open; the light nearly blinded her.

—You have grand manners, Davie Condon, I always knew that about you, Brendan Coughlin shouted, as the door shut behind her and their laughter faded. She sighed and crossed the yard to the pony and cart, the basket numbing her arm. She laid the basket on the cart and untied the pony, and she then sat up on the cart, surprised at how firm her hands were, as she gripped the reins and led the pony into the quiet road. When she rounded the bend in the road she felt safe, imagining the boiled egg in the eggcup, beside the mug of hot tea that the old woman would have waiting for her.

———

—Are you any good at all in the garden? the old woman asked that evening in the cow house doorway. Alice was milking.

—I did a bit in the convent, Mam, and the nuns said I did a good job.

—You'll dig it then next week. You have that fine strength, said the old woman. —It hasn't been dug in a long while, not since James himself did it ages ago.

The old woman was fiddling with the knot on her scarf. —You're keeping an eye on that hen.

—I looked in on her before the cows and fed her, Mam.

—Right so, that was a fine bag of flour today.

—Yes, Mam.

—You're a good girl. That's the best bag we ever got out of that whelp, said she, and left.

Later, when Alice was standing in the paddock after putting the cows out, the old woman came and stood next to her. Alice had not heard her come up.

—I don't have the strength anymore to wash him, she said, —and you have all that fine strength.

The cows were sauntering down to the pond, where they would drink and then lie down close to the elms for the night. Alice watched them; then she gazed to the right of the crossroads, into a big field, where a herd of cows were grazing in the shadows of trees that grew on one of the ditches; the other three ditches were bare. A worn path ran next to where the cows were. The right corner of the field sloped upwards into a grove of poplars. Alice had often seen smoke rising there.

—Himself and the work itself, God help us, would wear the life out of anyone, the old woman poked the ground with her stick.

Alice raised her hand to her brow, for she noticed a man on the path.

—Sure, once a week is all, and it won't take you that long, said the old woman.

The man had disappeared, though Alice continued to stare at the path and the ditch. A noisy group of crows, on their way home to roost in the elms, flew low above her and the old woman.

—He's used to it on a Saturday, so that'll be the day you'll do it, the old woman raised the stick onto her shoulder.

—Sorry, Mam, said Alice. —What was it you said, Mam?

—You'll wash him, you will sure enough! the old woman turned abruptly and walked toward the elms.

—Wash who, Mam, said Alice, who now walked briskly at the old woman's heels.

—Were you not listening to a word I said? The old woman stabbed the stick into the ground and swung it back onto her shoulder.

—I'm sorry, Mam, Alice pleaded. —I was distracted by a man that I saw in the big field.

—Haven't you swept them flagstones yet? And what man are you talking about! What man and where, I ask you?

—It was a man I saw on the path in the big field over the road.

—Ha, there's only half a man in that place—now make sure you feed that hen and don't be paying attention to things beyond the paddock.

Alice ran dutifully through the trees, flapping her gabardine and calling the hens, who darted from the elms and the dung heap, where they dusted themselves. An hour later, she was sweeping the flagstones, and the old woman was watching the elms.

—That's Stephen Condon's place, and it was him who owned the bull that put James where he is today. He went over there that day, a foolish young fellow, and Condon told him the beast was a gentle one—are you not done sweeping yet?

—I'm nearly done, Mam.

The old woman crossed the yard toward the house. —Leave it, for God's sake, she waved her hands at Alice. —Come on in and eat and rest yourself, and pay attention to your work, and nothing more, and you'll be well looked after here with the two of us.

But the evening after, Alice watched for the man on the path. He appeared after the cows were milked, and she lingered in the paddock until he had left. The old woman hid in the elms, and the moment Alice entered the henhouse to count the hens, the old woman slipped out of the trees and went into the house to prepare supper.

On her way upstairs that night, Alice stopped to watch a dusty photograph hanging above the window, between the Sacred Heart and John F. Kennedy. She recognized the photo had been taken in the paddock, because of the shape of the elms against the sky. In the photo, seven young men and women stood around their seated parents. All were in their Sunday clothes. Alice leaned over the stair rail, pondering which girl was now the old woman, but she heard the doorknob rattling and turned to see, below her, Lena Tarpey standing at her brother's door, with the oil lamp.

—The one on the right side is myself. Most of us slept in the room you're in now, said the old woman. The flame of the lamp crackled around her worn face; she bid Alice a good night and opened the door enough to slip in. Alice watched the old woman's shadow trail reluctantly through the door after her, and then the door shut.

Alice went slowly upstairs, into her room, where she knelt at the chair and said her prayers. Then she undressed and draped her clothes across the back of the chair and slipped her nightgown on over her head. She crossed the room and stood before the dresser mirror and brushed her long black hair out, without looking into the mirror. She pulled the blankets back and got into bed and shut her eyes against the moonlight through the window—oh, but she was weary, though sleep did not come: Those people in the photographs were troubling her. Where did they go? To what corners of God's earth? Where in life do people go? She imagined that there would have been more than her bed in the room then; there were also the headboards she had seen in the henhouse, which the hens now perched on at night. Back then, the wardrobe was filled with their clothes—the sound of their feet on the stairs and their cries and laughter echoing in the house and the yard, their voices filling the paddock and the now silent trees the old woman stared into every evening. Alice pulled the blanket up over her face and prayed to God to give her sleep, her mind straying to the man in the field. She longed for tomorrow evening, to see him walk out there again; such a thrill to sit there and look, without someone knowing, and not have to bow her head and hide.

———

Grass taller than she, thistles, nettles, and ragwort suffocated the patch of ground behind the chicken wire, next to the clothesline.

Alice knotted her mantilla tightly, bundled her skirt high between her thighs, and threw her leg across the chicken wire. She knelt at the edge of the patch, tucking her apron under her knees, to pillow them. With both hands she clutched the weed stems close to the ground, and heaved the weeds over her shoulder. Insects buzzed loudly around her ears, and stuck in her mantilla. She weeded her way to a strawberry patch, and plucked the weeds carefully around it. She located the corner of the garden where she would plant the potatoes and cabbage. When she had finished weeding, a bright and full moon was glowing above Tarpeys' farmhouse. She stood and took off her mantilla and shook the clay from it.

Her sister had left the mantilla to Alice. Her only sister, who had died when Alice was a baby, and Alice offered up the day's work for the repose of her sister's soul, as she offered up all the days to her sister. The mantilla, and one letter from her sister, was all that Alice possessed; the letter named the parish of Kilroan, where her sister had met the man, who later she waited for on a road at night.

Only two nuns knew about this, and the week before they sent Alice out to the Tarpeys, they brought her into the front room, where a girl was called to only on important occasions. The nuns sat at a round table opposite Alice. A pot of tea with a cozy, and a plate of biscuits, lay on the table; a fire blazed in the fireplace behind them. The largest crucifix Alice had ever seen hung above the fireplace.

Sister Catherine smiled and held the plate of biscuits up. Alice lowered her eyes, thanked the nun, and said she was grand. Sister Kathleen spoke kindly, telling Alice she once had had a sister, whose name was Margaret, and she died from pneumonia, when Alice was a baby, and she was unwed and with child when she died, and this was a frightful sin, but Alice must remember that God was all forgiving.

Sister Catherine pointed to the mantilla and the envelope, which had been opened. She asked Alice to pick up the mantilla, that Margaret herself had sewn it, and it would last Alice a lifetime. Alice spread the mantilla over her opening hands, her fingers working like a spider until one finger caught a tiny hole, and Alice dropped the mantilla onto the table, recoiled from it, joined her hands at her breasts, and cried out. Sister Catherine scowled and told her to straighten herself up; there was never a need for such a carry-on. Alice raised her damp eyes to the crucifix, but she did not see Jesus now; she saw a nearly naked man, his arms and body about to rip from each other, like they were only held together with thread.

She lowered her eyes to the hissing fire that was shooting sparks onto the hearth behind the nuns. Must not fall down, she prayed to him, Jesus, don't let me fall.

—You must be firmer than this, Alice. Your sister needs you, my child, she needs your daily prayers, Sister Catherine scolded her. —You are the fortunate one.

—You are that, and a very strong girl, too, Sister Kathleen said, and smiled. —And that strength is a gift from God, so raise your head up now like a good child and take them, and none of this carry-on. Take them. That's your duty.

Five days later, Sister Kathleen held the red suitcase and walked with Alice to the deserted train station in County Offaly. Alice wept, as the nun knelt before her, buttoning up the mackintosh, at the same time chastising Alice to not be a crybaby—the world had little time for it. The nun stood and tugged the sleeves over Alice's clenched and trembling hands. She told Alice to put the mantilla on.

—This will guard you from the sight of men who will try to take advantage of you, the nun said, fixing the peak of the mantilla low over Alice's face. —And it will remind you to not be foolish with men like your sister, God forgive her, the nun sighed.

That morning Sister Catherine had given Alice the shoes, and told her to get off the train at Limerick Junction. She embraced Alice, telling her God was her real family, and that the Tarpeys were fine people and Alice would be grand company for them, because they kept to themselves and bothered no one.

Before Alice's sister died, she was working at a grocery, in the village of Bruff, which was not too far from Kilroan. Margaret lived over the grocery, and one night at a dance in the Kilroan parish hall, she met Davie Condon, who was then twenty-three. He had sat on his own all evening, out of sight in a darkened corner, watching her from across the hall. Brendan Coughlin was one of the lads who had walked down the line of girls to ask her for a dance, and from across the hall, above the sound of the music, Davie heard Brendan laugh, as he walked away, when she had turned him down. Toward the end of the night, Davie stood and crossed the floor to her. He asked her if she would like to dance and if a bottle of lemonade was to her liking.

Margaret was thin, but hardy. She had an oval-shaped face, round hazel eyes, and short, curly brown hair. They danced at the other end of the hall, away from Brendan Coughlin and the other young men. She led Davie confidently through "The Rose of Moncoin"; and, as they were leaving the hall, she joked that she was so thirsty she could do with another bottle of lemonade. He said he, too, was out of breath. They walked from the lighted hall, into the dark, to fetch their bicycles. She forced his fingers open and pushed her fingers between his. She rested her cheek upon his arm. He playfully cautioned her that she was acting a bit brazen.

—When you're from outside a place, no one pays a bit of attention to you, she said. —They don't give a damn about you if you live or die, she added.

They went out for four months and kept their attachment a secret: Davie did not want to hear talk from the neighbors, or feel the cold, suspicious looks from his mother, listen to the jokes from Brendan Coughlin and his likes.

Margaret told him she was born in County Offaly and her parents had contracted TB a year ago and died within a few weeks of each other and she had a baby sister in the care of the nuns. The nuns had got her the job at the grocery, which she appreciated very much, but everyone she met on the street in Bruff ignored her. He told her that it was only a matter of time before those people got used to her, and his own father had died four years ago, which his mother and sister had never got over, things being much more difficult at home than he'd like them to be, but he didn't see a thing he could do to change it.

They met on Sunday afternoons, in the oldest part of the grave-yard, in Kilroan, where the ground sloped down to a stone wall. He slipped his hand underneath her dress, fingered her petticoat, then the waistband of her knickers. She laughed and rolled down the slope to the wall. He crawled after her, leaned on one elbow, kissed her and told her that she was lovely, and never had he imagined he could be so lucky as to meet someone like her. He slipped the sus-penders from his shoulders, unfastened the clasp of his trousers and lay out on the grass. She undid the buttons of his trousers and put her hand inside. He shut his eyes, and the birds, the cows and trees, fields, gaps and fences all disappeared; his love for his sister faded, his mother and her mourning clothes, and his dead father, whose grave lay on the other side of the graveyard, the world empty of all of them and their ceaseless demands; but then his eyes were flickering open, and they were all back again, solid as ever, and Margaret had stood up, was nervously patting her dress into place, pulling the blades of grass from her hair, complaining that she was late in get-ting back to sweep the grocery and stock the shelves and they'd be mad at her, and he stood quickly, slipped his suspenders onto his shoulders, buttoned himself up.

On those Sunday afternoons, Lena Tarpey was one of the few people to visit the graveyard; she came to pray at her father and mother's grave, which was near the entrance of the graveyard, and not once did Davie and Margaret notice her coming and going.

The day after his father's funeral, Davie Condon's mother locked their bedroom door and moved into her daughter's bedroom to sleep in the same bed with her, and so began the daily visits to his father's grave. Davie's mother lost all interest in the running of the farm and his sister, Nora, who had never spoken a word in her life, accompa-nied their mother everywhere, opening and closing doors and gates before and after her. Nora gathered the eggs, lit the fire in the morning, and baked bread in the afternoon. She washed all the clothes, and every Saturday night she washed and combed her mother's hair for Mass. She then washed her mother's feet, and she made efforts to wash Davie's feet, but he would never let her.

Nora left notes for her brother, on his pillow. She wrote them in pencil, on newspapers he had already read.

> *Noticed white cow is sick. Has not eaten a bite all day.*
> *The brown hen hatched. Bring bacon for Sunday dinner.*
> *Leave your things for wash on the bed.*
> *Pray to St. Joseph for help.*

After their father died, she ended each note this way, but Davie did not pray anymore; nor would he ever kneel at his father's grave, and his mother would not speak to him because of this.

The afternoon he left Alice at the crossroads, Davie sat at the kitchen table, staring at their locked door, his mind drifting again to a night he was never too far from, when he was a boy and disturbed by a dream he had long ago forgotten: He had pushed open the door and stood crying in the glow of the oil lamp on the table beside them; his father was on top of his mother, his father's reddened face and tense mouth, the whites of his eyes shining and the light from the lamp shining on his bulging arms, his fringe hanging straight down from his forehead. Davie held the doorknob, crying, Mama, Mama, there's a thing I saw in my head, but his mother had turned her face from him, had done that the moment she heard the door creak open. Her legs were spread, her knees raised, the light gleaming on the white flesh of her thighs, and the nightdress bundled about her waist. The two of them were one throbbing shadow on the wall above their bed.

—Get out! Get out! Don't you ever cross this threshold again, his father shouted.

As a child, Davie Condon used to sit on the flagstone outside the cow house door, while his father and mother milked, and point down the path to the empty road, saying, Look. Look. His father asked his mother, What's troubling him? What is he looking at there? Sure there's not a thing there to look at. And his mother's only response ever, as she wept in the flank of the cow she was milking, I don't know, it's the way that God meant it.

When Davie finished National school, he took to working the farm; being an only boy, he didn't have a choice. In the evening, after the cows were milked, he went to his room, shut the door, and did not sit at the fire with them. The day he turned eighteen, his father asked him if he'd like to go to Powers, but Davie said he'd no interest; his father never asked again. As Davie grew older, the family, the neighbors, too, saw him as being a bit different; that was all, and you could be if you did your jobs, which he did—a bit of an odd one, all right, that young fella of the Condons is, but a hard worker, the neighbors said.

Nor could you locate the quietness that opened up in the Condon family to a specific moment. It was the way they were: The father, who wore an enduring frown, was never a talker; neither was the mother, and they weren't the kind of people to try to make sense of such things, because doing those jobs was what life was about, and if you got those done, you couldn't ask for or expect much else; so, morning and night, father and son milked the cows together; in spring, they planted the potatoes, spread manure on the meadows; they saved the hay in summer, topped the wines, and brought them into the barn with the horse and float, and the only talk between father and son were the father's commands and instruction: Hand me that hammer over there. We'll start putting in the spuds tomorrow. A bit of fencing to do in the rock field. Did you edge the scythe? Are you ready to go we're late for Mass. Kneel down there and we'll say the Rosary.

I did yeah. All right so. I did do it yes. Right so.

At night, they all knelt and recited the Rosary; they went to Mass together on Sundays, and to confession and the first Fridays, and there were happy times, too, like when cattle were sold at the market in autumn, and the father brought home a cake for tea. The four of them sat around the kitchen table then, and the father, not a regular drinker, was made jolly and chatty by the few drinks, and he'd tell Nora what a fine-looking girl she was, as she stood there at his shoulder, smiling and pouring his tea, and he'd look across the table at his son, tell him that nothing on the farm would work without him. He'd say to his wife that the day they married was the luckiest one of his life, and he couldn't be happier on a different piece of land, and the father and mother told the children how they first met, in Tipperary town, after a Fair; they had passed each other on the street, then turned around at the same time to say, Hello there; and sure God had his hand in that, both parents agreed; most certainly, it was his doing.

What Davie wondered, in these moments, was why life was not like this more often, and he felt ashamed, because he realized that love was what he really felt for them, and he was living the life he was supposed to be living, with the people he was supposed to be living with, and the distance that had grown between him and his father and mother was all his own doing, but the next morning his father's face was stony, as he walked past his son in the yard without a nod or a hello, his father's flat and bloodless shadow falling across him, and he understood once again that yesterday wasn't real; today was what was real and yesterday was a trick.

Beginning at a young age, though, Davie found a way to manage it: He imagined himself sitting at a desk, wearing an ironed shirt, the sleeves rolled up to the elbows, and he wrote with a pen, over and back on a blank page. Every evening, he walked down a busy street lined with buildings, the newspaper tucked under his arm, head raised, through the crowd, and he walked from that street to a smaller street lined with houses; small brick houses, they were, with potted plants on their windowsills and baskets hanging above their doorways, spilling over with flowers, and the happy cries of children playing in the middle of the street, and he walked down this street to a stained-glass door, where he put a key in and pushed open the door, and walked up a stairs; the walls around him were a sparkling white, and at the first landing there was a large window looking onto a back garden, a tall hedge bordering it, and a rose of Sharon bush in the middle of the garden; and, at the top of the stairs, there was a beautiful woman; she wore a maroon dress, a red cardigan, and she smiled when he came around the turn in the stairs; her hair was coal black and long, but sometimes her hair was red and long, then black again and only curled at the ends, and she had a long and beautiful neck, dark speckled eyes, and a sharp and striking nose, and he was living in a different body, and the woman called him by another name, and he pushed his hand between her opening legs and stroked the curly black hair, the red hair, and they rode each other under the sheets and on top of the sheets, but he was kneeling on one knee, and his father was close by, his father's tired breath clouding the cold air, the only light a candle flame, in the middle of a February night, shivering in the channel of the stone cow house and gripping the feet of a wet calf, pulling it from its mother, who lay on her side and moaned, her tail stiff and raised over her back, the swollen udder forcing her legs wide open like you would a compass, and then he was spreading manure with a dung fork along potato drills, in April; it was drizzling rain; the tops of the trees had disappeared in the mist, and his father's fart cut through the moldy air, and then he was on his own, with a billhook in his hands, cleaving briars on a ditch; it was cold and he needed to put his jumper on, and he was on his own, too, when he cut weeds with a scythe in the field beyond the house; he was drenched with sweat and it was raining again, but he kept chopping the fleshy weeds down, and then he was walking on his own through a mucky gap, a cold and beautiful winter sky overhead, where iron-colored clouds raced toward the mountains, and a woman was calling his name: *David. David.* She had painted lips and shining hair and she wore perfume that drifted down the stairs to him, but his mother was calling him and his father to come in for the dinner, and he walked into the warm, steam-filled kitchen, the fire blazing, the smell of boiled bacon and cabbage, and his sister winking and smiling at him; she was laying the table and he smiled back at her. *Everything's grand. Everything's all right. The rain will stop and the kitchen is warm. Winter does not last forever.* His mother standing silently over the cooker, as she stirred the food in bruised pots, while his father sat into his chair at the hearth and pulled his wellingtons off.

His father died in late autumn, when Davie was not yet twenty, and before he died, he asked Davie to come to his bedside. —Look after your mother and sister, that's all you have to do. And look after the land. You're me now, the father said.

Davie blessed himself, and left the room. His mother followed him into the kitchen, pleading with him to come back and say a decade of the Rosary with her and Nora, who was kneeling at her father's bedside. But he did not turn, but took his cap and coat from the back of a chair and walked from the house. In the yard, the chickens gathered at his feet. He fed them, then walked from the yard, onto the path to the big field. It was nearly time to bring in the cows for milking. No more dreams from now on, he told himself. That's the end of them. It's dreams that make a man mad, change him into something he's not—he knew he could do forever what he had been doing every day for as long as he could remember; this was not hard; in his sleep, he could do it, made easier now, too, with only himself to handle.

After the funeral, Davie's mother and sister took the horse and cart home. The men and Davie went into Powers. They sat in the circle of chairs around the hearth. Stephen Power lifted the shutter, and walked out from behind the bar.

—What are ye having, lads? he asked, shaking hands with Davie.
—I'm very sorry for your troubles, he added.

Brendan Coughlin sat beside Davie. He told Davie to not hesitate if he ever needed a hand with anything, to just say the word. John Kane was one of the elderly men sitting there, and all listened, as he told the story about the afternoon Stephen Condon faced Ahern's Whitehead bull that had broken into Condon's meadow. Davie's father had only a hayfork, but he raised it up, standing directly in front of the bull, shouting at him to either get out of his field or he would break his head. The bull pawed the ground and snorted, but Stephen Condon moved closer and shouted louder until the bull finally turned and ran from the field. John Kane said he saw it all himself; and, for as long as he lived, he would never forget how the bull turned and ran from Stephen Condon, ran away from him the way a spring calf would. Brendan Coughlin remarked that they didn't make men of that type anymore, and all nodded in agreement. Later in the evening, Brendan sang "Slievenamon." John Kane turned to Davie and said, Your father's safe in Heaven now. You have those fine few acres, and what more could you ever want.

—That's the truth, John, Davie nodded his head earnestly. —That's the God's honest truth. I couldn't ever ask for more.

The next morning, Davie told his mother he would, till the day he died, do the best he could for her and Nora, do whatever needed to be done outside, but he would never visit his father's grave. His mother was sitting on the edge of her and his father's bed, she in a black dress, her face wet from crying, and she did not raise her face or say a word to Davie. She had stripped the sheets from the mattress. They were neatly folded on her lap, her hands joined and shivering upon the sheets.

That Friday evening, Davie went to confession for the last time. He told the priest he would not ever pray at his father's grave, and there was no more to say about it. He stood and left the confessional before the priest had a chance to say a word. Outside, it had begun to rain. Davie stood in the doorway of the church and pulled the cap from his pocket and put it on. He buttoned his coat up, pushed his hands into his pockets, and walked across the churchyard to the statue of Saint Joseph. He stood at the base of the statue and gazed up, but he could not make out the saint's features against the dark. Davie held his hand out, was about to touch Saint Joseph's feet, but he drew his hand away, and turned his back on the statue and walked into the rain and the dark.

After Sunday Mass, when Davie was a boy, he used to kiss Saint Joseph's perfect feet, while his parents chatted with neighbors in the churchyard. Nora stood there with him, and on winter nights then, when it rained, he did not sleep, for he imagined the cold rain dripping from the saint's beard, rain beating his opened eyes and flowing over his naked feet, the rain changing to ice between his toes. Davie and Nora used to chip the ice from the statue's toes; Nora left notes on her brother's pillow on Saturday nights.

Jack Frost outside. Don't forget St. Joseph after Mass.

Margaret and Davie had sex twice: The first time was in the graveyard, and the last was on a Sunday afternoon a week after, when they had not planned to meet, but Margaret had walked across the fields from Bruff, and happened upon Davie, in the big field. She was wearing a blue summer dress, and had powdered her cheeks; her shoes were polished, the daisy petals and grass seeds sticking to them. She told him she was on a Sunday ramble, and running into him was a pure coincidence. When they were lying together under the trees, she told him she could not sleep the night before; she had the urge not only to see him but to touch him.

When Davie told his mother two months later that a grocery girl from the village of Bruff was carrying his baby, and he wanted to marry her and bring her home, his mother picked up a bread roller, turned from the kitchen table, and hit him once on the shoulder. He stumbled back, and raised his hands before his face.

—You will not bring a tramp from outside into this house and this land, after the way you disrespected your father, his mother said, —You won't, I tell you, over my dead body will you!

—But Mama! he pleaded, gasping. —Those years are over. Behind us now. He's not coming back. Can't you see that he's gone for good and forever.

—May God forgive you, she said, and raised the bread roller high. He clenched his fists and stepped back from her. —To have the cheek to talk to me like that in this house. You know nothing about it. You know or care for nothing or nobody here, the selfish person that you are, living in your own world every day of your life. Get yourself away from my house. Go on outside and do your jobs. Go into the fields with the beasts. That's where you really belong!

He ran through the yard, the hens dispersed; he took the path to the top field, ran off the path and under the trees, where he stood waist deep in the tall grass and docleaves that were still wet from last night's rain. The sopping leaves were withering, rotting on top of the grass. It was somewhere here he had lain with her on that warm Sunday afternoon, but now the rain from the grass and docleaves seeped through his trousers; that day, her dress had lifted in the breeze, as he sat and unlaced his boots, slipped them off, then his shirt, trousers, and drawers; they had flattened the long, dry grass to make a bed, and when he had woken up, he was hard again, and mad to go at it, their clothes heaped there on the grass beside them, her blue dress and her frayed knickers strewn on top of his yellowing drawers, and in his head now those clothes were aflame, burning to ashes in a wind that scattered them like the hawthorn petals in spring, but the air, that afternoon, when he awoke, was heavy with the smell of summer fields and her sweat and his sweat, and when he had put his hands underneath her, to lift her, and shove all the way inside of her, she moaned and tore at the grass, flinging the ripped grass onto his back, but now he was gazing up at the nearly bare trees along the ditch, their leaves spilling around him.

—Where, where, he cried at the trees, while swiping at the leaves. —Where was it! Didn't that happen. Didn't I feel it! He began to rip furiously at the long grass, the weeds and the docleaves, stumbling under the trees and panting. —It was here! It was here! No, no, it was not here. It did happen. No, it couldn't happen. It couldn't happen here. The ash was above me when we woke. Our bed below the ash tree. No, not the ash, but the elm—aha!

His boots were sinking into the wet ground, and he turned from the ditch, walked back onto the path and down to the yard, to the dairy, where he sat on an upturned bucket he always sat on, exhausted, his eyes drying, the mind settling down. Think of the jobs that needed to be done; that was the thing to do. Think of them. He'd go back out there soon; he'd be able to manage it. He'd not go near that ditch, not even look over there, when he gathered the cows for milking.

That night, when he had milked the cows, he walked across the fields to the village of Bruff. He found the back path to Margaret's room, above the grocery. He picked up a few pebbles and threw them at her window. The shadow of a fire was reflected upon the glass. She sneaked down the back stairs to him, shivering in her nightdress, her feet bare. He ran to the door to greet her, and she stepped into his arms. He held her and told her they would have to leave, have to leave if they were to ever be together.

—We'll take the train to Dublin in a week or so, he whispered. —Find our way from there.

He then told her he just had to make sure there was enough fodder for the cows, his mother and sister fine for the winter.

—We'll be fine, Davie, Margaret whispered into his ear. —We'll be away from here. We can go to London, Davie. No one will know us there. No one there will be against us.

—Yes, Margaret. Yes, my dear Margaret, he said, and pressed his face into her hair.

She asked him to come up to her room, warm himself at the fire; she had brewed a fresh pot of tea less than twenty minutes ago, and she had a packet of biscuits they had given her from the shop. He said that he had to go back home for now; his mother might find out that he was gone.

—It's always them, Margaret began to cry, always them it is, she said, as she tried to pull away from him, her curls shaking, but he wouldn't let her tear from his arms. —What about me, Davie, she cried. —I don't have anyone, not a one now, but this baby—God forgive me. Do you know what it's like to have no one, Davie? Do you?

—Whist, I do, Margaret, whist, I know it only too well. Please now, Margaret, go on up before you get your death of cold. I have to go back and do a few jobs.

—No, you don't know what it's like at all, she cried, trying again to break from his arms, but he held her tightly. —You think you do, but you don't. You have them and they have you. You have no idea what you have and you don't appreciate a bit of it. That's what your problem is—

Her talk made him angry, and he told her to stop it immediately, and that she didn't have a clue what she was talking about, and sooner than she could imagine it would be different for them, but for now she should go on up to the fire, for she and the baby would get their death of cold, and he had jobs to do at home.

She gave up, and pressed her head upon his chest, saying he was right, that she was sorry for causing him all the trouble, but she was tired and frightened of being on her own and thinking about him always.

—Go on up now, Margaret, he whispered. —I'll be back in a few days. Things will be fine. Things won't be like this for too long more.

Two weeks later, Margaret waited for him behind the ditch, down the road from where the hawthorn trees were. They had arranged to meet there at half eight and then cross the fields to the train station, get on the night train to Dublin. Davie left the kitchen before the Rosary, left his mother and Nora sitting at the hearth, and went and sat on the upturned bucket in the pitch-dark dairy. He eventually stood up from the bucket, and slipped on his father's overcoat that hung on a nail behind the dairy door. He dusted cobwebs from the sleeves, as he opened the dairy door, shut it after him, walked through the yard, past the silent henhouse, taking the path to the big field, the sleeves of the overcoat covering his hands. The moon kept coming and going from behind the sparse clouds; it was a very cold evening. As he walked, he shut his eyes to the image of Nora, her eagerness every Saturday night, as he gently pushed her hands away, as she tried to unknot his laces, her tears falling onto the toes of his boots—Christ, oh, Christ, but he could not leave her with his mother and all them jobs to be done. He couldn't do that to his own family. Only a pure bastard would do such a thing. He'd be cursed for life, if he did that, blasted and miserable, hiding his face from everyone, till the day he died. He had promised his father. Promised every one of them. And what use would he be in a city like London with a wife and child to take care of?

He turned to watch the path he had walked on. The moon had come from behind a cloud. His father and he, the cows and the horse, had made that path; without knowing it, they had, on their daily journey, back and forth and back and forth for years and years. A small piece of the earth, but his piece of the earth. He raised his face to the moon, which all of a sudden looked new to him, like it was his first time seeing it; this moonlight shining for him only, and wasn't this place really his life? Fooling himself that it could be otherwise. What was he thinking? Doing? Dreaming? And he blocked his ears to the whistle of the train, as it departed Limerick Junction.

He never mentioned or heard from Margaret again; he learned to put it out of his head, though less than a year later he began to make those evening journeys to the ditch, but he was not thinking about her at all. He walked up and down under the trees, planning the jobs that needed to be done. He walked the perimeter of the field, examined the fences, as he had done with his father; he watched the sky for rain, and felt which way the wind blew. He walked out of the field, crossed the fence into the meadows to look at the grass, pondering when it would be ready to be cut.

He slept in the bed he slept in as a boy, his mother and sister next door, their black dresses and shawls and stockings piled on the chair. He lay awake, the blanket pushed back, his drawers around his knees; after, he ran his fingertips along the damp wall, as he had been doing since he was a boy.

Every afternoon, when he returned from the creamery and fed the hens, he put the two hard-boiled eggs his sister had boiled for him in one pocket and a few slices of bread in the other and went to the dairy. (His mother and Nora never returned from the graveyard until around two.) He sat on the upturned bucket, next to the swart turner. It was dark there, even in daylight, apart from the narrow beams of light that shone vigorously through cracks in the wooden wall behind him and from the cracks in the roof. He spread sheets of newspaper at his feet, to gather the eggshells and crumbs. He threw the crusts of bread through the doorway and watched the cock and the hens rip them asunder.

A few weeks after he had met Alice on the road, he was woken by a dream, on a Monday night, in which his father and Margaret, on a cold January day, are driving a horse and cart; the road is churned to muck, but they are finely dressed, on their way to the train station, their suitcases piled high on the cart behind them. His father is wearing his Mass suit, the one they waked him in, his hair slicked behind his ears. The cart is sunk to the axle in the muck, but his father and Margaret are laughing, his father urging the sweating, steaming horse on, the reins leaping wildly along the horse's back, the horse eventually pulling the cart free from the muck.

It will pass, Christ, fuck, 'twill, he told himself, as he threw back the wet sheets and sat on the edge of the bed. Hold on now, he told himself, hold on. Because every Tuesday morning, likewise on Friday, he waited for the door to open, her shadow to fall, the shape of her black mantilla along the floor before him, as she stepped through the door, the wicker shopping basket on the crook of her arm—he got back into bed again, and pulled the blankets up to his neck; it will pass, he told himself, the winter becoming the spring was the fault of it; the ground heating up; his misfortune to have met her that day on the road—but he could hardly wait for the night to end, to tremble the moment the door opened and her shadow fell, and his own ugly and wretched body forgotten then—aha, but he needed to put the spuds in. He should have started them this week. He had wasted the week moping around the field, and sitting in the dairy. There was bound to be looks from the mother: *I hope you're paying attention to your jobs?*

The following morning, he stood at the window, reading the paper; John Kane stood next to him. The door opened, and Davie let the paper drop a few inches. Then the shadow, she standing still for a moment, before she walked to the counter. The haloes of cigarette smoke swimming above her, in the light from the window behind him, and that bostoon, Brendan Coughlin, getting to stand there beside her.

—Go on Brendan, one of the men pushed him from behind. Brendan Coughlin poked her shoulder with his finger twice, but she did not stir.

—You need to give her a better poke than that, Coughlin, one of them laughed.

—If she'd take off the bloody Communion veil, Gerald Clohessy laughed, and sure maybe you could make a decision on her. Sure you have no idea what's under there at all, what do you think, Brendan?

—The very thing, Gerald, Brendan Coughlin said. —It's that black Communion veil. I've never seen the likes of it before. It must be the fashion someplace.

John Kane was saying something to Davie about how grand the seed spuds were this year, when she turned from the counter—the seed spuds, oh, the blighted seed spuds, Davie thought, as he stepped toward the door and opened it, then shivered with delight, when she passed by him, her shadow touching his body. The men at the counter were laughing. Gerald Clohessy banged the counter with his fist.

That night Davie awoke from a dream, in which his father's cold lips are crushed against his—Davie flung the blankets out onto the floor, ran his tongue across his lips, wiped them rapidly with the back of his hand, hearing his father's laugh and Brendan Coughlin's laugh, the jingling of traces and the dying roar of a slaughtered bull. Davie had stumbled out of the bed, thinking he had woken up in a strange place; he tripped through the blankets; so terribly frightened, he was, till his hands touched the cool, familiar wall, and the comforting dampness sank into his blood.

The curtain covered the window completely, blocking all light, the dust so thickened upon it that the first Saturday Alice saw it in the lamplight, she thought it was part of the wall. The damp, foul smell made her gasp, and she felt as though she had stepped inside a tomb. The wall above his bed was bare, the mortar having fallen away in large and small patches.

This was her second Saturday to wash him. He was hidden beneath the blankets, his back to her. She had laid the oil lamp on the nightstand, and had brought in the basin of hot water, which she put on a chair, next to his bed. She lifted her eyes to the shadow of his bare head now throbbing on the wall, her own shadow rigid along the bed. She rolled her sleeves up and sat cautiously on the edge of the bed. Dirt had crusted under her nails, from being in the garden all morning; she noticed, as she squeezed out the cloth.

—My own hands haven't done a tap of work with years, he spoke in a coarse whisper—these were his very first words to her, she, rubbing the cloth down his arm; and she stopped, dipped the cloth into the water, rinsed it out, imagining that the sound she heard was a ripple in the water, maybe the oil light playing tricks, or those hens beyond the window. She had begun to unbutton his vest. An old smell, that was new to her, escaped, as she undid each button, his flesh warm against her fingers. She slipped the vest from his shoulders, managing somehow to get it over his hands, drag it from underneath him, without lifting him. She dropped the vest onto the floor.

There was no excess flesh around his waist or stomach, his ribs visible against the skin. A line of gray hair ran from his neck, down to his stomach, his skin so pale that she thought to even look at it would hurt him. She ran the cloth down him; he opened his legs and she ran the cloth between his legs. She rinsed the cloth out and touched it to his breast.

—How's that garden coming, child? Many a long day has gone by since I seen it.

She stopped and bowed her head, stammering that she was sorry.

—It used to be a fine plot, he murmured. —Aha, yes, a long time ago now that was. His Adam's apple shifted, and he gulped, his lips and eyes tightly shut.

—The garden, child, I hear you in the garden beyond the wall, he whispered. —Sure don't I smell it from you. Don't I smell the clay.

She stood quickly and dropped the cloth into the basin.

—Please, sir, she cried, —I am just doing my duty, your sister is in the village but will be back soon.

—I dug it myself as a young fellow, I had the strawberries and all, he said. —I hear you out there. I hear you every day and evening. Sure don't I know nearly every word you're thinking.

He had turned his head from her, to the wall, the top of his head shining, the throbbing shadow. —I've been traveling here all these years, she heard him chuckle, as he watched the patches of mortar. —Islands, he whispered. —These are my islands, they are—can't you come back here beside, child, he said, gently drumming the quilt with his fingertips. She sat back on the edge of the bed. —Don't worry, for God's sake, I won't do a thing to you, he said.

—I have to milk soon, she said. —Mam will be back from the village. She'll be waiting out there for me in the cow house.

His turned his head, his eyes now on her, then darting along the wall again—the surprised and liquid eyes of a child.

—I should put on your fresh vest, sir.

—You've time enough for that, child, he said. —Your hair is grand and dark. I didn't think when I heard you talk that it'd be so dark.

—But I have to go out and turn them cows in, she said, touching her hair, about to rise.

—You put in the manure, I suppose, he sighed.

—Yes, sir, she said.

—Yes, he whispered, —it is that time of the year again, child, and sure you belong here now and no place else.

That July the weather was warm; from the paddock, Alice watched the meadows beyond the crossroads, the horses pulling the wheel rakes, the swart-turners and mowers, the men and women turning the hay; Alice longed to be there with them; the man walked to the ditch. The old woman hid in the elms.

At the creamery, Alice overheard the men talk about how good the hay crop was, but they also feared the weather might break. The one group of men continued to make fun of her, but she was becoming used to their caffling.

One Tuesday, at the counter, Brendan Coughlin said, —I heard that old man of the Tarpeys is a fine bull. The young men and the grocer laughed. Then Brendan Coughlin took his cap off and bowed, calling Alice, your more than royal highness.

She dropped the messages into her basket and headed for the door. Davie opened, and asked, How're you, Alice? a question he had been asking for a few weeks. She thanked him for opening the door, but she never looked at his face.

She loved the journey back home, the silence, the warm air, being away from the men and their vulgarity, but there was the one kind man who opened the door. She pushed the mantilla from her head, recalling his voice. She had begun to look forward to hearing this question, see his hand on the doorknob. It was one of the things that made her feel safe and wanted. The Tarpeys were kind, of course; she could not want more; they appreciated all the work she did for them, but she knew it was all God's will, as all of her happiness was, and it was him she thanked for it.

Alice turned the old man on his side and ran the damp cloth along his lower back, which was golden in the lamplight.

—There, oh, God, 'twas there. She stopped; he again said, —There, his voice rasping like the rusty hinge on the henhouse door. She wiped her hot forehead and eyes with the damp cloth.

—I'm very tired, please, I am. She had stood up.

He whispered, —Come back here to me, child, it was there—

—What? Where, sir? I have too many jobs to do, please, she implored.

—Don't worry about them jobs—the animal, child, it was right there.

She sat back on the edge of the bed, watching his back. Then her hand was moving, as though drawn by a magnet, until her trembling fingertips touched the raised, purple scar on his lower back. Her eyes were filling with tears; she heard the bees outside, a cow lowing in the paddock. She felt faint and lay down there beside him, and those sounds from outside faded from her ears.

—Go to sleep then for a while, he whispered. —That garden and all them jobs will be the end of you, child. Rest yourself. Them jobs can wait for a lifetime.

She had shut her eyes, was asking God to give her sleep—then she was opening her eyes, and someone was calling her name, Alice, Alice, are you all right, child? For a moment, she thought that it was nighttime, and she was in her bed upstairs, and it was years ago, and it was one of the boys in the photograph who was calling her.

—I'm awake, sir, she said, but she did not move. —I must go outside immediately.

—Stay there a while, child, till I tell you this one, he cleared his throat. —Wasn't I bringing the bull through the crossroads there beyond. Stephen Condon's bull it was—there was a girl, Mary Dwyer, I was great with at the time. We were going to marry, but I did not know how to tell my sister. Mary Dwyer was a grand girl, though. She was all I ever thought of then, being a young fella. I would wake up thinking of her and go through the day only with her on my mind, and my life was never better, when I was thinking about her. In fact, thinking about her was the only life I wanted. She had fine, black hair. But as I said I did not know how to tell Lena I wanted to marry this girl, nor did I want to leave Lena—so I wasn't paying much attention that day to the beast I was leading—a shorthorn bull, with big shoulders and his nose flaring and him snorting and the spit trailing onto the road, and I a young man that day, my mother and father not too long dead, and the rest of them gone away to God knows where, me leading the bull through the crossroads and he must have noticed the cows in the field outside and he bawled like the devil himself, and pucked me one good one at the same time. I didn't know what in God's name was happening to me, but I was lifted off the ground like I was a petal and I landed in the dust at his feet, and didn't he push me before him with his forehead and beat the living daylights out of me, beat me into the ditch. He trampled down on me and his spit dripping onto my face. I was crying out for Lena. The hens were wild in the road and the cows had gone wild and ran down to the ditch, trying to get onto the road. My sister was running down the road as fast as her legs could carry her, screaming and wailing and waving her scarf about in the air. The bull lifted his head from me to watch her and ran back through the crossroads, bellowing once and she cursing him. She got on her knees by me and held my head on her lap, asking me not to leave her, that I was all she had, she wailing and shaking. I couldn't even open my mouth. It was full of blood and I couldn't feel my feet. They had left me and they would never come back again and I knew it there and then that they would never come back to me, and I thought that nothing good could ever happen to me again, that my life was over, but then here you are, child, beside me now, child. Sure he sent you to me and haven't I been waiting here all these years for you.

The dying wick of the lamp flickered, and in that strange light Alice saw a young, helpless body curled up, bloody and defiled in the dust, a girl kneeling over him, her face to the heavens, pleading. Alice pressed her face between the old man's shoulder blades and kissed him; his warm, brittle skin tasted of salt, dust, and the stale cloth that needed washing. She listened to his heart, the quiet breath going in and going out of him. He was silent for a while; then he whispered that he never again saw Mary Dwyer, she went away, and Lena would not put him in a home, though he had pleaded with her to do that, but she said she would not put her own flesh and blood in a home.

The old man reached his hand back; she held his hand, his fingers tightening around hers. She needed to put his clean vest on, and go to the cow house. She had yet to start the wash, and yesterday's clothes, on the line, were well dry by now; she needed to bring them in.

—Aren't you lucky to be safe at home here with me, child, he whispered.

—I am, sir, she squeezed his hand.

One Friday morning, after a sleepless night, Davie Condon walked up to Alice's cart and asked her how the Tarpeys were. She was about to leave the creamery yard, was sitting in the cart, but she let the reins slacken.

—They're fine, sir.

—Are you still doing a bit of gardening? he asked, noticing the dirt under her nails. She folded her hands across her lap.

—Yes, sir, she said. The mantilla was peaked over her face; she was wearing the gabardine. Her lips were exactly as Davie had remembered, but he still could not see her eyes.

—Sir, the woman will be waiting for me. Beg your pardon, but I have to go.

She flicked the reins, and he stepped back from the slow-moving cart.

—Alice, he called, walking behind the cart, —Alice, he called again, following the cart into the road. She ordered the pony to halt.

—I picked you up that day in the road, my name is Davie Condon. He stood next to her and took his cap off and shoved it nervously into his pocket.

—Is that who you are? she glanced, seeing briefly his broad face, his large eyes with the eyebrows joined—so this was the man she watched every evening in the field, whose father owned that awful bull, the kind man who opened the door, asked her how she was.

—You called me sir, and I told you there was no need to do that. You were wearing a coat and it was a warm day.

—I couldn't fit it in the suitcase, she politely said, her head bent again, not looking at him.

She thought about how she had trudged around the bend that day, exhausted from all the walking, holding the red suitcase, and it was so hot, but then cool in the shadow of the hawthorn trees, the blossoms blowing at her feet, and she was very frightened, thinking she'd never find the house at the crossroads, praying to be rescued; then behind her she heard the clinking traces; his strange ways, him watching out for her—she raised her head now and looked down the road, saw the bend she was now familiar with, that she had first walked around, then the road straightening out, the hawthorn trees lining the ditch. She felt as if she had known them her whole life, that he had created them especially for her.

—I must be going home, she said. —They'll be wondering where I am.

—God bless, so, Alice, he said.

—And you, too, she said.

Davie stood in the road and watched the cart shifting from side to side, the tracks marking the dust. The empty milk churn shining in the sunlight. As she neared the bend, she pushed the mantilla from her head. A flock of sparrows shot from the ditch and spread out like a gray sheet above the cart.

Her hair is black, he squinted, so black I hardly knew she was not wearing it anymore—

—You'll be round to give a hand in the meadow, Davie. I asked a few other lads inside.

Davie turned to see Brendan Coughlin walking toward him.

—Oh, I'll be there, sure enough, Brendan, Davie said earnestly.

Brendan offered Davie a cigarette; they lit up, standing side by side, then they turned and stared down the road.

—How old do you think that young one at the Tarpeys' is? asked Brendan.

—Eighteen or nineteen, Davie replied.

—She's a fine girl, well able for all of us, it looks like.

—And a hardworking girl, too—

—Your mother and sister are in good form, Davie?

—They're grand, thanks, Brendan—he would never tell him or anyone else around that he rarely said a word to his mother; and this had been the case for years —and your own mother? Davie inquired.

—Aha, sure she's not too good, Davie, but you never know. She might outlive the whole lot of us. You know yourself the way they are.

They were silent for a while, smoking, watching the empty road.

—She must be a relation, the Tarpey girl, do you think?

—Sure no one knows. There's a few of them away all right—ever hear a word from the brother?

—Aha, the mother gets a letter from him every now and then. Married with children now, too, living in New York, he is, in the police, I believe.

—Tell the mother I mentioned him.

—I will—she must be a tough one, all right.

—What, Brendan, Davie was confused.

—That girl at the Tarpeys', who do you think!

—Aye, Davie said, —aye, indeed, I thought you were talking about your mother.

The two men laughed.

—She'd be grand all right, though, Brendan lowered his voice. —I do be only codding with her, and if she can put up with me she can put up with anyone—and the bravest I've ever seen here abouts, ha. Stood up to himself inside. The first one I ever saw doing it.

—Aye, she would be that, too, I suppose, Davie began to walk away.

—Sure, I'll see you in the meadow then, with God's help, Brendan said after him.

—I'll be the very first one there, Davie said.

—Grand job altogether, Davie, Brendan said.

———————

Three mornings later the old woman stood in the road and watched the pony and cart trundle through the crossroads. She noticing this was the second morning Alice had not worn her mantilla.

The old woman left the road and went to the yard, where she watched the elms for a moment, muttering. She blessed herself, as she walked into the house, went to the fire, and boiled a kettle to make tea for her and her brother. She boiled an egg for him and put the mug of tea, the egg, sugar, butter, and salt, on the tray. She lit the oil lamp, opened his door, walked in, and put the oil lamp on the table. She came back out and brought in the tray and laid it by the lamp. She did not know if he was awake or asleep, but sat on the chair and took her scarf off and spread it along her lap. Her hair fell around her shoulders. It was iron gray and tangled in places. She hummed, and rocked, pulling at strands of her hair. He had turned around, was staring at the ceiling. She stood and poured the tea, put in a few spoons of sugar and stirred it. He sat up and took the mug of tea, and sipped.

—Is the tea hot enough? she sat back down.

—It's grand, thank you.

—I have written someone about buying the hay.

—Good, sure, what's the weather like today?

—It's a fine day, thank God.

—Is she doing a good job in the garden?

—A fine job, she whispered.

—She's a grand girl, he said. —Worth her weight in gold, she is.

—Yes, she is, and honest, too.

—God-fearing, I hear her praying out there all the time, he said.

—Sent by the man above, surely. Sure there wouldn't be no one more honest than she in the whole wide world.

She stood and opened the egg, put in a spoon of butter and a pinch of salt, placed the egg on the tray, then the tray on his lap. She pushed the pillow low on his back, so that he could sit up higher; she straightened his collar. She sat down, sighed, and took a drink from her own mug. His vest was fine and clean, which pleased her greatly.

—She sat out there for a while last evening again and waited for him, the old woman lowered her eyes and wound a strand of hair tightly around her fingers.

—And she won't get over it, he whispered.

—She's young, she whispered. —It'll only get worse, if you ask me.

—And you have no idea who the man is?

He had asked that to her many times, and she had always said no, afraid if she mentioned the name Condon, it would disturb him.

Lena was the youngest of the Tarpey children. She had always been plain-looking and very shy. James was the next youngest, and as children they played together in the paddock, built a swing in the elms, and went for walks along the roads and into the fields in the evening. They milked cows together, and saved the hay. Sometimes she helped him in the garden. Their older brothers and sisters were grown and gone abroad by the time they were out of their teens. Their mother died then and a year later their father died. Lena and James were in their mid-twenties by this time. Their three older brothers lived in Manchester, San Francisco, and Chicago; a sister lived in Sydney; only a brother living in London made it back for the funerals.

—She might get over it, he whispered, —people do, like a sickness, you know.

—Not likely, she sighed, —not likely at all. The way she stands out there watching. You'd never know what she'd do, being so young and everything. I might not be around for too long more—

—Stop that talk, can't you, he said crossly.

—Talk you can call it, but we have to face facts, too, she scowled.
—A man will only ruin a girl like her—she's well looked after here,
and what more could she want.

—Sure it must be terrible to have neither a father nor mother, a
brother or sister. That must be the very worst thing of all, he said,
watching the ceiling.

—God bless that poor child, the old woman said. She was putting
her scarf on, fingering the long strands of hair back underneath it,
while watching the light flickering on the patches of mortar.

—And the cows, he whispered.

—There're all fine, but that old pony can't last too long more.

—God help us all, he said.

—Which one is that one today? She had pointed a crooked finger
at one of the patches of mortar on the wall.

—Aha, he said, that one is Newfoundland, it looks like to me.

—Where in God's name is that?

—It's close enough to Canada, he said. —I remember that from
school. A few from here landed there.

—Any news from there now?

—I haven't heard a word yet, but I'll let you know later on, please
God.

—Well, finish your egg whatever you do. You'll need some suste-
nance with all that traveling you're doing.

—I will so.

—Another mouthful of tea.

—I'm grand, thank you, and you can quench that lamp if you
want.

She blew the flame out, and sat there in silence, sipping her tea.
He was snoring when she stood, lifted the tray from his lap, and left
his room.

<hr />

Climbing the stairs to Alice's room, Lena Tarpey whispered an Act
of Contrition. She had read Margaret's letter to Alice before. Alice

kept it in a zipped pocket inside the red suitcase; the old woman had come across it there, and a week ago, while Alice was at the creamery, the old woman found the letter under Alice's pillow. Some of the words were blotted out. From tears, the poor child, the old women guessed.

She crossed the room and opened the wardrobe. The mantilla was hanging over the rail. She reached down and took out the small red suitcase, unclasped it and took the letter out; she put the letter inside the top of her dress.

She had seen Margaret Gilmartin on a few occasions, in the graveyard years ago; she had seen her and Davie Condon embrace on the grass and noticed their bikes hidden in the bushes. She knew Davie Condon's bike. She had watched him, from the paddock, cycle with the Coughlin brothers, to and from National school. She had seen Margaret at Mass, in Bruff, on many Sundays, as that was where the old woman went; a woman had told her after Mass once that the girl was working in the village grocery, and her name was Margaret Gilmartin. She did not think that Margaret and Alice resembled each other. She had never seen or heard Alice laugh, but she had heard Margaret's laughter a few times, down the slope of the graveyard, on those Sunday afternoons. She knew, too, that Mrs. Condon and her daughter went to the graveyard every day for hours. She had seen them crossing the fields, and knew the time they left and the time they came home.

Nobody ever takes much notice of old women, she thought as she came back down the stairs, but she would do what was necessary to protect Alice from them Condons, who had once nearly taken everything she had in the world, and it was her duty to make sure a Condon wasn't going to do it again.

Dear Alice

I am your only sister Margaret Gilmartin. You are my only family and all I have to talk to and say good-bye to. I tried to live my life according to God but made one big mistake with a man. I am with child and you must never make that mistake for you might end up like me. God forgive me. I made a big mistake with a man. I am very sick now and the nuns tell me to ask God for forgiveness and I ask you to not be ashamed of me for there is only us in the world our father and mother God rest them gone these last few years. The man was not a tinker but an upstanding man. I want you to know that. He is from the parish of Kilroan in west Tipp. I waited for him on a dark night behind a gate and he did not come. The nuns say that is how I am sick. I made my mistake and got punished for it and I suffered for it and asked God every night to forgive me. You must live in the light of the Sacred Heart and not think about the past that is me for you are a different person. You must be a good woman. I have nothing to give you but the mantilla I sewed it myself and this letter. God forgive me, you must remember me daily in your prayers and forgive me your only family. God rest our father and mother and protect you always and forgive me for what you and I will always suffer for.

———

—I've never seen anything the likes of it around here before, John Kane whispered into Davie's ear, the Tuesday morning Alice appeared in the store without her mantilla.

Davie did not say a word. When the door opened and he had seen her shadow, he thought it was not her—he had only known the shadow of her mantilla, where now shiny black hair fell close to her shoulders. Brendan Coughlin did not come close to her, but stood up straight, took his cap off, and politely said, Good morning to you, Alice. She did not look down the counter, but shyly nodded her head. Davie watched the grocer fumbling, as he got her the messages and wrote them down in his book. When she turned from the counter, the men were silent, watching. She lowered her head, as she walked toward the door; her long, pale forehead, her eyes, revealed to Davie at last: round, blue, and shining, in the light of the door he had opened. Those eyes, that forehead, reminded him of someone else; and he believed, for some reason, that the person must be his sister.

—Thank you, she said, as she walked through, he stepping away from the door.

That night, long after bedtime, Davie stood at his opened bedroom window. All afternoon, he had been cutting hay. In two days, Brendan Coughlin and a few other neighbors would help him. He needed to oil the wheels of the swart-turner—but her image would not leave him be for a moment, would not let him sleep a wink. A breeze, with the scent of hay, blew around him. On Friday, he would ask her to meet him on Sunday afternoon. He would make his move; he believed that he didn't have any other choice.

When he was a boy, he had stood alone at this window on many summer nights. He now remembered going to his room after the Rosary, shutting the door behind him, and Nora bringing him a slice of bread and jam, a mug of milk. She used to open his school satchel, do his sums for him, write him notes then, too, concerning his mother and father. The dusty crucifix, above his bed, she had given him on the morning of his Confirmation. His father's stiff overcoat, on a nail behind the door, she had hung there a long time ago; there was only the one night Davie had worn it.

He came away from the window and lay on the bed, and when he shut his eyes he saw the blossoms floating between the cart wheels, a girl whose eyes he had just seen for the first time, but could he bring her into this room, would she want that? Would they stop him again? Don't think about that part of it, he assured himself. He'd cross those bridges when he came to them.

So, on Friday morning, in the creamery yard, he asked Alice would she meet him on Sunday afternoon, around half-two. He said he was almost finished with piking the hay, and Coughlins' meadow would be finished tomorrow. He told her to walk down the road beyond the crossroads; he would wait there for her in the ditch.

—The Tarpeys sleep on a Sunday, Alice said, and I have the day off, apart from the milking, so no harm at all.

—Not a bit, Alice, Davie said, and said good-bye; she said good-bye to him, leading the pony into the road. He went quickly to his horse and cart; he needed to be in the meadow. He had a good bit of work to do before Sunday.

That afternoon, as Alice was cleaning out the henhouse, the old woman stood in the doorway and said she had to make a journey to the post office.

—Listen, in case James needs anything, the old woman said.

—Yes, Mam, Alice replied.

The old woman hummed as she walked down the road, and turned right at the crossroads. She was wearing her good Sunday scarf and a light yellow raincoat she also wore to Mass; her sister had posted it to her twenty years ago, and the old woman had taken great care of it—it still looked new, but from another time altogether.

The *Irish Independent* was spread at Davie's feet, the pieces of eggshells littered on it. He was sitting on the bucket. The hens were going mad in the yard, which he believed was a crow bothering them. Then the doorway darkened a little, the thin figure of a woman there.

—Is that you, Mama?—but wasn't she at the graveyard? He stood, immediately recognizing the woman of the Tarpeys—the yellow coat did it.

—Leave mine alone, she said, her voice shrill and hoarse, as something landed at Davie's feet, which he believed had fallen from above, because he did not notice her fling anything. He gazed down at the envelope, then raised his face to an empty doorway.

—Excuse me, he exclaimed, the hens had gone deadly silent.

He sat down slowly on the bucket, and flicked the eggshells from around the faded envelope; he picked it up; he sifted his fingers through the flap, taking note of the tear stains, as he unfolded the brittle paper that had almost separated at a middle fold. . . . *Dear Alice . . . only sister Margaret Gilmartin . . . my only family . . . God forgive me . . . parish of Kilroan . . . on a dark night behind a gate . . . what you and I will always suffer for . . .*

And her voice again, as though she were there beside him, reciting each line, her thrilling voice as it was in the graveyard and in the field, her voice and her smell drifting down a back stairs in Bruff, the sound of her feet coming toward him, like laughter, on the stairs, a voice he believed was lost forever, part of another life—oh, God, oh, why God—it was a mistake, God, a mistake a different, younger person made years ago; he smelled the letter, it was old, all right, it was very old—

He had work to do in the meadow; he had wasted enough time, and should have been in the meadow an hour ago, not sitting here; he tried to stand, like anyone would try to stand, do it without thinking, but he could not stand, for he had no legs, he had no back, because he was hollow, hollow and hard as the metal bucket he was sitting on; hollowness was all he was filled with, that and emptiness —he had killed her and their baby. Killed them dead and cursed them for all eternity.

—You must be happy now, Father, that I'm talking to you, you must be very happy, he shouted at the roof, a strange voice, one he did not recognize, echoing down at him through the dust and the sunlight. —You must be happy now like you never were, but I deny you, I deny you, I do!

He clenched his teeth, hung his head down, his arms loose and his tears sounding like raindrops on the newspaper. —I deny you, he trembled, sliding from the bucket, then curled up and the newspaper ripping underneath him, as he writhed from side to side. —All of you, he cried, squeezing his eyes shut, every one of you. Please leave me alone. Just leave me alone. Leave me be.

Then Nora was kneeling by him, and gently shaking his shoulder. How long she was shaking him and how long he had lain there he didn't know, the hot sun through the roof, his hands joined and pressed between his thighs, his legs pulled up, the crushed eggshells against his cheek.

—You'll have to do it yourself, Nora, he cried, not lifting his face from the newspaper. —You'll have to do it all. I cannot do it, my life is gone. My life is empty and useless. I have done a terrible wrong, you'll have to look after it, all of it, you'll have to. I'm so sorry, Nora. I'm sorry for all of it, sorry I was the way I am.

He went silent, weeping, his face contorting like a child's, as his sister stroked his shoulder. She suddenly stopped, pulled a pen from the pocket of her cardigan, and began to write on the newspaper close to his face. She wrote quickly, then put the pen back in her pocket, kissed him once on the cheek, and rose and left. He waited a while before he sat up. He wiped his eyes, leaned over and read.

> *I can do everything here. For God's sake go. Go away from here.*
> *I will pray for you and your happiness. Write to me when you can.*
> *You have done no wrong at all. I know that.*
> *Pray to St. Joseph.*

He tore her words from the newspaper, and stood up; he shoved the piece of paper into his pocket. Her picked up the letter, and gently put it in his pocket. He would keep it, then one day post it back to Alice; one day, a long way away from now. He would live so that he could do it. Live to confess to Alice, ask her for forgiveness— but now he could go away, go far away to finally become the other person he really was.

On Friday and Saturday evening, Alice watched for him, but he did not walk to the ditch. She walked back through the trees, calling the hens and the new chickens, and when she was sweeping the flagstones, the old woman turned from the trees.

—You were out in the paddock a long time, is the old pony sick?

—No, Mam, not at all, the pony is fine, thank God.

—And them cows?

—All fine, Mam.

—Come on in and eat your supper, the old woman said. —You're working too hard, so why don't you go on to bed early.

—Thank you, Mam, said Alice, —I'm nearly finished here.

That Sunday afternoon the old woman stood at the bottom of the staircase, listening to Alice upstairs, the crackling of the hairbrush. When Alice appeared in the kitchen, she told the old woman she was going for a walk, because it was such a lovely day. Alice's hair was shining; she wore her brown Mass skirt and a white blouse, with a green cardigan that the old woman had never seen her wear before. The old woman warned Alice to be back on time to milk the cows.

—I won't be a bit late, Mam, said Alice, as she walked briskly through the door. The old woman went to the window, watching Alice skip across the flagstones and into the elms. She imagined for a moment that Alice was herself, herself as she once was, years ago, running and laughing through the elms with her brother, and she felt the feeling of warm sunshine on her hair, which now caused her to smile. She came away from the window and lowered the kettle over the fire. She whispered an Act of Contrition, and turned to look at the pictures on the wall. She'd take them down tomorrow and give them a good cleaning; she'd let them go for far too long. When the tea was brewed, she got the tray out; she would not bother with sleeping this Sunday, but go and sit with her brother. She was eager to tell him how grand the garden was and there'd be strawberries soon, strawberries for him after all these years.

———

—Friday night they say, Alice heard the grocer tell the men at the counter on Tuesday morning. —Friday night they say Davie Condon went off across the fields after dark, he did, a mystery if there ever was one, left a note to his mother and sister on the table. I always knew there was something missing in that young fella—who, only a madman, would do that?

The grocer walked up the counter and handed Alice the pound of butter and the tea. —Who's going to open that door for you now, Alice? He leaned forward and grinned, his mustache twitching.

She bowed her head and dropped the butter and tea into the basket, and turned from the counter. She walked, the men quiet, and watching. Her legs trembled, and she wanted to cry, but she would not show herself before them, not a thing; she walked, thinking about how she had waited on the road for him that Sunday, how she had watched for him in the field these evenings; busy in the meadow, was what she had then thought, the jobs having to be done before anything else—then she was startled, because the door was opened for her, opened by a man, who asked, How're you, Alice? She thanked him, but did not look at him, but walked on, into the yard, the door shutting behind her; she had recognized the man's voice, though: He was the one who had stood at the end of the counter and pestered her; she had heard them call him Brendan.

She stood alone in the creamery yard and gazed at Davie Condon's horse and cart, tied up close to her own. A woman, the first one Alice had ever seen at the creamery, was adjusting the traces on the cart. Alice began to cry, and the woman turned. All Alice saw was a blurred, long and white face—beneath it, a puddle of blackness. The woman stared at Alice for a moment and then sat onto the horse and cart and, without saying a word to the horse, she flicked the reins and the horse went into the road.

Alice placed the basket on the cart, managed to sit up on it, and lead the pony into the road, but on the way home, she knew her strength had abandoned her; that's what was really happening; the reins were heavy and strange in her hands—she should never have trusted a man to bring her happiness, should not have given up her strength to him, allowed herself to be led astray, because happiness came only from God, and she knew he was punishing her now; she had not been listening much to him of late, paying too much attention to the moment she lived in, too much time spent before the mirror, watching for him in the field, his voice, hand on the door, not praying enough for her sister, so now she must bear this. She cried, as she urged the sluggish pony on, not feeling the sunshine he had given her, not hearing the birds and seeing the fields and meadows; she did not taste the dust of the road or feel the cool breeze when the pony and cart passed into the shadow of the hawthorn trees, as though a black veil had fallen between her and all of them.

She tied the pony up, and went into the kitchen, glad that the old woman was not there. She did not care about the hungry hens in the yard—how could she be expected to, without her strength? She sat at her seat, at the table, and sobbed; even those few steps upstairs would defeat her, although she wanted to be in her room and close the door, lie on the bed, be away from all of them. Then she heard him call her: Alice, Alice, he called gently. She raised her head.

—Child, come on in here to me. She knew who it was, and she dutifully rose, went to the brown door and slowly turned the rattling doorknob, pushed the door open. She had not prepared the oil lamp, so she could not see him, the light from the kitchen only reaching the edge of his bed. —What is it, child, he asked. —Come on in here to me and shut that door after you. She shut the door and stood there in the dark. —What is it, he asked again. —I hear you crying out there.

She heard him tap the empty space next to him, and she lay down there beside him. His arm caressed her; she pressed her head to his side, and sobbed, —He's gone forever. He's gone from me forever and I'll never see and hear from him again. I won't see him every evening in the field. They're all gone, all of them.

—You're at home now, child, don't worry, you're safe now, what else is there to be worried about? They're not all gone at all. All of them are still here. Still here forever.

—I have been a pure disgrace. I have not done my jobs. I don't think I'm able to do a thing anymore. I can't face them people at the creamery tomorrow.

—You poor child, you can, he said. —It'll all go away in time. I promise you it will.

—But I'm going to die, she said. —I feel that is what's going to happen to me. I'm only a stranger who is going to die.

—God does not want you to die yet. You have too many things to do, and you're only young—but sure don't I know myself what you are going on about.

—You do, she sobbed.

—Indeed, I know it very well, child, he sniffled.

She raised herself up, leaning on her elbow, and she reached her hand out into the darkness, then lowered her hand and touched his nose, the tears on his cheeks, his wet eyes. She then lay down and put her arm across his chest, pressing her face, again, to his side, his chest lifting her arm up and down.

—I had a sister, she said. —I had one but didn't know her. She died a long time ago, and done an awful wrong.

—Don't be worrying about that, he said. —We have to look after the living, too—how's the garden, child?

She was quiet for a moment, then said, —It's grand, thank God, there's a bit of weeding I could be doing.

—Time enough now for all that, he sighed. —Time enough, the day is long, and you're a grand girl, and you'll pull down that old curtain on your way out. It's been in that same place for long enough.

—I will so, she said.

—This could be a grand room in time, with the lick of paint, it could be.

—Yes, she said. —I'd paint them walls blue and paint that ceiling white.

—Blue's a grand color. You'd never see a nicer color than that, he said. Then, —Go to sleep there now, child, and don't be worrying about things you can't do a thing about.

So, she held him. The hens clucked in the yard and the light moved across the fields and the meadows. In time, she would bring him strawberries, feed them to him, and she would wash him and he would tell her about his islands and the people who lived there, tell her, too, about the people who once lived in Kilroan, Bruff, and Pallas, but for now she would sleep safely, her arm across him, the afternoon becoming the evening, and all that he had planned for her, waiting.

The Postman's Cottage

EVERY THIRD OR FOURTH FRIDAY, UP TILL THIRTY OR forty years ago, which is long before milking machines were even heard of, and places not even too far in from the road still didn't have electricity, there used to be autumn Fairs in the village of Pallas. After morning milking, the farmers who were selling would gather their heifers and bullocks and hunt them down the fields, along the byroads and the main road to the square in Pallas. For miles around you could hear the cattle lowing along the roads, although louder than them were the shouts of the farmers themselves swinging at and hitting the often restless beasts with their ash sticks.

It was to one of these Fairs that Mrs. O'Rourke sent five fat bullocks one Friday morning on the verge of autumn. The O'Rourkes lived back up in the hills. There were ten children. Eoin was twenty-four, the eldest, who had recently taken charge of the fifteen-acre farm, their father not having survived the flu that spring.

The morning of the Fair his mother boiled him two eggs over the fire, and before her son had eaten the eggs, she had heated a few kettles of water so he could wash and shave himself. His brother, Michael, who was less than a year younger, was to say later that his brother was in a fierce hurry finishing up the milking that morning, and was whistling like mad, as he was known to do when he became excited, which was natural enough, for it wasn't every day you got the chance to go to the Fair, not to mention have fine bullocks to sell.

Michael also said that his brother took those long strides of his, hunting the cows before him while he combed his black hair out, telling Michael between whistles that the earlier you were at the Fair the better chance you had of getting a good price.

When Eoin sat at the hearth less than an hour later there was no hurry in him as he slipped on his freshly ironed drawers, while his mother, who was frantically ironing his Sunday trousers and shirt on the kitchen table, appealed to him to get a move on and to make sure he left instructions for his brothers and sisters with regards to what jobs they should be doing around the farm and what livestock they needed to keep an eye on while he was in Pallas. Eoin stood up from the hearth whistling, saying to his mother that she should not worry about a thing, reminding her the bullocks were going to make a great price, and that he would have to go for a few jars with the lads after the Fair—you couldn't ever say no to the lads—but he also told her he would not waste too much time in the public house, as this had never been his way.

His brothers and sisters had hunted the bullocks down from the hill and cornered them against the middle gate in the boreen. Mrs. O'Rourke followed her son into the yard, sprinkling holy water on his cap, his back and neck and shoulders. Eoin blessed himself quickly. He began to whistle, then he grabbed the family pram and began pushing it carelessly around the yard, with the youngest child, Timmy, in it, who cried with delight. His mother warned him to stop his foolish carry-on, that he should not take too much for granted and to not forget on his journey back the road to say a prayer for the soul of his father. She was both needing and expecting her eldest to return home that evening with a good sum of money. It had been an exceptionally wet summer and much of the hay had rotted in pikes in the meadows.

That day the square in Pallas was crowded with people from all over selling not only cattle and horses and pigs but also chickens, ducks, turkeys, and eggs from all three. Makeshift stalls had been built around the square, directly across from Ryan's public house and grocery. Winter cabbage was for sale in a few stalls and a line had formed there from early on in the day. A few butchers from Tipperary town were selling bacon. The cattle Jobbers had arrived from all over Munster; they were known to be tough, particularly when they had drink taken, and it was said that without a moment's thought they'd break people's heads with their blackthorn sticks if you were to vex them, but most farmers knew that when it was getting closer to evening you didn't have any dealings or words with a Jobber, no matter what price you got.

Eoin O'Rourke sold the bullocks around one o'clock, he did get an outstanding price, and after the Fair he sauntered laughing through the door of Ryan's with his best friend, Tom Dillon, who at this time was making a living milking cows for the few bigger farmers around Kilroan. (On Saturday and Sunday afternoon he also put in a few hours at the grocers in the village of Kilroan.) In Ryan's, they joined in a round with two other friends from Kilroan: Francie Houlton and Jim Dwyer were their names. The four young men stood, crushed behind the door of the public house. Eoin's friends clapped him on the back; they called him a boyo and told him he was blessed, his mother would be awfully proud of him, he was a true son of his father's; he was the luckiest man alive in Pallas and Kilroan, or any other place in the world for that matter, and then like every other man in the bar and street they began to discuss the day's cattle prices and last Sunday's hurling match.

Rounds went by; the farmers from Kilroan came and went, chatting and laughing with the young men, on their way in and out the door. Evening drew on. The Pallas Square was washed and swept clean, the stalls had been taken down, and most of the Jobbers had left, when the four friends stopped drinking pints of porter and began to drink John Power's whiskey with water. It was pitch dark outside, around eight o'clock, when Houlton and Dwyer started to make fun of their two friends about Kate Welsh—a grand-looking girl, she was, one of the very best, they all agreed. She lived on a small farm in the townsland of Ballinlough, and over the past few weeks both Tom Dillon and Eoin O'Rourke had walked out with her, although it was presently well known that she was fonder of Tom Dillon, as she had said this openly, and he was cracked about her, which he has also said openly; and behind the door of Ryan's this night Eoin O'Rourke smiled broadly and stuck his face into Tom Dillon's face and told him he could have Kate Welsh for all he cared, and the very best of luck to him. Then the two friends raised their glasses, shook hands, laughed loudly, and Eoin O'Rourke turned to his other two friends and told them in a serious tone that he never had a bit of interest in Kate Welsh in the first place, that girl was not his type at all.

The talk going around at this time in Kilroan and Ballinlough was that Kate Welsh would be doing very well for herself to secure the likes of Dillon, for Dillon, being an only child, would inherit his father's noble cottage, which back then was named Dillon's Cottage. (Years before this it was known as The Butler's Mansion.) The whitewashed cottage was not really a cottage at all but a small house, because it had the two floors. It was located on the left side of the road, right outside of Kilroan village, no more than a ten-minute walk to the church and the grocers. At the back of the cottage was a semicircle of sycamores; at the front was a stone wall, with a hedge of laurels growing along the top. The cottage had been built by an English landlord—a rake, no doubt, who, it was said, amongst other things, won another man's wife in a card game, and she went off with him, too—anyway, at one time this landlord owned nearly all the land in Kilroan, but on both sides of the Irish Sea he drank and gambled his land and money away, and he'd ordered the cottage built for his coachman or butler, although no one around was fully sure what his job really was up at the landlord's big house. The so-called butler or coachman was a slight, immaculately groomed, polite Englishman, who planted the laurel hedge, grew a lovely flower and vegetable garden in the back, and attended first Mass in Kilroan every Sunday, even though it was plain that he dug with the other foot— but after the landlord had to abscond from Kilroan because of his losses, the Englishman left soon after, and the cottage lay abandoned for many years until Tom Dillon's father, John Joe, was fortunate enough to inherit a sizable amount of money from an old aunt, herself a sheep farmer in New South Wales, and he bought the cottage with the money. He was the gravedigger in Kilroan for thirty years, but apart from digging graves he was otherwise gifted with his hands, and knew well the foundation and the walls and rafters in The Butler's Mansion to be sound, so he went about fixing up the cottage.

When John Joe Dillon died, Tom gave up milking cows and working at the grocer's to take over his father's job as gravedigger, which he did until he landed the luckiest job of all, one he kept till the day he died, as anyone in their right mind would: He became the postman for Kilroan and the surrounding area, and never again did he have to dig a hole to make a living, and the younger lads coming up began referring to Dillon's Cottage as The Postman's Cottage. Tom was a good few years married to Kate Welsh when he became the postman, although their one son was not yet born; they were married five or six years before he appeared.

Around the time of the Pallas Fairs no one would say Tom Dillon was not a great catch, but they did openly admit that Eoin O'Rourke was by far the better-looking man; he also had a kinder nature than Dillon, so they said, but Eoin had no prospects, and this was what he really had against him, when you take into account the few acres on the hill, his mother, the brothers and sisters, who since their father's death fully counted on him.

They did maintain that Kate Welsh, who was nineteen or twenty at this time, was one of the finest-looking girls around, and a very smart young lady, too, although more than one or two people in Ballinlough remarked that she couldn't keep her nose out of other people's business, and when she was a pupil at Ballinlough National school, she was too forward for a girl of her age, and she never listened to those who were older than herself, who naturally knew better.

The morning after Eoin O'Rourke sold the five bullocks, Charlie

Ryan was hunting in his cows for milking and noticed a newspaper parcel tied together with string, left atop a big rock in the middle of his field, with a smaller rock on top of the parcel to keep it in place, or so it looked to him that that was what that rock was for. This field, where the Ryans grazed their cows after the hay pikes were in, was beyond the crossroads on the Pallas road, going toward Kilroan; it was large and rectangular and stretched all the way down to the bog and the Main Trench, which all summer had flooded its banks due to a deluge of rain, and the surrounding fields and meadows were under God knows how many feet of water.

Charlie Ryan took one look at the parcel and suspected that something was amiss. He left the cows and the parcel, ran home across the fields, hopped on his bike without saying a single word to his wife or the children, and cycled to the police barracks in Pallas to inform Sergeant Culley, who only a few weeks before had become the new sergeant.

Sergeant Culley, surrounded by the other guards in the barracks, opened the parcel and picked out a pair of drawers, a clean shirt, and a pair of Sunday trousers; in the pocket of the shirt he found a rather peculiar note, written in pencil, in large block letters: *Say a prayer for the awful thing I done. For the poor children who will come after me. Eoin O'Rourke.*

A few hours later, Mrs. O'Rourke read the note in the barracks, and raised her head and claimed to Sergeant Culley that, yes, it was indeed Eoin's handwriting, but the words were barely out of her mouth when she began to weep again, then admitting she had no clue if the handwriting was Eoin's or not, and she rightfully questioned the sergeant as to who in the name of God around here ever paid a bit of attention to how their children wrote, if they were even lucky enough to be able to write one word in the first place. She wiped her eyes and asked him if there was any sign of the money or Eoin's shoes and socks. The sergeant said they hadn't found a thing else. Mrs. O'Rourke dropped her head and cried once more.

That evening she took to the bed. She called Michael to her bedside and told him it was now his duty to run the farm. The parish priest in Kilroan then was Father Gill and he sat at Mrs. O'Rourke's bedside, trying to console and coax her to get out of the bed, explaining it would do her or none of the children any good for her to stay in it, but she told the priest she was too troubled to move; was it not enough to have lost her husband not so long ago, and now this encumbrance.

Was there a fight? Did you lads hear any words said to a stranger, a tinker, or a Jobber in that crowd at Ryan's on his way back and forth to relieve himself? Did you see him with a parcel, perhaps with a change of clothes in it?

These were the questions Sergeant Culley asked Francie Houlton, Jim Dwyer, and Tom Dillon in the barracks the day after Eoin's disappearance. No was their answer to all of them. The sergeant, with his notebook open, sat in a chair next to Tom Dillon and asked him whether young O'Rourke had said anything disturbing of late, had he hinted a word about traveling? A tearful and trembling Tom Dillon told the sergeant if Eoin had such plans he did not tell them to him, and the two of them were the best of friends, not the sort to keep things from each other, for they had known each other since they were barely able to get a solid word out. He then told the sergeant the last he saw and heard of Eoin was at the crossroads just outside of Pallas, where the two of them had walked together after they left Ryan's. Tom said that he took the right fork, cycled on to the graveyard in Ballinlough, a good bit late for his meeting with Kate Welsh, and Eoin walked off, whistling, on the road going toward Kilroan, shouting once into the dark, I'll see you after Mass on Sunday, Tom, please God.

The other two lads had stayed on in the public house. An accordion appeared from behind the bar and everyone gathered around Francie Houlton, urging him to play; they had to keep at him for half an hour, which was routine, but when his fingers finally touched the buttons, and the first few notes leaped out, he shut his eyes and drifted off into another world, and there was no stopping him till the publican Mike Ryan told everyone it was time for the whole lot of them to go on home, that the cows still had to be milked in the morning.

The sergeant questioned all three if they had a good few jars on them and they slowly nodded, as if to say, *well after all it was a Fair day God knows*. Francie Houlton broke down, and then wiped his eyes and nose with the sleeve of his shirt, and proclaimed that it was one of the best Fair days ever—he ended up playing all night. Jim Dwyer said this indeed was the bloody truth, and he dragged his cap off and muttered the truth was that God usually had contrary plans to your own and there was not a thing you or anyone else in the world could do about it, and those congregated in the barracks, including Sergeant Culley, bowed their heads and silently blessed themselves.

The following day Sergeant Culley was overheard saying on the street in Pallas that from his few short years of experience in Pallas he had come to believe that those lads who lived back up in the hills were lacking in more than a little bit upstairs.

—God knows what might go haywire in that young fellow after he had a few drinks taken and all that money in his pocket, the sergeant openly professed that same night in Ryan's, although he did have a good few jars on him when he said it.

In the barracks the next morning he announced his decisions regarding Eoin O'Rourke's disappearance: First things first, the sergeant, as everyone else had done already, dismissed the assumption that Eoin had gone for a drunken swim—you see, back then nobody could, because you couldn't do much swimming in narrow dikes and rivers of stolid water, choked with rushes, and, of course, you couldn't do much swimming either in the rushing waters of a flood. So, the sergeant suggested that Eoin, mad and heedless because of drink taken, walked into Ryan's field to relieve himself, and while he was in there he took a sudden fit, flung the clothes off of himself, and the *awful thing* was that he had run down through Ryan's field, with only his shoes and socks on, and threw himself into the trench; or, in a similar manner, O'Rourke stumbled out of the field, with only his shoes and socks on, and raced like a lunatic down the dark Kilroan road and hung himself from a tree somewhere in one of the fields by the roadside; finally, in a solemn voice, the sergeant recited another version of what he was reported to have said in Ryan's less than twelve hours before this: The recently rich young fellow had it all arranged, had the change of clothes hidden behind Ryan's ditch, and he switched clothes, left the queer note to throw people off, and presently young O'Rourke was becoming familiar with life in America, England, or Australia. When he was finished, those who sat around the table in the barracks bowed their heads and coughed, shoved their chairs back, and did not look at one another in the eye.

Sergeant Culley's accounts were related at the creamery in Pallas later the same morning and news traveled swiftly to the parish of Kilroan. The O'Rourke family and everyone else in Kilroan were livid: Hanging! Is that what he said? Hanging, of all the things that miserable bastard could think of; can you fathom it for one second? Worse even, the poor boy running mad without a stitch on a cold night along the road, and becoming familiar with life abroad, ha! And these people would tell you that they were smart men! God have mercy on us, to be stuck with Peelers like them, but there's the law for you, sure enough. What else could we ever expect?

According to them, Culley and his kind knew nothing, never in their life having seen or spoken one word to Eoin, the most good-natured young fellow God ever put breath in: A responsible, respectable young man like Eoin would never conduct himself in such a manner, bring such misery to his own family, his father's body barely cold in the grave.

—The law is the law, and oftentimes human beings don't behave like human beings, particularly those with certain dispositions, in rare situations they have never confronted before, was Sergeant Culley's arrogant reply, and under his instructions the guards walked in twos and threes with the coats of their uniforms fully unbuttoned, carrying billhooks, rakes, saws, canvas bags, and ropes far in from the roads to scrutinize the trees, thinking they'd find a naked Eoin O'Rourke, with his shoes and socks still on, the money thrown at his feet, hanging from an elm or poplar. They were having a field day for themselves, as the saying goes, and were going to draw it out as long as they could. They even had a bet for a few pints going between them at Ryan's as to whose land and what kind of a tree they'd eventually find him on, whether he would be wearing the shoes and socks or not, but they came across no body hanging from a tree, so the sergeant suggested they drag the ponds, where they also uncovered no body; then the sergeant told them to turn their attention to the rivers and dikes, where they only found the foul and sopping remains of aborted calves and drowned dogs and cats and other things rotted by water and muck beyond recognition.

They did the best they could when it came to searching the bog, and they could not get close to the Main Trench, for the water had spread out in a single enormous sheet, blanketing the meadows and fields, and the only way you could gauge its depth was when the tops of the rushes penetrated above the surface of the water, and this didn't tell you much about how soft the ground might be, and those guards were not knowledgeable about maneuvering through a bog, most of them not being from around Kilroan and Pallas, they not being farmers themselves.

They also searched the hay barns along the Kilroan road to look up at the rafters, but no trace of Eoin O'Rourke was found beyond the newspaper parcel on the rock and the queer note in the shirt pocket.

The next Sunday Father Gill said a special Mass for the safe return of Eoin O'Rourke. Mrs. O'Rourke unwillingly left the bed, only to weep throughout Mass. She and her sons and daughters knelt at the top of the church, as they had that spring, when their father's coffin lay inside the altar rails. The Tuesday after the Mass, Sergeant Culley widened the search of the local fields and hay barns, ponds, and dikes. Nothing. He halted all searches at the end of the week and he announced in the barracks he now definitely believed young

O'Rourke did run mad, screaming, splashing, and laughing, with the money in hand, into the bog, where the fierce waters of the Main Trench brought him to the Shannon and his body was dragged out like a coffin ship itself into the miserable and unforgiving Atlantic Ocean.

Most of the people in Pallas and Kilroan, apart from the O'Rourkes, were beginning to believe that this was most likely the truth. Eoin was certainly too kind a young fellow to turn his back on his family and make a run for it, and he was way too easygoing, easygoing and lazy, not gallant enough for such a spirited adventure, although several months later it was whispered amongst certain men in Kilroan (these were the men who knelt in the porch of the church and talked quietly during Mass and left after Holy Communion to head for Powers public house) that of course there was some truth to the fact that Eoin made off with the money; since, according to them, you could not blame a young man, with a fat purse warming his thigh, a few jars on him to give him a bit of Dutch courage, for no matter what your outlook on life is, honesty and God and family have very little to do with it, when you think about that same young man trudging up a cold and dark hill to a needy houseful, knowing what was before and around him for the rest of his life would change very little.

In the end the O'Rourkes had to live with it, because what else can be done when misfortune so cruel and devastating happens? None of them were known to ever again mention Eoin's name or his disappearance in public, and as time went on it felt as though Eoin O'Rourke never existed in the world in the first place, and people in Kilroan were considerate enough to not ever refer to him in the company of an O'Rourke. The same people, though, began to cease talking and speculating; like all news, it became old news. The winter was not far off and people had their own and their livestock to worry about and look after, and it had been such a frightful summer with all the rain.

The O'Rourkes pulled through the autumn and winter as best

they could, with the help of neighbors and Father Gill, who continued to visit Mrs. O'Rourke; he eventually cajoled her out of the bed, but never again did she frequent the village or attend Mass, but sat rocking in a chair by her bed; but there was also good news, for in a few short years Michael transformed the hill farm into a noble one, and despite the fact that all of his brothers and sisters had to leave the home place, similar to what everyone else had to do back then, they all married and all prospered in life.

The Fair in Pallas ended a year or two after the Eoin O'Rourke episode, which, in itself, had nothing to do with the Fair closing. The main reason the Fair ended was due to the cattle churning the then unpaved roads to mud with their hooves, their manure and urine splattered and pooled along the roads, and they trampled down the walls of the dikes, and the younger, wilder beasts were well able to leap across the dikes and escape over those ditches to run unhampered through the fields and meadows, and the unlucky farmers who owned those fields and meadows were left with mending fences that those contrary heifers and bullocks had traipsed before them, post and all, into his land; needless to say, this was one of the few drawbacks in those days, or any day for that matter, of having land next to the roadside, but these farmers were the happiest of all when the Fairs closed in the small country villages like Pallas and Emly and moved to the bigger places such as Tipperary town and Limerick City.

It was the whistling man pushing the food trolley into the train carriage that took Kate Dillon's attention from the passing countryside and made her raise her face up to look over the seat opposite her, where the slouched, dark-haired young man had been peacefully dozing since the train left Houston station. She pushed her red scarf halfway back her head and watched the few late-afternoon travelers up ahead stir awake. She knew it was the lively smell of the freshly brewed tea and coffee that was waking them, that and the fact that not too many could sleep through the man's frightfully loud whistling.

The young man sat up, hunched his shoulders, and blinked at the window light. She watched his brow wrinkle and it looked to her the way his eyes were blinking he had no idea who and where he was. She herself could neither read nor sleep on a train, not being used to it, for she had not spent four days away from home since her late husband, Tom, had taken her to Killarney on their honeymoon many years ago. More than anything else, she wouldn't mind the chat, but she was also enjoying watching the countryside between the towns and train stations. It was nearly May and outside of her train window, the fields and trees were green again.

The man pushing the cart was still whistling when he placed a paper napkin before her on the table. The exertion from pushing the trolley and the steam from the tall tanks of hot coffee and tea had reddened his face; his silver hair was tossed and damp, his forehead was shining. She took note of the patches of sweat underneath his arms, and his wrinkled white shirt, the tie tucked inside the shirt halfway down, above his heavy stomach. She knew it would be hard to keep a white shirt clean and fresh with the kind of job he had. He nodded politely, said Hello, Missus, and asked her if she would like a fresh cup of tea.

—No, thank you. She smiled up at him, respectfully nodding her head, as if to say the reason she did not want the tea was because she did not want to put him to all the trouble of pouring it.

—Fair enough, Missus, the man whistled once and turned his attention to the young man.

—And yourself, young fellow?

—Coffee, Mister, thanks very much, lovely day it is.

—Yes, indeed, thank God for it, said the whistling man. —I can bet you, too, that the sun will make an appearance later on.

He had a Cork accent, she now detected, and he was older than she had at first thought, when she had watched him pushing the trolley toward her. She now placed him in his early fifties, as she glanced at the fine wide wedding band on one of the thick hairy fingers gripping the handle of the trolley. She fingered her own wedding band, and turned to look at the young man.

He had put a crumpled pound note on the table, was half-lifted out of the seat, rooting around in his pocket for change, and talking away to the Corkman. She recognized this young man's accent as being from down around her way, but there was also something familiar about his face: a broad, handsome face, with a flicker of kindness in his large hazel eyes that had caused her to smile and feel safe the moment she sat into the seat opposite him at Houston station. She put his age at around seventeen or eighteen. She, herself, had been living for over thirty years in The Postman's Cottage and she guessed that the young man was from one of the many farming families who lived out in the country and came into Kilroan for Mass on Sunday.

Her one child, Christy, was twenty-four. He was a graduating engineering student at the university college in Dublin, and she had phoned him two weeks past, requesting that he come down for a visit, but, he had asked her, for once, would she not take the train up to Dublin and visit him: He said it would do her the world of good to get away from there for a few days, and he was very busy studying for his final exams, and there was his new Dublin girlfriend, Tracy, to consider, who was dying to meet her.

Seán Egan had proposed to Kate Dillon, and this was why she needed to confer with her son, but in her four days in the city, she neither found the courage nor the right moment to ask Christy a thing; in fact, at every twist and turn she felt she was a hindrance to him and the new girlfriend—the two of them were not apart from each other for more than a few minutes, and she could barely get a word in otherwise; then, this morning, while she and Christy were alone in the taxi, on their way to Houston station, he told her he had decided that he was going to work for an American engineering firm in Qatar for five years, said he was sorry that he had forgotten to mention it earlier on, but the money out there was very good and he'd send the few bob home to her, of course, so he and Tracy were heading off this summer, but would spend a few weeks at home before they go, because Tracy was dying to see Kilroan—never happier in my life, Ma, our future, Ma.

The Corkman had gone into the next carriage, although she could still hear a faint whistling. She fingered a paper hankie from underneath the sleeve of her cardigan and began to wipe the mist from the window. They were going through Kildare; outside her window were sweeping, flat fields, where handsome racehorses contentedly grazed. *Our future*—those words would not leave her be from the moment she kissed Christy good-bye and got onto the train, although she was more than well aware that it was herself who had drummed it into him, day after day, when he was going to National school and later when he went to the Secondary school in Hospital, that there was no life for him in Kilroan. Drove him like a workhorse from day one, she did, and the postman often telling her to leave the child alone, that she'd turn him into a pure stranger who had no idea who or where he was—nothing and everything to complain about, as usual, is what the postman would say to her at this moment, God rest him.

Seán Egan was Kate Dillon's age, and a bachelor all his life. He was not from Kilroan, but from the coast of Clare, and some fifteen years back he arrived in Kilroan to manage the creamery. A few weeks ago, at her kitchen table, was when he asked her to marry him. She sat across from him; they were drinking tea, like they did every evening when he stopped in on his way home, a habit that began a few weeks after the postman passed way. Seán Egan laid his mug down, interrupting her conversation about plans she had for the garden.

—Kate, would you think about marrying me, he said humbly, —you don't have to give me your word now, Kate, but would you think at all about it? I'm very fond of you and there's not a thing I'd like better in life, but it does not matter a bit if you don't.

He at once rose from his seat at the table and went to her back window, his back turned to her, as he leaned against the cooker and stared through the lace curtain at the rank garden and groaned. She watched his thick body, which she had come to cherish, sitting down and standing up at her table every afternoon, the blackened redness of his wrinkled neck above the stiff white collar, and his gray hair cropped so close that she could see his scalp, his thick, short legs a few feet apart, and his hands gripped so tightly in his pockets that they dragged his trousers up, the gray socks furrowed over his work boots, showing two inches of his white, hairy legs, his trousers clenched so tightly that it shaped his broad, round backside, and even from where he stood, that odd, particular smell of red soap and fresh milk drifting to her; she had first smelled it the afternoon she ran out onto the road and frantically stopped him on his bicycle, she weeping and frantically asking him to help her with the postman, who she said lay dead to the world in the garden.

—I'd have to see what Christy wants, Seán, I'd have to. I would have to go with whatever the son wants. She turned her eyes from him to the open back door that looked out upon the blooming syca-mores.

—Don't I understand that very well, Katie, he whispered, and del-icately, as though it were a nightgown, he lifted the edge of her cur-tain with his two fingers, and continued to silently stare out there for five more minutes.

Kate Dillon sighed and gave the window another quick wipe, while looking across at the handsome young man. She knew by his ruddy complexion, his robust chest straining the buttons of his blue shirt, the words he spoke to the Corkman and the way he had spo-ken them, how he had dragged that crumpled and soiled pound note from his pocket, that this young fellow before her was no student.

—How is the coffee, young fellow? she asked.

—It's grand, Missus, thank you, he nodded, —I usually drink tea, but on the train, I like coffee just for the change.

—I never touch it myself.

She smiled at him. The train had stopped at a station, whose name she had not got the chance to see. She craned her neck along the window. There wasn't a single soul on the platform but the stationmaster who was laughing and talking through the window to someone in the next carriage. At the entrance to the train station, an elderly farmer had halted his horse and cart; there were two small milk churns on the cart.

—Portlaoise, this is, Missus, where the big prison is, the young man said.

—Is that right, she said. —Didn't I forget that 'twas here that was.

—Oh, I'm dead sure it's here, Missus, he nodded, watching through the window.

—Your man is coming very late from the creamery, at this hour of the day, she said, pointing to the elderly farmer.

—That's a fact, Missus, but you know the way men like your man will keep talking for hours long after the creamery is long closed.

—You're dead right there, young fellow, God knows.

One or two like him went by her cottage every afternoon. From her kitchen she'd hear the hooves of the ponies clopping leisurely on the road, the muffled voices of the men talking to their ponies. She knew those men by name, and if she happened to be out on the road, out trimming the hedge, they'd stop and have a few words with her. They'd reminisce about what a great man the postman was, how the new postman wasn't half as good, even though he had that nice, comfortable van and all. They'd inquire about the young fellow at the university, and tell her that he was a credit to her, and they'd say how much happier and better off everyone was in the olden days, in spite of how little people had then.

The train began to pull away; the elderly man lifted his cap and waved it high in the air. Kate Dillon and the young man smiled and waved back. The time slipped passed her on the station clock. Seán would have locked up the creamery and be cycling past her cottage around now. He would lean his bicycle against the whitewashed wall and look over the gate at the flowers and walk up the path and look in the windows back and front to make sure everything was in its rightful place. She imagined his face pressed against the glass, his darkened shadow stretching into her kitchen. She had given him the key and told him to go in and make himself a cup of tea and a sandwich; she had walked up to the grocers and filled the fridge for this very reason, but he had told her that sitting at her table wouldn't be the same without her sitting across from him—he'd only feel like a stranger in a strange house.

—The forecast is very good, young fellow. There won't be any rain for a long while, she was looking again at the young man, —I heard that on the radio this morning early.

—Sure it's fine weather all right, Missus. He was gazing at a cloudless sky over the hills. —I'm going home to help my father for a few days in the garden.

—God bless the work, she said, her eyes opened wide with admiration. —You're a very good boy. You work yourself in the city.

—I do, Missus, in the buildings, I do.

—A fine job for a young fellow like yourself, she said, now knowing where those fine strong arms on him came from. —Sure it is far healthier working outside than inside. My husband was the postman, you know, worked outdoors every day of his life.

—Well, Missus, I work indoors, too, I'm a tiler by trade, but I can do everything and anything in that line.

—You can't beat a good honest day's work like that, not many are doing it now, she said mindfully, —and it's good to be earning your own few bob, and half the country out of work and on the dole, but I often think if they really needed the work, they'd find it for themselves.

—Aha, the devil knows. He shook his head at the passing fields, then turned to face her, and wiped his eyes, yawned, without covering his mouth.

—You're putting it aside, I hope. She brought her hand to her mouth, coughed, and sat up stiffly.

—I am, Missus, I take every second of overtime going—

—I have a son up there in the university, she cut him off, —the only one I have, a brand new man those years have made him. You wouldn't even know him if you saw him. He got so tall and every-thing these last few years. I didn't know him for a moment myself when he came to meet me at Kingsbridge a few days ago. Of course, he had a new girl with him who I never had met before. Tracy is her name. Never met anyone with that name before, only on the TV.

—Fine job, altogether, Missus, he smiled. —Fine job.

Ballybrophy was the next stop she remembered from the journey up. The young fellow placed his elbows on the table, and took a slug from the paper cup. A stream of coffee dribbled onto the front of his shirt. He did not notice this at all, but kept the cup to his mouth, watching out the window on the other side of the aisle. The seats there were empty. She immediately wanted to tell him about that coffee stain. He could go into the toilet and wash it out and with the heat from the sun through the window, it would be dry before he reached home. Young fellow needs a haircut badly, too. It was too long above his forehead and oiled down around his ears, not tidy the way she'd have it, the way Christy wore his. But the light through the train window put a shiny, clean tint on the young man's hair. She ad-mired the way a few wisps stuck out across his forehead.

—I've worked around that side of the city where the university is a few times, the young man said. He was rearranging his feet and ac-cidentally touched her shin. His ears turned bright red.

—Sure, my son, Christy, is very lucky to go there, she said in haste, —and I don't know if he appreciates all we went through for him, although the postman and me had only the one and that made it an awful lot easier. But I understand too well that he would not be running back home to me. It's not that I'm a pure fool, young fellow. He was always a very good boy to me, mind you, did what he was told, he did, but you yourself wouldn't understand what I'm talking about at all, being too close to being a boy yourself, but that's all be-fore you.

A burst of sunshine through the window made her shift in her seat. She opened a button in her gray cardigan, and she reached her hands up and fully pushed the scarf from her head. She had a long, narrow face and a high forehead. Her hair was jet black and tied back tightly in a bun. She had fine cheekbones, and the tip of her nose went up a little. She tilted her head to the side, and brought her joined hands from her lap and placed them on the table.

—Where are you and your people from? If you don't mind my asking, young fellow.

—Toward Oola, Missus, he turned from the aisle to her.

—Well now, she burst out, well, well. She eyed him—her mind drifting in the second as to where she saw a face like his before.

—I could tell from the moment I saw and heard you that you were from down around my way. I'm from Kilroan myself, not too far from you, and for the life of me I can't think of anyone I know in Pallas anymore, but sure years ago I must have known many. You're a bit young to know anything about the way things and people were back then.

—Well, Missus, my father's family is from up around Kilroan way, but that old place was sold long before my time. There was only the few acres. All are gone from there a long while ago.

She leaned closer to him. He pushed the empty coffee cup to the edge of the table and wiped his mouth and fingers and shoved the napkin into the empty cup. She noted the sun had dried the stain on his shirt.

—And where exactly would the home place be?

—Well, it's a good ways from the village, so I heard my father say once. There was a big family of them, all over the place they are now.

—The truth is young fellow is that I'm not from Kilroan myself, but I've lived there for more years than I can remember, but the postman himself, God rest him, had the family cottage there.

She sighed and cast her eyes down, squeezed them shut, and brought her hands from the table and joined them on her lap.

—God rest him, the young man whispered and sat up straight. His foot touched her shin again, and he reverently bowed his head. She opened her eyes to a troubled look on his face, a look she immediately wanted to take away.

—Aha, for God's sake, don't let a woman like myself be worrying you at all, young fellow, she waved her hand. —Things could be an awful lot worse. We had a good, long life, the two of us did, thanks be to God for it, and I'm still young and in good health, only a touch of the arthritis in places, but what else can you expect from a woman like myself, after all that I've been through and seen.

—Well, I'm very sorry for your troubles, Missus.

—Well, thank you very much, she smiled and nodded. —I don't know now if I should be telling you things like this at all, but sure what harm. You're old enough to hear such things, but didn't I find him in the garden, five year ago it was. I lifted the curtain and looked out the kitchen window to call him in for his tea and didn't I think at first he was lying down in the drills resting, but I knew the way the spade was lying across him that there was something not right, but lucky for me, God was looking down on me, for didn't Seán Egan, who manages the creamery, happen to be cycling by on the road at that time, because in fright, the first thing I did was run out onto the road to look for someone, and how lucky I was that in the darkest hour of my life a neighbor was there to help me, and help me he did. God does not close a door without opening a window, as that saying goes. My husband died in his favorite place in the whole world, that's what everyone was saying to me at the funeral. A huge funeral it was, too, one of the biggest ever in Kilroan, he being the postman— but God took him in his favorite place, Kate Welsh, they all kept saying to me after—couldn't ask for more, they were saying what more could he or me wish for. We had a fine, healthy son, who's do- ing very well for himself. I suppose that's the truth. Never sick a day in his life the postman wasn't, but there you are now; he was, in- deed, a great man in the garden. That's for sure, exactly like yourself, I'm sure.

—My uncle Michael says I'm the best of the lot in the garden—

She did not let him finish, but wagged her finger at him the way a schoolteacher might. —But my son didn't like the garden, and that was a big disappointment to the postman. He thought that the young fellow thought that he was too good for working in the garden and working for the farmers in summertime, which he never did, being good at school and all, that was the only way the postman could see it, but that was not it at all I was tired of telling the postman my whole life. You can't have it every way I used to repeat to him over and over. There's only one talent God will give you and he gave one to my son, and I made sure he found it, young fellow, and only a few of us have a chance in the first place to even find out he gave us one. You do good work yourself in your job; it sounds to me like you're an honest enough young fellow.

—I do the best I can, Missus, he nodded.

—Good enough, then, she said, —my own son was saying a few years ago when the postman passed away that I should go and live with him in Dublin, and I said I was not leaving my fine, safe cottage and neighbors, no matter what, and now he's off to some foreign place with a stranger of a girl, who could not once look me in the eye when I met her a few days ago, like I was a foreigner myself—but I did the right thing not to leave home, and God knows when I'll see him ever again but sure he was top of his class always, and what more could a woman like myself ask for. I'm very proud of him is the truth of it—and I don't say that out loud ever, to be very honest with you.

—They all come home so easy now, all of them, he spoke at the window.

—No one ever spoke a truer word, he will come home to his home and his mother, she said, —sure it's not like it was years ago at all.

She felt happy as Larry, safe and relieved—and how blessed she was to meet such a smart and kind young fellow.

—Your father farms, she said.

—Yes, Missus, said he solemnly, turning from the sunlit fields. —They're not easy times for farmers now, not according to my own father, that's for sure. There's talk they're going to shut down all the creameries. I don't mind the farming myself at all. But my father thinks there's no life in it for a young person, that that day is long over, although my uncle Michael has a massive farm back in Bruff, with the milking parlor and the silage and slurry-pit and everything. His son is looking after it now.

She had heard about shutting down the creameries from Seán; he had said, too, that there was no avoiding it, but he had a good pension coming to him.

—On the small side then, young fellow, she said, knowing well she was being too nosey.

He looked from her and blinked at the passing fields.

—Well, now, she said hoarsely, bringing her hand to her mouth, —I'm terribly sorry, but didn't I forget to ask you your father's name—I don't know if I've already told you myself that I am not from Kilroan at all. My real home was in the townsland of Ballinlough, although I was not too sad to leave it. In fact, I was lucky enough to leave when I did. I'm from a small place myself, and don't miss milking cows one bit, that's for sure.

—Can't blame anyone for that, he said, —but as I said earlier they have the machines now. It's all much easier.

—You're right there, everything is easier, she sighed. —I haven't been thinking of this journey at all. The chat is a great help, and I had an awful lot on my mind, but I'm feeling an awful lot better, and am dying to be back home. I'm not used to the trains and being away from my own place, but there's nothing grander than meeting a stranger on a strange journey who's not a stranger at all.

The train had stopped and moved on from Ballybrophy, without either of them noticing. It was now at the platform, in Templemore. A few people stood and left the carriage. No one came in. She watched the few country people walking past, a boy and a girl running and laughing around them, a woman shouting, who she could not see. *Mind them tracks. You'll knock people down or get killed dead with that kind of carry-on.* The porter wheeling a trolley full of boxes and parcels, his jacket fully open, his tie loosened, and it struck her what a lovely day it had turned into. It would still be daylight when she reached Limerick Junction, maybe even be warm. The young man gazed at the platform, too. His eyes were motionless, and the look on his face shook her for an instant. His mouth had fallen to one side, like he was biting down on his back teeth. She hoped that she had not upset him with her talk, but all the chatting was making her feel light and girlish.

The children ran up to the window and gawked and stuck their tongues out, then laughed and ran off.

—There's children for you, he sat up and laughed; the look vanished.

—God bless them, she smiled, —I only had one myself, as I told you, but that was more than enough for any woman, and as I said it's all in front of you. That's where life always is, as my friend Seán keeps reminding me, and to be honest I would not want to go back to any of it again.

—This is where they train the gardai, Missus.

—Is that right. She sat up attentively, —I thought it was the other place we passed through above.

—No, Missus; I'm fully sure it's here, didn't I think about joining them myself a year or so ago.

—And you didn't.

—No, I didn't, no.

He was waving and smiling at the children, who had run again to the window. He rolled his eyes and made faces at them. She held back telling him she had once thought that her son should join the gardai, but the postman was insistent that Christy Dillon had too good a head on his shoulders for that work, said that the guards were not as good as people cracked them up to be.

—You'd be fed and found with the gardai is the only thing, and you'd never have to leave home, she said, —and there might even be a bit of excitement.

—There could be, I suppose. He had stopped watching the children and was watching her.

—Not much ever happens for the gardai down our way, mind you.

—It's all in the cities, Missus, robbers, guns, and the drugs, the guards are kept busy there.

—Don't I read that every day in the paper, young fellow, and hear it on the news every morning, sure it's a woefully dangerous job, when I think about it. I am so lucky to be living where I'm living. I would not feel safe in any other place in the whole world, only in my own cottage.

—To be honest, Missus, the marks weren't good enough for the guards, I didn't have much interest in school. I couldn't wait to get away from school is the truth.

—Oh, she said compassionately, slowly, —don't I understand only too well myself that it's not for everyone. When we were young, none of us got a chance to go at all. Only a small few. Those who had the land and the money only had the luxury to care about schooling. There was always too many jobs to be done at home around the farm was the problem, too many jobs and too many mouths to feed, and our mothers and fathers not having the time and patience to think about what was going to happen to a single one of us in a few years.

—Missus, he said, sitting up and smiling broadly, —O' Rourke's my name, by the way, Timmy O'Rourke, after my father.

He put his hand out, and she shook his hand. His fingers were almost too thick for her hand to hold.

—O'Rourke.

Her mouth opened wide. She sat up stiffly, pressed her palms upon the table, and leaned forward.

—From Kilroan, did you say! Which one now did you say your father was?

—Timmy, Missus. According to my mother, he's the younger of them.

—He's a brother to Michael—

—The very man, he threw his head back and laughed. —I can't believe you heard of them. That was my uncle Michael I was talking about earlier with the big farm in Bruff. He had a stroke a few years back but is doing all right. And sure my uncle Eoin went to America years and years ago, and we never hear a word from him, not even a Christmas card do we get.

She squinted at him. How could she tell him? It certainly wasn't her place to—but this is what the O'Rourkes are telling their children? In the name of God, the awful shame of it, to have your own fooling you, but she couldn't tell the young fellow: Your uncle Eoin drowned in the Main Trench, God rest him, the summer it would not stop raining and everyone believed, after, that the deluge had come because God was punishing them; this is what Father Gill told them from the altar—nor could she say, your uncle Eoin was on his way home from the Pallas Fair, and he drowned with all the money, his body pulled into the Atlantic, and not one of your uncles and aunts were the same after; they never got over it, and your poor grandmother died in St. Joseph's Mental Hospital, would not leave the chair in the room; no, indeed, could she ever tell this young fellow a single word of it.

—My husband, God rest him, she said calmly, —my husband, he would have known your uncle Eoin, when they were your age, they were friendly the way young people are at that age. I don't know your father at all or any of your uncles and aunts—but tell me now Timmy, will your uncle Eoin ever come home and visit us?

She could not, for the life of her, help but inquire.

—That'll never happen, unless a miracle, he was barely able to get those words out.

—Who could blame your uncle Eoin, going out there in very hard times, they were, as most people did. Not like it is today, as you said yourself earlier, Timmy.

—What would I know about any of them, Missus. It's not like they'll tell you.

A lonesomeness had crept into his voice. His face was toward the table, his cheeks heavy. Strands of his hair had loosened and were falling over his forehead. His mouth tightened into a straight line.

—My father and mother would kill me dead, Missus, if they found out I even mentioned his name to anyone outside the house, he said sorrowfully. —They'd go stone mad. My father only talks about him at Christmas, telling us we have an uncle in America, although at the same time he says he's too young to remember him going away, but he remembers well them talking about it after, so he says, and my mother like a mad woman tells him to keep his mouth shut about those things and not be fooling us, and my father shuts his mouth when my mother tells him to.

He had not lifted his face, but was making circles on the table with his finger, pressing his finger hard so that the tip was bent back. —You know the way them older people are, can't say a word or ask them anything ever, excuse me now for saying so, Missus.

—Well, you're right there, was all she could say.

He lifted his face. With the palm of his hand, he pushed the stiff strands of hair from his forehead and turned to the passing fields.

—We shouldn't and won't say another word about any of it, Timmy. Let bygones be bygones, as my husband, God rest him, and my friend Seán says. I've only one thing to tell you about your uncle Eoin, Timmy.

He sat up, turned to her, was all ears.

—Well, when I was a girl, around your age, and like yourself, being too young to know a single thing about anything, and let me tell you you shouldn't be bothering yourself with things you can't know or do a thing about, I walked out once or twice with your uncle Eoin.

—You did not, Missus, his eyes opened wide, innocent as a child's looking out of a pram on a summer's day. —You did not, he repeated it more slowly.

—Oh, I tell you now, I did, Timmy, she said cheerfully. —Well now, I only met him twice now, as I said to you, Timmy, I'd cycle down from Ballinlough after the cows were out in the evening and I'd meet him at the gully not too far beyond Kilroan. Of course he had the few cows to milk himself, but he brought me Bulls Eyes, and he'd put one or two in the pocket of my cardigan out of devilment, knowing they'd stick to the pocket, and I'd find them stuck in there a day or two later, but I have to admit that I'd pull the threads off them and suck away on them. He was a funny one, all right, your uncle Eoin was, a great one for the joking and the whistling—so there was only the three or four times. Small enough world, as they say. You know he told me he was planning to cross the water so that put a stop to us very quickly, and we were only foolish young people then, like yourself is now.

Timmy O' Rourke sat back and looked out, a drifting look on his face, his body shaking to the gentle motion of the train—thank God she'd be home soon. At least she had told the young fellow something of the truth, and what did it matter what she told him anyway, because fairy tales was what all the past was now—but God forgive her for telling him the bare-faced lie about his uncle's plans to cross the water, she fooling him herself like everyone else was, but she could not tell Timmy O'Rourke that on a summer's evening years ago his uncle Eoin stood in front of her bicycle and gripped the handlebars, and he was crying, asking her to give him a chance; there was spittle on his lips, tears rolling down his reddened face, and he was wearing his yellow Sunday shirt, with the wide suspenders, that all the boys had back then, and because of all the rain, the water was loud, tumbling underneath the gully, so that they had to shout, he shouting that things were going good on the hill, there was the bullocks to sell, and when she eventually was able to cycle away from him, she was crying so hard that she could not see the road, crying, *What can I do, Eoin, what in the name of God can I do, my mother and father won't let me, they won't, they won't ever let me,* and he ran up the road after her, gripped the carrier of her bike and she crying, *Please, Eoin, let me go, let me go, Eoin, please, I can't go against them, God forgive me,* peddling as fast as she could, afraid that she might fall into the blurring ditch, and he running after her, beseeching of her for that chance—can't tell Timmy O'Rourke a single word of that either, unless you're fully off your head you can't. She didn't tell a soul about it back then, not the postman—definitely not him!—that same autumn they began to walk out in a serious way.

Christ Jesus, she prayed, Christ Jesus, forgive me, forgive me and take me home to my home. She meekly glanced up at young Timmy. The sun shone radiantly on his face, on his blue shirt and thick hair.

Christ Jesus, but he was the image of Eoin, the same eyes, that sad mouth going sideways, the fine set of teeth; she caught her breath now, just as she caught it back then, when she saw his uncle smoking and laughing with all the lads outside of Sunday Mass, when he cycled, whistling, under the trees toward her on late, warm August evenings, the dust from the road smothering the sunlight under the elm trees where the gully is—the dreadful innocence of a young man's whistle.

She kept her hands as they were and crossed her legs and drew them tightly underneath the seat. She spoke in a quivering voice. —You'll find out, Timmy, that sometimes you don't do the right thing, even when you feel and know in your heart and soul that it's the right thing and you'll find out, too, that many times they won't let you do the right thing. Mark my words now, young Timmy O'Rourke, and that's the best advice I can give to a grand young fellow like yourself.

—But thank you very much for telling me about him, Missus, and I have something now that I was just thinking about to tell you.

—Go on, like a good boy, she managed a quick smile.

—Well, I haven't told this to anyone, not even to my own father and mother.

—Grand, I won't open my mouth to anyone, go ahead now with it, like a good boy, because we're nearly in Thurles, and although I'm enjoying the chat young Timmy, thank God we're close to home.

He started by telling her about Uncle Michael getting the stroke a few years ago. Uncle Michael's wife found him out by the silage pit one morning in January. There was snow that morning, and when Uncle Michael's wife came upon him, she thought he was dead; his hands were that cold and stiff. Snow covering his face and he lying on his back in the liquid muck that runs off the silage pits, so he was rushed to the Regional in Limerick. Timmy rang in Oola, Alice and Mary rang in England, Joe and Jack, not spoken to in years, were rang in Australia, Jimmy married in Tramore, Lena and Kathleen married in Dublin.

Timmy O'Rourke held his hand up before his face, counting off his fingers to make sure he mentioned all of them.

—They had the tubes stuck into him and the mask on his face, the tank set up, and the curtain pulled around him, Missus. And we all thought we'd seen the last of him. But then a miracle happened. He rallied, you could not believe it how he did but he did. The doctor said he himself had never seen the likes of his recovery. On the fourth day, he ate a bit; on the sixth, he was able to sit up. The family was rang back all over the place, told to not worry. No need anymore to make the journey.

Then Timmy O'Rourke told Kate Dillon that one afternoon, not too long after the stroke, he ventured in to see his uncle in the hospital. Uncle Michael was very fond of Timmy, Timmy being a very hard worker, good in a garden and good with the cows. They talked about the usual: weather and cows and the hay and silage and the football and the hurling and the dishonest and greedy politicians the country was eternally saddled with and jobs so hard to come by and everyone leaving all over again, like they always did, and the dead Hunger Strikers and that heartless and bitter woman Mrs. Thatcher. Then Michael O'Rourke stopped talking and the right side of his face started jerking; his eyes spun around to white, he foaming at the mouth the way a tired-out horse would.

—He was taking a fit, Missus, and not a nurse in sight, when you need them.

He told her about the uncle snorting through his nose, then barking like a mad dog out the side of his mouth, barking at Timmy that it was him who should have died. He had luck enough for five people in his life. He reached out his hand and gripped Timmy's wrist, his eyes spinning again and his uncle hisses that one of the friends did it, and the bastard guards in Pallas paid off. He growled at his nephew that he knew that much, that it was one of the bastard friends, his head going from side to side, and he drooling all over the blanket and Timmy's hand, that he would not let go of.

—I'm fully sure now, Missus, that he was talking about an episode he saw on the television, he was mad about John Wayne and Zane Grey and the Virginian and Trampas and Mannix and Steve McGarrett, and used to never stop talking to us about them when we were children. Then he went on like a madman again, Missus, that it was the friend and no one else, says then he saw that friend after, saw it in his eyes, the way they had changed, saw the awful badness in them, saw right down into him—that was all you ever needed to see to know, so my uncle Michael said, but then suddenly, Missus, he put his hand up before his face and stammered, *Enough of that now, not a word, not a word to your father, ever,* his voice settling down a bit, becoming more normal.

—And when men like Uncle Michael say enough that is what they mean, and you know yourself what I mean, and he told me to promise him again that I would never say a word to anyone in the family, especially not to my own father and mother, or uncles and aunts, who I never see anyway—and then the nurses rushed in like an army, Missus, pushed me back and said it was a storm in the brain, delirious, they said. Delirious, I'd never seen him or anyone else like that. It was an episode stuck in his head, stuck in there and never turned off. Behaving like he was in the Mental and not the Regional. A man delirious, they kept saying—but he got over it, is in good enough form now, but in the wheelchair, mind you, but still looks at the television all the time, looks at it and smokes away and says only a few words, and I never said a word to him afterward, but didn't he whisper in my ear a few days after: *Say a prayer for your own who came before you and never forget them, son, never forget them.*

—Never forget them, but what exactly are you supposed to remember, I ask you, he spoke boldly, —I can't often help thinking, Missus.

She stared at him, her dry lips parted a little. He wiped his mouth with the back of his hand, settled back, touched the glass with his fingertips, and pressed his face to it.

Thanks be to God he was done with it. Her elbows and knees had become frightfully sore from being in the same place for too long; she had not taken her tablets, for the joints. He had been speaking too fast and she had drifted in and out of his yarn, he putting his uncle's mad words together for the sake of the story itself, since a young fellow hungry for stories from long ago was who Timmy O'Rourke really was. She could see that now; now when it was too late. Never able to keep your trap shut, is what the postman would say, as he had so often said to her—Christy, from the second he first found words, never asked her or the postman one solid thing about what went on years back, like nothing happened or mattered before the day he was born.

Never forget them. The postman told her when they were first married that Michael O'Rourke was a queer one and to keep out of his way, that he couldn't be trusted one bit, so years ago, if he was walking toward her on the street in Kilroan, she pretended not to see him, and bowed her head and crossed the street.

Jim Dwyer was one of those boys, he went off to America not too long after she married the postman; he became a fireman in New York, lived in Queens and married an American girl, and the postman and he did not keep in touch beyond the Christmas cards they posted to each other for the first two or three years he went over, and when the postman died, there was no word from Jim Dwyer—but who would have told him, how in God's name would he have known?

Francie Houlton married an older woman; she had a big farm and a public house, up Longford or Leitrim way. She and the postman were not even invited to the wedding; that quick it was, and if Francie Houlton were to walk down the aisle of the Dublin train now she wouldn't know him from Adam.

Those two men were at her wedding, though. Francie Houlton played the accordion; he played it even better than his father used to play it, and the young and old got up to dance. Jim Dwyer got up on the stage and sang "Shanagolden"—but what was she thinking, because they weren't men then, no more than the young fellow across from her was now; young fellows was all they were, and full of devilment and feckless like all young fellows are, wanting each other only, though mad to marry, too, start what they thought would be lives of their own.

The young fellow sitting across from her would marry in a few short years. He'd become an altogether different person and forget completely about his uncle Eoin, and no one would ever tell Timmy O'Rourke, since no one knew anyway, why his uncle flung himself into the Main Trench, ended up down in the sandy mud and the rushes, but it did not matter one bit whether they did or didn't, because like the dead themselves, those who went then were never seen or heard from again.

—Is it dreaming you are?—Wake up, Missus, we're nearly here, said Timmy O'Rourke. He was shaking her left arm above the elbow. She opened her eyes, trembled and straightened herself up. She felt her face reddening as he withdrew his hand and sat back.

—Here I am now, indeed, on the train, that's where I am and no place else, Timmy, is the truth. I'm only tired, I usually lie down for an hour or two in the afternoon, and I couldn't do that today of course.

She released her arms and legs and pulled her scarf down low over her forehead, managing somehow to tie the knot, though she did not feel her fingers working. —When you're around as long as I am, you get to see and hear too much, some of it is good news and some is sad, she said, reaching her hand along the table, gently squeezing the back of his warm hand. She had the urge to tell him that he was the image of his uncle Eoin, but she did not want to stir all that up again. —I should have had that cup of tea the Corkman was offering earlier, she said, —and I forgot to take a few tablets. Are we in Thurles yet, Timmy?

—Thurles, Missus, we passed through there a while back. We're close to the Junction, I'm telling you. We're at home.

—I'm going to get married, Timmy, that's what I've been thinking. I am and you're the first one to know, and no one can stop me from doing it this time.

But he had not heard a word of what she had said; too occupied, he was, with the passing countryside, the fields and trees and dung heaps he must know like the back of his own hand, though he stared so hard into them, as if they were vanishing forever, and this was his last chance to take them all in. She squinted at the sunlight bursting along his determined face, the warm April sunlight rippling quickly across both of them. His fixed, unblinking eyes. The speeding, rattling train.

—Thank God we're safe home, can you believe it, Timmy O'Rourke. She leaned forward, whispering, tapping the back of his still hand. —You'll help me with my bag to the taxi, Timmy; it's up in the rack up above me. My son Christy said to sit across from a country fellow because he'd help with the bag. The reason I sat here in the first place. When I first laid my eyes on you I knew that was who you were, and there's not much in the bag at all, mind you.

He turned from the long row of bushes that grew on the ditch next to the tracks; the white fences of the racecourse gleamed in the distance. He leaned his elbows on the table. —Not a bother, Missus, I was just thinking that I still can't believe you knew him in the flesh. You knew him when he was only my own age, but you know what else I was just thinking, too, Missus, he spoke earnestly. —That this is the happiest part of the journey home for me, nearly being here but not rightly here, and not knowing what things are going to be like, but being so close that you think you can see what'll happen and then you turn around and go away again and home and all you thought it was never happened at all. Home never is what you thought it was in the first place.

He groaned then, and sat upright, the sulky look she had noticed earlier fixing itself upon him—in God's name, what else was he going to unearth upon her and where, I ask you, did a young fellow like himself find such talk? Beneath her the train screeched; then it lurched, pushing and pulling her, and then it abruptly slowed and slipped awkwardly into the inner rail. The platform suddenly rose up to the window like a brick wall; she squeezed her eyes shut and opened her eyes to people standing close to the crawling train; other people stood farther back, smoking and leaning against the pillars, suitcases and bags stretched along the platform like sleeping cats and dogs. The evening light covered the front part of the platform at a straight angle, the back part in shadow, cigarette smoke billowing through the light like steam from the teapot every day at her back window. The big tub of red geraniums blooming. She had leaned over four days ago and smelled them. Thank God they were still there, and time had done nothing to them. They were glorious, washed in April sunshine.

—We're at home, Timmy, it looks like, we're safe now.

—Indeed we are, Missus, we're stopped.

He stood tall in the aisle, rolling his sleeves down, buttoning his cuffs, while examining his reflection in the train window, then brushing his hair into place with the palms of his hands; he tightened his belt a notch, pulled at the collar of his shirt, and patted his stomach with both hands. —Right you are, Missus, he said, his eyes shifting from the window to her who yet had to stand up. —We must go on out, he smiled, —unless you want to end up with that whistling fella in Cork, ha. I have your bag here safe with me. We had a great chat, all right. I didn't feel all that time going by one bit, Missus, and I'm sure you yourself didn't feel a bit of it either.

The pounding rain and a dream woke her. The shadowy light at the curtain told her it was around half-six or seven. She heard rain on the flagstone path, rain on the road, and in the sycamore trees. She thought she heard Tony Hartigan hunting his cows. If she didn't, she would hear him any minute now. She had heard different generations of the Hartigans hunting cows every morning since she moved into the cottage.

She needed to get up and make a pot of tea. Seán had dropped a note through the letterbox, saying that he'd stop in before the creamery to see how the journey went, and to make sure she was safe. She knew he would be too polite to ask her about Christy's answer; he'd wait for her to say something. She had knelt at her bedside last night and thanked God for bringing her home safe, thanked him for Christy's good fortune, and asked him to guide her, prayed for the soul of the postman. After she rose, she decided to write a letter to Christy over the next few days; she'd tell him that she was going to marry Seán Egan.

She turned the blanket back and brought her legs out slowly to the floor. Timmy O'Rourke's face was in her dreams, the face frozen against the fields passing the window. She thought at first that it was Christy or the postman's face; it felt that familiar, a face she had kissed and wiped. In the dream also was the aroma of freshly brewed coffee, and she heard a man whistling, then the smell of dirty bog water—Seán would knock at the front door, and she imagined herself opening the door to the rain rippling off his umbrella, he in his green raincoat and wellingtons, and his clean-shaven, red jaw, his generous and timid smile.

She went into the toilet and washed her face and lightly powdered it. She brushed her hair back into a bun. She put on her underclothes and housecoat and went downstairs, turned left under the stairs, and into her son's small bedroom to check on the two begonias that had begun to bloom in pots on the windowsill. She pressed her fingertips into the clay in both pots, and it was moist. There was the famous picture of Einstein, next to the U2 *Boy* poster, pinned above her son's single, perfectly dressed bed. Against the opposite wall was a tall dresser John Joe Dillon had made years back. This room was her favorite in the house because of the unusual patterns the sycamore leaves cast in spring and summer along the floor and the bed. She sat on the edge of the bed and stroked the cold quilt. So many mornings she had gently shook the curled-up figure, the growing boy, sat there then and stared, stunned at how swiftly his body grew bigger, as though each night he took one more step away from her.

She came out of Christy's room and shut the door. She walked past the stairs, and opened the door to the kitchen. She went to the sink at the back window and filled a kettle of water. She put it on the cooker, and returned to the window and lifted the curtain. The rain had lightened off a bit, thank God. Thrushes and blackbirds were singing. Raindrops dripped from the sycamores, and from clothes on the clothesline she had, before she left, forgotten to bring in: a shabby old housecoat she had washed a million times, an old towel that she should have thrown away ages ago, and a few good shirts belonging to the postman that she had decided to give to Seán. While she had been away, Seán had dug a section of the garden next to the clothesline. He had been saying to her for a long time how sinful it was to let such a fertile piece of ground go to waste.

She had never mentioned Eoin O'Rourke's name to Seán, but Seán would have heard his name spoken of at Powers, that is if none of the O'Rourkes were in there at the time, for Eoin's name would have come up when one of the older men recollected the summer the Main Trench was transformed into a lake; they would say that was the same time young O'Rourke did away with himself, and the conversation would end at that.

The postman never liked to delve into those olden times. *They're done with for a reason,* was what he had to say about them. This was exactly what Kate Dillon's mother liked about Tom Dillon in the first place. She told her daughter he was a man who was looking ahead, which was the only and right place to look. In the same conversation, her mother never neglected to mention John Joe Dillon's fine cottage.

In the evenings, when Christy was still a child, she'd watch through the window in the front room for the postman's return from work. First, she'd see his hand fumbling with the bolt in the gate, then the front wheel of the bicycle as he maneuvered it onto the flagstone path. Then himself, with his uniform open, his cap sticking out of his pocket and his shoulders drooped, his face to the flagstones, walking the path toward her. She'd have the dinner ready. The paper was laid neatly by his place at the kitchen table. She'd run to the kitchen and pick up anything of Christy's that was left lying around the floor. (He was not allowed to play in the front room.) Then she would tell Christy to go into his room and do his sums, and not to come out unless he was asked, or until all of the sums were done, and to look over the next lesson and try his hand at them. She had to discern what kind of mood the postman was in; most often there was no need for this, but Kate Dillon was the kind of woman who took precautions.

Where's the young fellow?

He's in his room with his books.

What's he doing in there at this hour of the evening, can't he come in and say hello to his own father.

I'll get him, then. Christy, don't be so badly mannered, take your face out of them books and come out here and talk to your father! Them old books don't tell you everything, you know.

Moods and tempers were what she called them—when the mood was good, she could not ask for more: He would let Christy sit on his knee, while he himself sat on in the front room and read the paper, and after he finished with the paper, he'd put the boy on the bar of the bike and take him for rides around the silent country roads outside the village of Kilroan, the boy and himself laughing loudly, the wind making music in the bicycle spokes; then they'd cycle back through the village, where he'd buy the boy and his mother an ice cream cone at the grocers, then back on the bike again, past the church and down the hill to where the graveyard was, as he boasted to his son what a mighty, hardworking man his grandfather John Joe Dillon was, a man who made sure that a whole generation in Kilroan had dry and safe graves that would not cave-in in a million years, ready forever for the Resurrection.

But on more grim occasions he would walk in from work, enter the kitchen without a word, a deadened, distant, and glassy look in his eyes, and his wife and son and the objects around him, such as doors or stairs, that she had spent all day polishing, were invisible, he, impervious to the four sturdy walls that held him, the woman and the boy who loved and wanted only to please him. On those evenings, he'd sit at his place at the table and eat his dinner in silence; she would not say a word, but serve him his dinner and listen to him chewing. After, he'd go to the front room, sit into the armchair and hold the paper over his face for hours. She did not think that he was reading it.

Five years into the marriage he became the postman. But she was not unhappy or ungrateful; she would not have ever considered or imagined a different life, a life without him, not putting up with his way, not carrying out her duty to him; after all, this was the way God had willed it. So she washed her son's clothes and the postman's uniforms; she prepared delicious lunches and dinners for the two of them. She cleaned and scrubbed the house from top to bottom, and swept and washed the flagstone path. She tended her flowers, and cut the sycamore branches out back when they grew low to the ground. (Christy had run out of the house once and ran right into one, while she and the postman watched in horror from the kitchen table.) Every spring she whitewashed the piers and the gate and trimmed the laurel hedge. In the evenings, while he read the paper in the front room, she sat with Christy for hours in his room and made sure he did all of his homework. It's that job your father has that drives him mad. Being on his own all day. It would drive anyone mad. She had many women friends in Kilroan village, who she spoke to daily when she shopped for groceries. She had the men coming from the creamery in the afternoon who stopped in the road to tell her what news they heard that morning.

There was only the one time he pushed her. It was a few days before Christmas and he'd been delivering all day. People were filling him up with whiskey, and not being used to the drink, it made him irritable, made his behavior unpredictable, and on top of that he'd fallen on the path with the bike on the way in, and then she had made the mistake of serving the young fellow his dinner first, for he had brought home the good news that he had, once again, come in top of his class, and the teacher announced that he was the best student ever to attend Kilroan National School. The postman stood up from the kitchen table and threw the paper aside. He walked over to the cooker, pushed her from it, raised the wooden spoon, and shook it fiercely in her face.

Daddy, Christy shrieked at the table, *Daddy.*

But the postman paid no attention to him. His face had changed bright red, as he bit down on his tongue and shouted: If you only had one solid iota what I have done for you, Kate Welsh, you might not be standing where you are in that nice kitchen.

Later that evening, from behind the paper, he cried in the armchair, and said the business of the season was getting to him, that his legs and back were killing him, and he was frightfully sorry for his ungodly behavior to herself and the child, and that he was going to go to confession tomorrow evening. Was it the surfeit of love she gave so easily to the young fellow? she had often wondered then. Would it have been better if God had blessed them with another child? At night, in bed, he had often lamented that he would dearly love another child, a baby girl this time, but he also said that he was more than lucky to get what God had already given him.

In that nice kitchen. She sat at the table, sipping her tea, eager for Seán's knock on the door, and listening to one of the Hartigans hunting the cows in the field she could not see behind the sycamores. She watched through the back door the rain dripping from the still sycamores. It was at this hour of the morning that she thanked God for her life. She was indeed blessed and she was lucky. She knew many had it an awful lot worse. She had come to understand that what she thought of as her whole life was now becoming a part of it, the two empty places beside her at the table, nobody presently needing anything from anyone. If Christy only knew, indeed, understood it from beginning to end, if he had seen or asked about the thatched cottage she came out of in Ballinlough, most of her brothers and sisters living in England and America. Nobody ever said and did enough good, she knew that; nobody ever had simply goodness in them—that, too.

If Christy had only asked, indeed; all he had not asked and all that she had not told him, like the time years ago, when he was still in the pram, and she discovered the money under the floorboards in their bedroom upstairs. She was cleaning, the postman was at work, and Christy was sleeping in his own room. She had taken the curtains down to wash them. The room was fully lit, and she had dragged the bed out across the floor to sweep under it. When she was dragging the bed, a board underneath the bed came loose. She bent down and lifted up a small square board. And directly beneath the board was an old Halpin's tea canister, the kind people used years ago. She plucked the canister out, and dragged the lid open with her nails. Inside was a large roll of the old money, which went out years ago, wound tightly in two wide elastic bands. She knew the postman was good at saving, was cautious about rainy days in the future, but what surprised her was that he had not put the money in the post office or the bank for safety, for he was usually wise in this way.

When he came home that evening, she tried to coax him out. It was after dinner, and she brought the tea into the front room to him. She put the tea on the hearth beside the armchair and mentioned that when she was sweeping the bedroom upstairs one of the boards came loose on the floor. She watched the legs crossed, the one slipper dangling from the right foot, and the paper covering the upper half of him like he had pulled a curtain. Then she said the board was right under the bed, not a big board at all, just a small square one. An odd one out in the whole lot, it looked like, but it was well hidden, for she had never noticed it before in all her cleaning.

I'll fix it later on when I'm finished with reading this, said he from behind the paper, which did not drop an inch from his face, the top corners of the front pages curled over like pig's ears. Then she broke down and asked him why he kept such important things concerning herself and Christy's welfare from her, and without shifting the paper, he said he had no idea whatsoever what she was going on about now, and she could do her complaining later on when he was finished with reading the paper; didn't he, at least, deserve these few moments' peace, and what did he ever do but love the two of them the best way that he could, and what more could men do for women, and she was not fooling him with that stupid talk about herself never keeping a thing from him; didn't he know well about her gossiping on about everyone else's business with strangers in the road, and then he said that he knew her likes better than she knew her own self.

But I found all that money, she blurted, and now the paper slides quickly to the left.

All what money, I have no idea what you're talking about, woman, is it stone mad you are?

And it took him less than five minutes to sort the whole thing out; it was his own father, of course: John Joe Dillon himself had planted the money there years back, and because he had died suddenly, he did not get the chance to tell a soul about it. It was not until then that the postman told her his father made a prisoner of every penny he ever came across in his life, and he and his mother were lucky if they had butter on their bread more than two times a week, and the postman said he would never have his own live in that way. She suggested they immediately take that money and put it in the post office in Kilroan, but he said they didn't want the Reilly woman, who ran the post office, knowing their business, and they should take the money to the AIB in Tipperary town, where no one would know or care who they were.

Which was exactly what they did, and it was not touched until Christy turned eighteen, when every penny of it went toward his education. She had thought about it often in the years. A blessing, it was. Thank God that old John Joe Dillon was such a miser.

She would tell Seán all this by-and-by; she would tell and it would be a relief to do so—he was running a bit late, because of the rain? She finished her tea and went into the front room and began to dust the photographs beneath the picture of the Sacred Heart on the crowded mantelpiece, right above the postman's armchair. She did this every other week. There was a photograph of them on their wedding day outside the new church in Kilroan. Photographs of

Christy on his Communion and Confirmation days, the two of them, chins way up, standing next to him, her hat with the feathers, cocked to the left, his good cap to the right, her wearing a fox fur. A black-and-white photograph of the two of them with their backs to her newly whitewashed piers, and the laurel hedge she had trimmed the day before, Christy standing before the whitewashed gate, with his school satchel at his feet. There was a photograph of her own father and mother taken outside their thatched cottage in Ballinlough some thirty-five years ago, and a photo that would have been taken around the same time of the postman—he was not a postman then—with the Kilroan hurling team. Mrs. Hartigan had given her this photograph last Christmas as a gift. (Every Christmas the Dillons gave the Hartigans a box of Jacob's biscuits.) The photograph was in black and white, naturally enough. It was cracked, faded, and out of focus. She had never paid much attention to it because she knew so few of those boys on the team; she was still living in Ballinlough at this time.

The postman was kneeling on one knee in the first row, the hurling stick between his legs, resting against his thigh. She wiped the glass and thought that a youth standing in the back row might very well be Jim Dwyer. She now recalled that, like the youth in the photograph, he did have front teeth like a rabbit—buckteeth, as they'd say. She scanned the line of men, searching for Francis Houlton, but if he were amongst them, she did not recognize him, but there at the very end of the back row was Michael O'Rourke. It was certainly him. The hair and eyes, the way when they smiled their mouths dropped to the right, and she would never have recognized him if she had not met Timmy on the train yesterday. In the photograph, Michael O'Rourke had his arms tightly folded. He clutched his hurling stick across his chest—the exaggerated, high, thick fringe, the wide, thick shoulders Eoin never had that Timmy had inherited. A mysterious smirk on Michael O'Rourke's face?

She would not yet have met the postman at the time the photograph was taken, but not too long after. Every one of the lads in the photograph would have gone to the Fairs in Pallas, whether they were selling or buying, farmers or not. They would have gone for a day out, the opportunity to laugh in a world with so few of them. They would go cracked with drink and fight, often with their best friends; fight over nothing, things said that they could not even remember, had no significance whatsoever the following day, when all was completely forgotten and forgiven, and yesterday's words, no matter how harmful, were changed into a pure laugh. There was always talk in the villages the day after the Fair about how badly the young men had behaved, though everyone understood that it was natural for young men to conduct themselves in such a way—that the young men had earned and deserved their boyish diversions.

The night Timmy O'Rourke's uncle disappeared forever, the postman was barely able to cycle his bike. He wouldn't, mind you, have been a bit different from any other young fellow who had spent the day in Pallas. She had sat waiting for him for an hour on the low wall of the graveyard in Ballinlough. She knew right well what was happening, what those boys were up to. And when he appeared, he was bent sideways, leading the wobbling bike, his left elbow resting on the saddle. His pants, the shirt and boots, were drenched and covered in muck. There were bits of grass and rushes stuck to his clothes and tossed hair. He let the bike fall onto the road, and stumbled over to the wall to her, telling her they had a great day at the Fair, and Eoin got a great price for the bullocks, and never had he seen a man more satisfied. When she asked him why his clothes were in such a mess, he laughed and told her that he had fallen, bike and all, into the dike on the road beyond the crossroads, that it was so dark he could not even see his own hand in front of him. The battery in his lamp was damp and would not work. He then began to cry. He tottered before her, pulled her to him, and kissed her fervently on the face and mouth, his two mucky hands clutching her head and soiling her scarf. She finally got his hands off her head and persuaded him to sit on the graveyard wall. She told him he'd get sick from being so wet and she took off her scarf and began to wipe the muck from his face and hair and hands, picking the grass and rushes from his jumper. She rubbed his hands in hers, in an attempt to warm him, but he squeezed her hands tightly, and cried loudly, I love you, Katie. You're mine, Katie, and no one else's, now and forever, you'll never again need no one else.

The loud knock on her front door frightened her. She felt her body shrinking, the house vanishing—she had gently taken him by the shoulders and sat him on that graveyard wall and pulled the rushes from his jumper, plucked them from him like quills from naked and dead chickens and turkeys. But wasn't it very dark? Wasn't it frightfully dark? But weren't they only young and wasn't it a very long time ago and wasn't it only grass? Didn't rushes grow in the dikes, too? The cursed rushes, the cold and miserable bog, the shouting and the splashing, the crying and the fighting, his warm and naked young body swallowed under. God having his revenge. A young man, a good-natured boy, who must have cried and cried not to die like that in the dark, without his mother, calling against that beaten, cruel, and bloody land, and not a soul there to help him. Christ Jesus. Christ Jesus.

She was standing behind the front door of the postman's cottage. Turning the key was always difficult; it got stuck halfway, and she had to grip the doorknob, pull the door hard toward her, but she lost her will and began to bang as hard as she could on the inside of her own door, with her two fragile fists, as if she were trying to escape. Banging on the cottage door and leaning her forehead against the postman's threadbare uniform coat she might have thrown away a long time ago, she cried, Seán, will you please, please go around to the back, Seán, for God's sake, yes, for God's sake, yes, go around the back, that door's open.

That's Our Name

1.

THE PLACE WAS NOT CALLED LOOBY'S HILL AT THE TIME this happened; that name was to come a long time later, after Tommy Looby was dead for many years, but at this time he owned all the fields and meadows up there. I remember him well, from when I was a boy. Old Looby—my father and mother used to call him, so that's what I called him—our closest neighbor, to whom my father owed a large amount of money on card games long outstanding until this one morning in July he appeared in our yard.

My father had just come home from the creamery and my sheepdog, Toby, started growling, and my father and I turned from cleaning out the churns to see Toby jumping up, barking like mad, and swinging his tail at Old Looby, who took no more notice of Toby than you would a fly, but stood there with his shabby hat cocked sideways, the collar of his coat turned up, a stick in his hand, watching over at us. My father took his cap off to scratch his hair; he flicked one of his braces onto his shoulder and blew a single stream of breath hard out, then said under his breath, God forgive me, Marty, but I wonder what this miserable old bastard wants, I can bet you he wants what I don't have to give him.

Old Looby had been sending his cows onto the hill an hour earlier and seen the young woman hanging from the elm on the ditch at the corner of his field, the same way I saw her myself a few hours later with Old Looby and my father. The most beautiful young woman we were ever to see around these parts—everyone called her the Yank. Her own people born around here, but not buried here, buried in America, and their daughter born there but came back here for I don't know how long she intended—but God is a jealous God, and wanted her back, and she never did belong in a place like here anyway.

That field narrowed into a corner; the ground there was wet and soggy, and thick rushes grew there, and only the one tree that still grows on the ditch. Her blue sock dangled off the end of her left foot, and her other foot naked. Then I saw that other sock tangled in the briars high up. Her legs were all bloody from the briars. She wore a torn, dirty white nightdress. Her head had fallen into her chest and her short curled-up hair fell over her purple, swollen face. A lovely face that was, once. A red ribbon hung from her hair. She looked like a bloodied-up statue. They hanged her from the lowest branch, those two boys did, two boys who ran away, and were never caught for it.

Liam and Denis Gleason were their names, a few years older than I was then. Liam was the younger, a bit soft; he could not talk and had some problem with the hearing. A tall bulking young fellow who followed his brother around. Whenever I saw them up at the creamery, Liam would be hiding behind the red-headed one, Denis, who had wild-looking eyes, and he was the one I ran into the night my father and Old Looby burned the Yank's cottage to the ground, with her dead body on her bedroom floor—I never ever told anyone I ran into him, not even my own mother, and the next day those two boys disappeared and were never heard from again. The people around here put two and two together; they knew the young fellow Denis spent many an evening in her house with her, while his brother sat out in the middle of the yard, and didn't their own father boast down in the pub at that time that his young fellow was having his way with the Yank, that this young fellow was her very favorite.

Their father wasn't much, either. In summer he sometimes worked with Old Looby making hay, as he did with the other farmers; a strong, hard worker he was, though, a wiry-looking devil with a long sharp nose like a beak and the cap on him tilted to the left and his hair all slicked down with Brylcreem when he lifted his cap to wipe the sweat from his forehead. A nightly drinker, cursed with it, and you'd have to keep your eye on him for if what you had wasn't nailed down he'd be off with it. I never saw their mother but I heard she was a bit soft like the young fellow, but why wouldn't she be with a man like him for a husband.

Those two boys never went to school or Mass. The whole family was the kind of people no one ever cared much about or noticed.

Old Looby came back to our yard that night when it was getting dark. He took off his cap, shoved it into his pocket, and had to bend his head down to go in that henhouse door. You could not see a thing in that henhouse, even in daylight, for it was so dark. The hens went mad inside when he walked in and some of them darted out between his legs, and I had to chase them about the yard and put them in again. My father stood a little back from that henhouse door, but stood very solid, looking into that dark henhouse that evening. His eyes did not avert from that blank doorway, as he listened to Old Looby breathing inside. Her body had lain there on the henhouse floor since late morning—very much against my mother's wishes had the body lain there all day on the floor of the filthy henhouse, but my mother had my father to contend with—Old Looby came out with her body wrapped in canvas and slung over his shoulder. He would not have us tackle the horse and cart again like we had done that morning to bring her in from the tree. He said: I'll take her to that cursed house of hers myself.

—Suit yourself, my father said, and the three of us walked through the yard and set out across the hill to where her house was on the other side. The stars were out, and low in the sky, and God looked down; I remember thinking that, me an innocent young fellow then, God's looking down upon us, me saying a prayer for the re-

pose of the soul of the young woman, while Old Looby and my father, who I could barely see in the dark, walked along the hill in front
of me, whispering to each other, but I could hear Old Looby's
breathing, the weight of the girl's body on his shoulder.

Old Looby threw her on the floor of her house and unwrapped
her from the canvas like she was a side of bacon. Him and my father
would not even turn the light on, but only lit a candle. They dumped
paraffin all along her bedroom wall, pulled paintings off the wall,
and dragged her modern clothes from America out of the wardrobe
and flung them in a heap on the floor. A few pairs of her shoes clat-
tered against the wall. My father, bent over, with his head poked inside her wardrobe, threw her books out between his legs. Big books,
and copybooks. Then he pushed the wardrobe over into the heap.
The two of them pulled the nice curtains from the windows and
then they dragged her suitcase with New York City stamped on its
lid from the wardrobe. They unzipped the lid back, and emptied
whatever was inside into that pile on her bedroom floor; they
splashed paraffin all over her bed, and drizzled it along the walls and
onto a bedside cabinet. My father told me to get on my knees and
look under the bed to see if there was anything there that would
burn. I ran my hand along the floor and pulled out a pair of her small
white socks that were wrapped into a ball and I threw them behind
me, onto the heap.

All around me that night, the sound and heat of fire. Old Looby
dumped paraffin on her body, wetting the front of her nightdress, up
and down her whole body he sprinkled it, and when my father saw
me staring at Old Looby bent over the young woman, he came and
stood between them and me, and then the flames started to get out
of control; they burst through the wardrobe, and flames flowing up
the walls, and my father turned and shouted at me above the roiling
flames, as loud as he ever did or would, his eyes green and huge and
wild-looking as a mad dog's.

—Get the hell out of this house, was what he shouted and took a huge step forward and slapped me so hard on the face that I was flung backwards against her bedroom doorway; he stumbled toward me in her doorway, his arms out, his hands in fists, and his face red, shouting, —Get out! You don't see this! Get the hell out of this house! Run home to your mother! Do not look at her! She is not alive! She is not ours, a bad woman, not anything, not ours, a stranger! We do not know her! I feel his mad eyes on me still, and he's gone a long time himself, and the shadows of the flames along his red face, as he stumbled toward me that night, and behind my father the shadow of Old Looby swelling along the burning wall of her cottage, a fury within my father that had never raged before, and never would again, his awful eagerness, his fear, too, knowing, I now think, that he'd set the stakes with Old Looby, and had to go through with what was started; that was my father's nature—Christ forgive us all! Me in tears in her doorway, the way a young fellow will be when hurt by those he loves the most, felt my way out of her small house, with my hands around the wall that was melting beneath my fingers, and my father's wild and animal mouth screaming, me wetting my trousers. The house burned, she burned.

I ran like I had never run before, through her hall, feeling the terrible heat on my back, ran so hard through her yard and into the trees, where I ran right into him, who was crouched there in the trees, and I toppled over him, and he jumped up, and then I did; he looked at me and I looked at him, the shadow of the burning house inside his two eyes. The heat from the house was making my whole body shiver, me feeling I was burning there along with the house and her, and all that she owned, and my father's slap stinging me, and nothing ever again would sting like that, and her body in the flames, and then the Gleason boy running into the trees, running forever from me and her burning house.

They all knew and said it a few days later at the creamery that it was the Gleason young fellows who burned the house with her in it because, by then, they all knew those lads had gone from home, ran overnight, it was reported, their father crying his eyes out in the pub like the fool he was, telling everyone his poor young lads had run away from home without saying a word to him or their mother—

Old Looby, who I never saw in our yard before this morning and never would again after, although many the night my father was over at his house playing cards with a few of the men around. I heard those card games always came down to my father and Old Looby in the end. My father never told me so himself, but that's still legend around these parts. I remember my mother sitting in the dark kitchen after putting me to sleep; she would sit there without light and wait for that latch to lift, and when it did, and he was finally home, there would be loud sharp whispers between them—but I saw the young woman hanging from the elm with the rushes below her; my father and Old Looby were standing on the ditch, cutting the rope. My father did not look at me once but looked away; my father who had no idea what we were about to see on that ditch that morning, my father, dead a long time ago, who was always kind to me and my mother, but he had a hard side, too, I know it, because all them old people had a hard side, and when he and Old Looby finally cut the woman down, she toppled into the briars first and her body rested there for a moment, and then she rolled like a stone from the ditch and landed in the rushes. Water splashed out; the horse startled and I shaded the horse's eyes, told him to whist. There was dried dirt stuck to the woman's face; her hair was muddied up. Some of the briars had stuck in her hair; stains of dried blood on her nightdress, and her eyes bulged out huge and round. Her face was purple, her sock stuck in the briars. My father walked through the rushes and went back up on the ditch and sifted his hand through the briars to untangle the sock that he then shoved in his pocket, and I can bet you he left the sock in the burning house that evening.

Old Looby wrapped that woman's body in the canvas bag, and lifted her onto the waiting cart. My father never touched her body. I looked at the ground and dug the heel of my boot into it.

—Bring the horse on in, Marty, for Christ's sake before we all get sick, my father said, and turned and walked off across the hill before me; Old Looby walked next to the cart wheel with his head down, his right hand laid flat on the body covered in canvas.

Everyone knew my father was a thief: It was a joke amongst the farmers when they gathered at the creamery, where my brother and I used to stand around in the summer, hoping to get a day's work making hay for one of those farmers, who knew if a spade went missing from their dairy house overnight, or a hay fork disappeared, or a bag of grain was not to be found that it was my father, Jack Gleason, who did it.

My brother and I used to wake in the morning to see spades and shovels against the wall of the kitchen, tools farmers stored in sheds and dairies. Grain for cattle or pigs that was no good to us, so my father would sell that grain for nothing to some dishonest farmer, and they were not hard to find. The tools he would sell to them also. Once, I saw a mattress. That was only around for a day. I don't know how he had hauled that home on his back, or where he had found it, but beer and whiskey gave my father great courage.

This is how my brother and I came about: My parents were given a plot of land, which the government was doling out to poor people in the fifties. This was after the war. My brother and I were born in Dublin City, yet I do not have any memory of living there; my first memory is of a house in Tipperary, the fields around us, and the weeds five-foot tall in the yard. And I remember my father singing at night, stumbling up the path through the sycamore trees that disappeared in the dark—there's no darkness like the darkness in the country. The Galtee mountains were behind our small house, but far off, and those mountains shone in the morning when the fog evaporated. My brother was born deaf and dumb, but he has massive strength. I see him every day; he works at the church down the road. He wrote me a note once, which I keep in my desk: *We are forgiven* is what he wrote. It was me, anyway, not him. Because I led him to the elm tree on Looby's Hill—Looby's Hill, God, funny they would name a place after such a man; to call any place after him after what he did.

My mother used to sit at the back window and smoke and look out at the mountains. She's dead now, and so is my father. She did make sure, though, that my brother and I were fed. She kept a few chickens for eggs, and she would often kill a chicken; with the chicken's neck tight between my mother's two fingers, and with a swift downward twist of her wrist, she would break the chicken's neck.

Liam and I were raised on those few acres big enough for five or six cows and a garden where one could grow potatoes, cabbage, and carrots, though we grew nothing. We lived far in off the road—a mile, or more. You drive down the narrow paved road with the Galtees to your left; you come to a U, and beyond the U, on the left side, lies a clump of sycamores, with an unpaved, dusty path between them, a drop down in the road onto the path. No one lived on that path, only my family. Everyone around thought they were better than we were, and they would walk on the other side of the road if they saw my brother and me walking the road toward them. We had no grace. We looked like dirt. We were dirty, our clothes were. We were shit, we were shamed.

I was seventeen. My father never bought the cows he said he would, never grew the potatoes he said he would, never stopped drinking the way he said he would. He worked for the local farmers and drank at night. He thieved and my mother smoked his stolen cigarettes and listened to a stolen wireless, and Liam and I grew up.

They called her the Yank; her name was Madeleine. She told me she was the lover of some gangster from New York, and he had sent her away for a while. Her parents were born around where I grew up, but had emigrated many years before. She did not speak to them, she said, but when the gangster asked her to leave the country for a bit she told him she wanted to go to Tipperary. She thought she would be safe there.

She lived in a cottage three or four fields from our house. I walked through her yard one day that summer, with a hayfork over my shoulder, on my way to make a few bob helping a farmer turn hay. I came upon her in her yard, as she was reaching up to a clothesline. She turned with a clothespin in her mouth and said, Hello there, and the clothespin fell from her mouth. Her nice clothes on the line filled with wind. Music from a wireless, through her door. That day she wore a polka-dotted dress that flared out a little beyond her waist, and barely covered her knees.

She had more than one visitor that summer, but Looby was the main one. Him and his friends were. My brother and I hanged her at a dipped corner of Looby's fields, but she was dead, though, when we did it—it was easy for my brother and I to find rope; my father had things like rope about—I wanted Looby to pay, but of course my brother and I were nothing against Looby and his ilk; we were like the dust that someone swept from his floor daily.

It was nighttime. Looby and her were dancing in her kitchen. My brother and I stood outside the window. Looby wore a white starched shirt with the collar open. His braces hung down. She had a red ribbon tied around her hair. She always had ribbons wrapped around her bedposts. She wore the nightdress that swept the ground, that one. They danced over and back before us at the window. He swung her around, held her hand above her head, and twirled her. He held her in a gentle way, his hand low on her back, her hand resting on his shoulder. I could vaguely hear the music from the wireless. My brother stood beside me, his hand squeezing my shoulder. Looby and her were both smiling and looking into each other's eyes. Over and back they danced, the dresser behind them. One leg up, then the other leg up. Then her kicking her leg back, falling into him. Then their laughing. I watched the expressions on their faces. She undid the buttons of his shirt and ran her hand across his head. His eyes were closed. He had his body pressed into her so close— they swung around.

Then they stopped. Very sudden the way they stopped. She turned her back on him and raised her hands up. Looby said something very loud; I'll never know what those words were, but he went for her, grabbed her elbow, was pulling her, trying to spin her around, tried to bring her face to his. She jerked her arm away, and tried to escape from him, went toward her bedroom. As she moved, he hit her a box to the side of her face, the way one would hit a man. Looby, an old man, but a strong one. She stood hunched, clutching her head. Then he pushed her. She fell toward the dresser. Her head came down sideways, hitting the corner of the dresser. There were plates on the bottom shelf that rolled down to the floor, and shattered. A large serving plate on the top shelf shook, but did not fall. I jumped for her doorway, but my brother wrapped me in his arms and lifted me clean off the ground and covered my mouth with his hand, for I was about to roar.

He dragged me away from the window and into the dark trees at the edge of her yard, there where the lilac bush was. My legs swung, not touching the ground, kicking his shins with my heels, but he kept his hand over my mouth. I bit into his palm as if I were biting into an apple. A trickle of his blood ran into my mouth. I closed my eyes. His blood trickled along my hand, down my shirt. I sucked his blood into my nose, sucked my tears into my mouth. A door opened and shut in the night. Still, though, my brother did not loosen me, but kept his hand tight over my mouth, as I kicked and kicked backwards at his shins—

HE SHALL SPARE THE POOR AND THE NEEDY
AND SHALL SAVE THE SOULS OF THE NEEDY.
HE SHALL REDEEM THEIR SOUL FROM DECEIT AND VIOLENCE:
AND PRECIOUS SHALL THEIR BLOOD BE IN HIS SIGHT.

She'd read that to me; she, a reader, and the notebooks in her wardrobe that she wrote in. Now, all burned. Birds whistled in the bushes and my brother sat in the yard when she read that one verse to me. She sat opposite me in a chair on one of those summer evenings, wearing that white nightdress that swept the floor behind her on standing, her wireless on low, the door open. I knelt on the ground before her, and she lifted her nightdress with her two hands. I closed my eyes and went under as if going into a tent and kissed her there over and over, while she rested both her hands on my head and threw her head back, and cast one leg over the arm of the chair, while I clutched her ankles. That's what we did every evening. Sometimes, I dozed off in the chair as she read; she would wake me at dusk, touching me gently, stroking my bare arm, and shaking me, as though I were a child. I'd wake then to her face above mine, her lovely smell, a face so fresh, open, a face such as hers I had never seen before. How can one say what a face such as hers looks like? Is that not love, to say I don't know? And the way she would stroke my arm in such a loving way, as I made my way out of sleep. —Wake up, baby, wake up, you must go, I have some old friends coming.

No one calls anyone Baby where I come from.

All my young life my mother sat before that window with all her disappointments, the window around her like a cage, the mountains rising in the distance. Her chair creaked when I entered. —Is that you, Denis? There's food on the cooker. Her voice, barely audible, the cigarette smoke circling her head, bouncing against the window-panes. Smoke rising from around my mother, her right hand holding the cigarette, the lifted arm. Her few words: *Is that you?* Watching her mountains. She was a young woman then. I watched the back of her neck, a neck that no one ever cared about or caressed, the wrin-kled skin between her hair and the loose, broken collar of a gray homemade dress, with tears of chicken blood on its front.

Who would love those two boys? A drunken, thieving man, and a woman gazing out the window to the mountains. Her two filthy boys. Her failed husband, and father. Sodden, always sodden. To honor the two of them, to honor. Who would love those graceless boys? The dust gathered on the floor, a scrawny chicken simmered in a pot. Plumes of white, bloody feathers in a dusty yard. That was a hot summer. Her dream of mountains, her home done with. Ah, yes: *Is that you, Denis?*

My brother and me first went to London, and after a few years there, we arrived here in New York. I have three children, who are grown, and have brought me no grief. The journey of one's life can be peculiar, that much I know. My wife left me many years ago; our marriage was ordinary, and it fell the way the ordinary fall.

A loaf was baking. My father sat in his chair, at the table. My mother was kneeling, crying between the cooker and the window. He went on eating his boiled egg. I could hear his spoon scraping the wall of the shell, like the sound a baby chicken makes when it pecks to get out.

—Don't do it, my mother pleaded, —why are you involved in this? You'll bring nothing but trouble on this house. You'll end up in jail again is what's going to happen, and leave me here on my own with that young boy to raise.

She had spent all morning in the garden; her cheeks were red from the sun—but there she was on her knees, her back to him and me, and her head tilted up. She was wearing a white, unstained apron that she had just brought in from the clothesline, and her dark hair was tied back with a ribbon. I was sitting at the hearth. Toby was stretched out and sleeping; his head rested on my bare feet. We had brought the girl's body in a few hours earlier, and Old Looby had laid it on the floor of the henhouse.

That morning, when Old Looby eventually walked over to us at the churns and said those few words to my father, my father sent me off to feed the hens, but they were talking for no more than five minutes when my father shouted to me across the yard to bring the pony in and tackle him, so I went and got the winkers; then I called Toby and we walked out by the pond, where the midges danced in a cloud atop the water. The sun burned the back of my neck. Toby ran off, his tongue out and panting, hoping to get a few rabbits, he was. The pony raised his head when he saw me and came over. I slipped on the winkers and brought him down into the yard. My father and Old

Looby were still over by the milk churns. I led the pony under the evergreen tree and went to the dairy house and got him a pan of Parata. While he was eating, I slipped the collar under his neck, which was hard enough for me to do then, me being only a young fellow. I put the collar on and lifted the saddle onto his back. I put the britchin on, and I went and got the traces and hitched the cart up, and all this time Toby was lying out under the pony. Even in wintertime, in the hard frost, Toby lay there when I tackled. Aha, poor Toby, he didn't live too long more after this—my father had bought Toby from a Tinker for a few bob a year or so before I was born—

But my mother was kneeling, my father slowly eating his egg, like nothing was astray inside or outside the house, my father, a law unto himself, his round face and green eyes that you think should be blue. He did not look up from the egg at my mother or me, but kept dipping the spoon in, scraping every last bite from it.

My father was no poltroon.

—For God's sake, she pleaded, not turning to us or rising from her knees, —For God's sake, I know you owe him, you—you cursed with that affliction, but he's a neighbor, and we can get it to him in time, with God's help, we will—this is pure madness! That's someone's child lying on the floor of that henhouse. Do you hear me! It's someone's child! she said again, her shadow on the door of the cooker, the geranium full and blooming red above her on the windowsill, and she then asked him to immediately go to the Peelers, and to get the priest to pray over the body of the girl and to pray for all.

—Too late now, he said. —I let myself into this. I'll stand my ground. There's no other way out of it now. I don't want to end up back in it again, and I owe that bastard too much. Won't leave my family down, won't do that.

He laid the spoon next to the empty egg, his teeth grinding a little; then he picked up the spoon and raised it above his head and slid his chair back and dropped that spoon onto the table. Toby's ears shot up but he did not open his eyes. My mother didn't stir. —The damage is done, my father said to her back. Toby growled in his sleep. —I don't want any of my family to be worrying about it, he said. —All I owe Looby is now paid without paying.

Those were his very words: *Paid without paying.*

—She was a wild thing, that Yank was, he blurted. —The way she behaved, wasn't every good-for-nothing around visiting her house. Sure she even entertained the likes of them young Gleasons.

—Shut up, shut up! You're a fine one to talk, she said, and rose from her knees, turned around and looked at him, but she did not move, and he did not look at her, but looked down at the eggshell. —Do not bring your gambling talk and your judgments into my home with my young son there at the fire, isn't that a grand example you're showing that young boy—

—I didn't know, you know that, he stammered, then raised his head up to look at her, —I didn't know a thing till I went out there to that ditch—

—Didn't know a thing, did you not! said she, and took a few steps toward him; her shadow crossing him, and the head of her shadow touching me at the fireplace, and touching Toby, too, whose eyelids shivered and blinked, and whose body twitched, dreaming his dog dreams by the unlit fire. My mother swung away from my father and stood again between the cooker and the window. She watched sideways through the window, the two of them silent, and her shadow fluttering across the white cooker door, shimmering in the heat that escaped through the door. She laid her right hand on one of the curtains and put her other hand on a geranium leaf and rubbed the leaf between her fingers. I smelled the baking bread. He leaned his chair back, the chair resting only on the back legs; he opened the top buttons of his trousers, and rested his hands behind his head. Then he turned to me and winked, winked twice—but who'll ever know what was inside my father's head, sitting there at the table, with her body in the henhouse, and who knows what plan him and Old Looby had come to that morning in the yard, or how much money was owed in the first place? And all of it paid off in that instant—

—Not a thing, she said again, —I ask you, and who did this to that child—was it that old man who did it? Was it him? Would he be the kind to do that? she said, so low that I could barely hear her.

—What? he said. —What are you making up now, for God's sake? He straightened his mouth up, and his face went frightened, childlike, and the chair came forward, all four legs now flat on the floor. —What, he said again, —Old Looby would never do a thing like that. He give me his word, a neighbor—Old Looby, to shit in his own yard, to shit that close, way too clever he is, him and his land and his money—it will all be over with this evening, you and Marty are fine, thank God, and only God himself knows who did that to that stranger—will you look at the kind of woman she was, anyway, what you reap you sow, and wasn't there a line to her door nearly every evening since the moment she arrived. I can bet you though that the likes of them Gleasons were in on it.

—You! You! You're the grand one to talk, I have told you to keep your filthy talk out of this house. People like you are far happier not to see things the way they are, the way your kind made them, so you can cross the hill when you want, go on playing your games that bring nothing but misery and misfortune on everyone else—may God forgive us this one. May he forgive us, but I don't know if even he can this!

He banged his fist on the table. She shuddered; the spoon hopped up, and the eggcup fell over, with the shell still in it, and rolled onto the floor, but only the eggshell broke. My father bent over and picked up the eggcup, placed it before him, cool as you like, before him where it was before. Toby's eyes had shot wide open, but then closed immediately. —I want to hear no more about it. Not a single word now, you hear me—it's done with. People like you and I can't do much to change anything. Can't go back to any of it and undo it. I didn't have a thing to do with that woman, and I can't raise the dead. Can't bring all them dead back, woman! Women! Never satisfied, never can do the right thing for them. Cannot!—I'll stand my ground is what I'll do, woman, he then said in a quieter voice, grinding his teeth again, —I'll hold my own, woman, I'll do that and not another word about it.

The tears streamed down my mother's cheeks, as she watched through the window, looking at what?—then my mother spun around and smelled the air.

—The loaf, she cried out, bringing her hands to her face. —God forgive me but I've burned the bread, and she knelt before the cooker and pulled the door open, waving her hands and flapping her apron, as she pulled the loaf from the oven with her apron.

—Oh, it's not burned at all, she said, —but perfect is what it is, thank God.

Old Looby was in serious trouble. I know it now, putting two and two together in the years. He'd been at the girl's house one night when the guards raided, him and a few other fellows, who, like Old Looby, are a long time dead and gone. People I did not know but my father did, and he told me yarns about them. There was goings on down at her small house. That was all people talked about that summer. I heard it said that she would dance for them and the night the guards raided her house wasn't it said that Old Looby was caught in his drawers. That was the story anyway—whether it's true or not, we'll never know. Old Looby, who was around sixty then, close enough to my own age now. Never married, Old Looby didn't. Too mean to marry, I heard my father say to my mother many times.

My father never went down there; he wasn't that sort—but his affliction, as my mother used to call it, was gambling. He was a terror for it, and he wanted to outdo Old Looby; there was always something between him and that old fella; for years, there was, and it didn't end with the burning cottage either, but then unexpectedly my father stopped; stop it, he did, about two years after the cottage was burned. I was sitting at the fire one morning, after putting the cows out, and he had not gotten out of the bed yet, which was very strange for him to be in bed this late in the day. Even if it was sick he was, he'd be out working, but he walked out of their bedroom in his drawers and the stockings half-hanging off the end of his feet, scratching his uncombed hair, his face long and white as a sheet. She was over at the cooker, stirring the porridge. She was very mad at him. I knew that by the angry way she stirred, when he appeared.

He sat into the chair at the table, put his face in his hands and began bawling crying into his hands.

—I'm sorry, I'm so sorry to God, the terrible wrong that I have done, but I give you my word now, so that I might be able to close my eyes at night, God, that I will never play another game again. I'm sorry. I give you my word before my own, all you have given me in this world. Please forgive me, forgive me, God.

A few stray tears fell through his fingers and onto the floor. She stopped stirring and, at this very moment, didn't Toby wander in the door, his tongue out and his tail wagging, and Toby went over to the table and began licking my father's hands, and my father did not take his hands from his face, but said, I'm sorry, Toby, for what I've done, I am so sorry, Toby.

And she, still stirring, says, —You need to be sorry to more than Toby around this house, and she stirred gently then after saying it.

That did put a stop to it for him, though. He did keep his word till the day he died and the next and last time he crossed the hill to Looby's house would have been to go to the old man's wake.

I remember, too, those sermons off the altar that summer about the young woman, well not exactly about her, more about foreigners bringing nothing but badness and sin upon us, but that was all directed at her, who walked up the church, bold and lovely, as you like, every head turning toward the aisle, to the left and right of all gathered, in the old church in Kilroan. All watched her, except my mother. I'd say she was the only one in the church who never turned to look. She kept her eyes lowered and her head dropped into her chest, reading her Mass book.

My father, like me, looked. A tall, young woman, twenty-five or -six. She was wearing tights and had on the first pair of sunglasses I ever saw around here. Father Gill mumbled and lost what he was saying, as she walked, her red dress above her knees and her thighs going into that tight dress, her hips rocking from side to side, and with each step, the click click click on the tiled aisle, walking toward the altar, the statues and pictures cold all around her and the windows high up filled with colored light.

A few Sundays after that first Sunday she appeared in Mass she walked up the church and knelt in the seat right by Old Looby. She was wearing a hat, tilted sideways on her head. And the flowers hung over the rim of her hat and the blossoms shook while she walked. Lilacs, they were; lilacs from her own yard, growing out of her hat. We all looked, except my mother. Never her, at such a display. It was said that Old Looby shook all through Mass that one morning. I could not see him, though, from where I knelt with my mother and father; he knelt far up the church, for the richer you were the closer you knelt to the priest and the altar—that old, ugly thing, Old Looby, beside one so young and lovely—

—Tell the bloody dog to stop, Marty, my father said to me that July morning long ago, as Old Looby walked across the yard toward us, tapping his stick on the flagstones and flattening the rim of his hat, and I threw the scrubbing brush aside and told Toby to stop his racket.

—I know you don't think much of me, Old Looby stood before my father, —but I am your neighbor, and this is the worst we've ever seen, and we'll never see anything like it again, and I need a neighbor's help very badly. I swear on my mother's grave that I did not do this that you will see—I swear it, on my own mother, God rest her.

My father and Old Looby watched one another for a long moment, their eyes locked upon each other—then Old Looby stammered, Do you believe me, John Hogan? Do you not believe me, John? This is not a game, I swear it, I need a neighbor's help. I'll back off on what is owed and give you a few more bob into the bargain. This is very bad. Christ, I did not do this. Believe me. I need a neighbor very badly—

—And will all of it be paid off? Will it? my father asked.

—Yes, yes, Old Looby said without a moment's haste. —All of it, I give you my word, but you must promise to help me and you must believe me that I did not do this.

—I will so help you then, Mr. Looby, my father said, and spit into his own right hand, then held that hand out to Old Looby, who sighed and shook my father's hand.

⸻

I spoke to my brother in the dark of our room. He lay huge and shapeless beside me in the bed. I felt heat from him, felt he would protect me all my life, felt as though I could live in the world if he were in it, he deaf and dumb as an animal, he, so huge in the nights of my childhood. I felt the awful pain of her. He smelled like new hay and dirt, the same smell that was on me. I heard my father stumble, mumbling, in the hall, my mother shifting in their bed. I did not know if my brother was awake or asleep, but always spoke to him who could not answer me. Told him we should leave those empty fields, and farmers, those mountains, those lilacs and elms and poplars, leave those who slept next door.

Madeleine touched me. She did, that first afternoon I walked into her yard, when she turned from the clothesline. That was the first time. I was nothing up to that. I was everyone else until then. She touched me. To not know that love existed, and then to find it. After, what would I settle for. Everything was dead and old. They were dead. The mountains and fields and trees were—

I crawled under her dress and the light from the door shone through her dress. And the smell of lilacs and cut hay outside. My brother sitting in the yard. The summer light died in the mountains; the light slipped out of the trees; the shadows stretched in the yard. Clouds rolled in, bringing a swift shower of evening rain. Cows hid under the trees, away from the rain. I would wake to the sound of the rain on her cobbled yard, and her face over me in the chair, my eyes blinking open: All that we rise above: *Baby, baby*, she called me, shaking me.

My brother and I walked in her door. My brother went to her, and swept the broken plates aside. He turned her body over. The blood from his hand stained her nightdress at the shoulder. I knelt by her, by him. He gathered her into his arms, and stood up. Her hand dropped down, and swung there. Her eyes were closed, and her hair had fallen over her face, the ribbon still hanging there. Her face was gray, not hers anymore. I reached out to stop her swinging hand. Her fingers were cold upon mine. Her other arm fell down. It swung for an instant. I would not touch her again. There was blood around her waist now, from his hand. He held her there before me, but I turned and walked out the door.

I only turned back to look when I stood beneath that tree on Looby's hill. He was only a few yards away from me, but I could hear no breath, just him walking toward me with her in his arms, holding her as if she were no more weight than a feather. He kept his face raised to the dark, turned a little to the left. He passed me, and then turned to face me; he laid her body at my feet. I could not see her face anymore for the dark. He left to go and bring back rope, and I sat down underneath the tree. I shut my eyes and prayed for her to wake and touch me. In vain, though, I prayed. She was beside me as she is now, every night, when I shut my eyes. Lay dead in that field. Hoped she would touch me, run her hand up my back, and say *Baby*, but she is dead and burned in the place I came from. A place I cannot return to. The chair, her books, her shoes, the nightdress. All burned, are nothing, as she is nothing, the flames rising at the window, the glass in the window exploding, flames crawling through the roof, climbing higher than the trees, that bruise when her head hit the dresser, that bruise I could not see that brought no blood. What do you do? What do you do when those you love die? When they cannot touch you, cannot raise their hands to you, when their eyes and mouth won't open? She lay in the grass without heat. I waited.

He returned with the rope. I would not touch her, but watched him haul her body onto the ditch, up to that elm branch. She was no weight to him who is so strong. No weight, nothing.

2.

It was around three in the afternoon, when Toby started barking; he had noticed a stirring behind the alder bushes at the corner of the garden. She was kneeling in the potato drills on a folded-over canvas bag; she got up, clutching a bunch of weeds in her right hand. She looked toward the corner of the garden, telling Toby to stop his barking, that he'd wake every child in the parish.

She cast the weeds into the headland, and brushed the clay from her hands. She hiked her dress up, as she stepped over the potato stalks, going toward the corner of the garden. She was wearing her faded purple dress, the one that billowed out and hung close to her ankles.

—Come here, Toby, can't you, come back here like a good dog, I'll tell Marty on you is what I'll do.

She walked carefully across the cabbage drills. She had weeded the cabbage yesterday morning; she glanced at them, reminding herself that they might need watering. She stepped through the carrots she had thinned a few days ago—they had stiffened back up nicely—when a rustling in the alders caused her to raise her head. Toby had started up an even greater racket.

An alder branch swung down and bounced back up; an arm came out of the bushes and then a boy appeared, then another boy did. She felt no fear, though. Toby was here after all, and she was now busy telling him that she'd lock him up in the dairy house if in future he did not do what she asked of him. He dropped his tail and sneaked back by her; he circled her, whimpering until he finally settled himself between her and the boys, his ears erect.

They were Tinker boys. They looked every bit of it, the state of them. Out to steal, as usual. Thank God for Toby.

The bigger one stood in front of the smaller one. A shiver went through her as she gazed into the bigger one's eyes. He had that look like nothing in the world could hurt him. He was well over six feet, with big ears and a round face, his right eye running all the way to the left, God bless the mark. His front teeth pushed his upper lip out. He wore a heavy winter coat and his stomach was putting pressure on the buttons. She groaned. It was unbearably hot, and how in the name of God could a young Tinker even have the strength to stand it?

The other boy had a coat tucked underneath his arm, and he carried a small suitcase that was held together with a piece of rope. He had fine—what she would call— smart features. His large eyes held a terrified gaze, though, the way they were on hers, like she had trapped him like you would a fox. Toby had stopped paying attention to the whole lot of them. He had stretched out and was now licking his front paws.

—We're not meaning to disturb you, Missus, the smaller one spoke.

—This is private property, she chastised them. —And the two of you Tinkers are trespassing.

—We were on our way home, Missus, but the dog, Missus—

She shook her finger at them, and said brazenly, —My husband and son are only five or six fields from here and if they see you two Tinkers, they'll—

—We're not Tinkers, Missus, the smaller said. —We live here. We're on our way home.

She felt stunned, terribly ashamed. To talk like that to a neighbor's child—what in the name of God was she thinking, but yesterday was a strange day, and every day from now on would be a bit like that.

—Oh, God forgive me then, she cheerfully clapped her hands, as if to say she was only joking about the Tinker remark. —This hot weather will drive us all to madness, she said. —Sure I'm out here all morning under the hot sun, and I'm not thinking rightly, not having slept a wink last night, God help us, and yer name would be?

—Gleason, Missus, the smaller one said. —That's our name.

—Oh, oh, is that a fact now, she said, —so that's who the two of you are then.

She took a deep breath. Gleason—by God—the very name her husband had mentioned yesterday afternoon at the table—and he had mentioned the name a few times in his sleep last night. Gleason, indeed, the drunken man who lived down the path where the syca-more grove was, close to the turn in the road. She frowned and her eyes narrowed—wasn't Gleason stuck in the public house nearly every day of his life.

She herself had seen him once, in Looby's big meadow, on a day last summer when she had taken a bottle of tea and bread and fried eggs out to her husband and Marty and the other men. She had taken the food out there because she knew right well Old Looby wouldn't feed anyone, too mean he was to even feed his own neigh-bors who helped him out with the hay.

She imagined her husband, turning the hay a few meadows away, his sleeves rolled up and the patches of dampness under his arms, Marty walking beside him, doing the best he could at his age with a pitchfork, copying his father's every move, looking up to him; the very same walk the two of them had, their round shoulders, heads down, the narrow backsides, two peas in a hanky—Marty, who, on going out the door this morning with his father, would not speak a word to her, not once turn his head to acknowledge her. Such bad luck, evil and pure devilment her husband had led all of them into— she must pray and pray for the bad luck to pass; she would need to pray for a long time. She had spent the morning praying, while she weeded, kneeling on the canvas bag. God is good. God is forever good and there was no other place to go but on. Marty had to grow up. Marty would be a good man. He had that in him.

She looked at the smaller boy before her. His eyes had not left her face, a boy a few years ahead of her own. The body of the girl had lain in the filthy henhouse yesterday. The stranger she had never seen, not lifted her head to, but had heard the clicking of her heels when she passed her in the pew on Sunday mornings. Her eyes went to the bigger boy; his eyes did and said nothing.

—I'm sorry, but I don't know your people, she said, feeling a catch in her throat, the fierceness of the sun on the back of her neck like it was the only place in the world it was then shining.

—We need to be going, Missus, the smaller one said. —Our father and mother will be wondering where we are. We told them we'd be back home hours ago.

Without turning, the two of them took a few steps back, toward the ditch. Toby growled and bared his teeth, his front shoulders hunched.

—Sure, you young fellows must need a mug of water on a day like this, the two of you are as red as beetroots, she said.

The bigger one turned back to the smaller one and nodded; the smaller one turned to her and said, Yes, please, thank you, Missus.

—Wait there then, she said, I'll bring you young lads out a full bottle, and you stay right where you are Toby.

He relaxed his shoulders and lay back down.

A full bucket of water stood next to the cooker. On the table, covered with a tea towel, was the loaf she had baked yesterday. She had cut half of it into slices that morning and given it to him and Marty. She had put a bit of ham on the slices, along with butter and a sprinkling of salt.

She shoved an empty lemonade bottle down into the water. She listened to the clock, the flies buzzing all over her kitchen. The fly-paper over the kitchen table, blackened completely with dead ones—there will be so much grief and misfortune; all around knew by now about the stranger's burning house—the Yank who came home. There will be much sorrow for a long time in her own home. It would never end. You have to live with grief like that for the rest of your life, every day, but she would pray to God to absolve her husband his devilish impulses, all the men their mistakes—to do that to your own and no one to ever know, only her own and Old Looby. Was that girl not God's child, just as Marty was?

That cheap suitcase the good-looking young lad in the garden was holding and the other one with that heavy winter coat; them two were not on their way home. They were on their way away, dressed and packed; she knew it the moment she laid eyes on them, if she were to think about it.

She lifted the full bottle of water out of the bucket—oh, but, in the meadow they are all speaking about the fire; they'll talk about the fire and the woman and the burning house for years and years to come. It made her dizzy, the heat, she needed to rest; it was over with, in the past. God made time; he made a dreadful amount of it. She corked the bottle, then walked over by the hearth to get the newspaper, and she brought the newspaper back, laid it flat on the table, next to the loaf, and laid the bottle flat on the table and rolled it in sheets of newspaper. Then, without thinking, she lifted the loaf and smelled it; it was a good loaf all right, had a firm feel. She could bake another one this evening, after the cows were milked. The garden would be fine until tomorrow; gardens don't change in the course of a day the way that people do.

She turned from the table and went back to the hearth for more sheets of newspaper. She came back and spread the sheets out on the table and put the loaf on top of them. All the times she had wrapped bread for her son, and once, only once, though, when he was very young, had he complained to her that the bread tasted of ink. She started to worry about that, that those boys might not like her bread; they might end up throwing the bread into a ditch somewhere on their journey away from Kilroan. She stopped wrapping. Her husband's coat hung on the back of the chair beside her, the chair he always sat in. The collar and the ends of the sleeves were frayed. She could see bits of the striped inner lining on each sleeve. She shut her eyes. The flies, the clock; the whole world was way too loud.

Last night she would not let him touch her, and he wanted to so badly. Last night, he was needing of her. He who was always so fear-less, but not last night, when he turned and tossed in the bed and the blankets fell onto the floor, and he cursing out loud like a lunatic, *Jesus God, not my child, Jesus God, not my own child, what in the name of God have I done to the child you gave me.* He made more than one attempt to get his hands underneath her slip and he tried to press her against the wall, grabbing her there, and trying to force her legs open. In the end, she took a blanket and slipped out of the bed. She looked in on her boy, who was sound asleep. She sat on the edge of his bed and gently she tightened the quilt around his neck. She sat for a while, watching him, listening to his breath, thanking God for him.

When she left his room and shut the door quietly behind her, it felt as though the ground beneath the house was trembling. God was looking down upon them, and they were cursed forever; they were wrong and no one else in the world was wrong the way they were, but God was good. She not only knew it, but felt it.

She went and sat in the kitchen, at the dark window. She cried, begging him for a new day: One more chance please! please! For all of them, imploring upon him as she had done her whole life for a world that was very different from the one she was born into.

She believed that around four o'clock he would not answer her; no new day would ever arrive, but the pony ran down from the hill; she heard him gallop underneath the evergreen trees, snorting and kick-ing up the hard clay and the dried-out pinecones that littered the ground there. She gripped the blanket across her shoulders and went to the window and pressed her face to the glass. She whispered the pony's name into the daylight. The pony neighed. A thrashing ma-chine spluttered awake in a meadow on the other side of the hill. The pure morning light arched above the evergreen trees.

She dipped her hand into the inside pocket of her husband's coat and took out his dark and worn wallet, which was a present from her own mother and father many years ago on their wedding day, in the old church in Kilroan. The wallet was nearly too fat for her hand to hold it. She did not want to look at those slips, did not want to see how much he owed and to whom it was owed to. So tired of it all. All those nights she sat in the dark kitchen, waiting for the sound of his thumb pressing down on the latch, wanting him there beside her in the bed, no matter what he had lost. No matter what.

She opened the wallet. There was more money in it than she had ever before seen. She took all of it out and placed it on top of the loaf; she folded the newspaper over and picked the parcel up, held it to her chest with one hand, the wrapped bottle of water in the other—men, may God forgive them the damage they have done to his earth, thinking like fools it is them who own it.

She raised her face to the clock. Look at the time it was already. She needed to get the dinner on; they'd be in soon, and be very hungry. They'd stroll through Looby's big meadow, with the pitchforks over their shoulders, and they'd cross the ditch into the rock field and hunt the cows before them, and she had yet to scald the churns and boil the straining cloth, but she had let the fire die. So she needed to start there, because you couldn't do much without fire, but not once all day had she thought about the fire in the hearth, although in the garden all morning and afternoon, and now in the shimmering evergreen trees, and on the flagstones in the yard she watched through the open door there was the smell of burning thatch tightening the air. The sour evening heat. How hard the heat must be on everyone around, the men in the meadows, the women having to sit under the cows for the second time like every other day of their lives, and there was the sad-looking boy outside in her own garden who had to endure the dreadful weight of that winter coat.